Greek Myths

A Compilation of the Life and Times of Eros Phanes

COMPILED BY HARRISON VANDERNOOT

Greek Myths - A Compilation of the Life and Times of Eros Phanes by Harrison VanDernoot

Reasonable credit goes to John Ronald Reuel Tolkien and his estate where such credit is due - for names or references to his brilliant works. Requiesce in pace.

Print ISBN: 979-8-218-16686-1

Ebook ISBN: 979-8-218-16685-4

Printed in the United States of America by Ingramspark

The Library of Congress has cataloged the hardcover edition as follows:

Greek Myths by Harrison VanDernoot.

Summary: The collected memoirs of Eros, who was sometimes known as Phanes, which were later compiled by Harrison VanDernoot. Eros and his relations go and have adventures as Greek primordial deities, while dealing with family issues.

[1. Magic—Fiction. 2. Greece—Fiction. 3. Households—Fiction. 4. Friendships—Fiction. 5. Olympus—Fiction.]

2023 [Fic]

V3.031

[printing details including paper type, font faces, art materials, and such]

To All the Primal Gods

Preface

What Experiences I Had With This Book, Even Though No One Asked

Ah. The preface. The part before the book. The part where the reader hasn't read the book yet but they need some background information.[1] The part where another famous author writes about their experience with the book, then finishes writing, walks out of their room, and is immediately paid a billion dollars by the author.[2] The preface is the part of the book where the author will write about writing the book for WAY too long.

[1] Not what the preface is.
[2] Not what the preface is.

You look at the preface and think, "That's not too long," and, "I better read this if I'm serious about the book." You then flip through the pages, reading all about every single detail of the book's creation, only for the author to spoil the entire book in a way that's subtle enough to not be pointed out when skimming, but explicit enough for you to realize it is a spoiler when you read it.

Nobody likes the preface. I myself didn't plan on writing a preface when I finished my memoirs. My memoirs were just going to be light-hearted tales of things that have happened to me.

But, when I went down to the publishing house, they were all like, "You gotta write a preface. If the readers aren't bored out of their minds at the beginning, what will entice them to read?" So they made me write one. And here it is. I hope you enjoy reading it as much as I enjoyed writing it, which I did not.

Blah blah blah blah blah blah blah blah blah blah, blah blah blah blah blah blah blah blah blah blah blah blah blah blah blah blah. Blah blah blah blah blah blah blah blah blah blah blah blah blah blah blah blah blah blah blah blah blah blah blah blah blah blah blah blah blah blah blah blah blah blah blah blah blah blah blah blah blah blah blah blah blah blah blah blah blah blah blah blah blah blah blah blah blah blah blah blah blah! Blah blah blah blah blah blah blah blah blah blah blah; blah blah blah blah blah blah blah blah, blah blah blah blah blah blah blah blah blah blah blah blah blah blah, blah blah blah blah blah blah blah blah blah blah blah blah blah blah blah blah blah blah blah blah blah blah blah blah blah blah blah blah blah.

Blah blah blah blah blah blah blah blah blah blah, blah blah blah blah blah blah blah blah blah blah blah blah blah blah blah blah. Blah blah blah blah blah blah blah blah blah blah blah blah blah blah blah blah blah blah blah blah blah blah blah blah blah blah blah blah blah blah blah blah blah blah blah blah blah blah blah blah blah blah blah blah blah blah blah blah blah blah blah blah blah blah blah blah blah blah blah blah blah! Blah blah blah blah blah

blah blah blah blah blah blah; blah blah blah blah blah blah blah blah, blah blah blah blah blah blah blah blah blah blah blah blah blah blah, blah blah blah blah blah blah blah blah blah blah blah blah blah blah blah blah blah blah blah blah blah blah blah blah blah blah blah blah blah blah blah blah.

Blah blah blah blah blah blah blah blah blah blah, blah blah blah blah blah blah blah blah blah blah blah blah blah blah blah blah. Blah blah blah blah blah blah blah blah blah blah blah blah blah blah blah blah blah blah blah blah blah blah blah blah blah blah blah blah blah blah blah blah blah blah blah blah blah blah blah blah blah blah blah blah blah blah blah blah blah blah blah blah blah blah blah blah blah blah blah blah blah blah! Blah blah blah blah blah blah blah blah blah blah blah; blah blah blah blah blah blah blah blah, blah blah blah blah blah blah blah blah blah blah blah blah blah blah, blah blah blah blah blah blah blah blah blah blah blah blah blah blah blah blah blah blah blah blah blah blah blah blah blah blah blah blah blah.

Blah.

Blah blah blah blah blah blah blah blah blah blah, blah blah blah blah blah blah blah blah blah blah blah blah blah blah blah blah. Blah blah blah blah blah blah blah blah blah blah blah blah blah blah blah blah blah blah blah blah blah blah blah blah blah blah blah blah blah blah blah blah blah blah blah blah blah blah blah blah blah blah blah blah blah blah blah blah blah blah blah blah blah blah blah blah blah blah blah blah blah blah! Blah blah blah blah blah blah blah blah blah blah blah; blah blah blah blah blah blah blah blah, blah blah blah blah blah blah blah blah blah blah blah blah blah blah, blah blah blah blah blah blah blah blah blah blah blah blah blah blah blah blah blah blah blah blah blah blah blah blah blah blah blah blah blah.

Blah blah blah blah blah blah blah blah blah blah blah blah blah blah blah blah blah blah blah blah blah blah blah blah blah blah blah blah blah blah blah blah blah blah blah blah blah blah blah blah blah blah blah blah blah blah blah blah blah blah blah

blah blah blah blah blah blah blah blah blah blah! Blah blah blah blah blah blah blah blah blah blah blah blah blah blah blah blah blah blah blah blah blah blah blah blah blah blah blah blah blah blah blah blah blah blah blah blah blah blah blah blah blah blah blah blah blah blah blah blah blah blah blah blah blah blah blah blah blah blah blah blah blah blah blah blah blah blah blah blah blah blah blah blah blah blah blah blah blah blah blah blah blah blah.

Blah blah.

RANDOM TABLE:

Blah blah blah blah blah blah1	Blah blah blah blah blah blah2	Blah blah blah blah blah blah3
Blah blah blah blah blah blah Results: Blah Blah.	Blah blah blah blah blah blah Results: Blah blah.	Blah blah blah blah blah blah Results: blah Blah.

Blah blah blah blah blah blah blah blah blah blah blah blah blah blah blah blah blah blah blah blah blah blah blah blah blah blah blah blah blah blah blah blah blah blah blah blah blah blah blah blah blah blah blah blah blah blah blah blah blah blah blah blah blah blah blah blah blah blah blah blah blah blah blah blah blah blah blah blah blah blah

blah blah blah blah blah blah blah blah blah blah blah blah blah blah blah blah blah blah blah blah blah blah blah blah blah blah blah blah blah blah blah blah blah blah blah blah blah blah blah blah blah blah blah blah blah blah blah blah blah blah blah blah blah blah blah blah blah blah blah blah blah blah blah blah blah blah blah blah blah blah blah.

Blah blah blah blah blah blah blah blah blah blah blah blah blah blah blah blah blah blah blah blah blah blah blah blah blah blah blah blah blah blah blah blah blah blah blah blah blah blah blah blah blah blah blah blah blah blah blah phanes blah blah blah blah blah blah blah blah blah blah blah blah blah blah blah blah blah blah blah blah blah blah blah blah blah blah blah blah blah blah blah blah blah blah blah blah blah blah kills blah blah blah blah blah blah blah blah blah blah blah blah blah kampe blah blah blah blah blah blah blah blah blah blah blah blah blah blah blah blah blah blah blah blah blah blah blah blah blah blah blah blah blah blah blah blah blah blah blah blah blah blah blah blah blah blah blah blah.

"Inspirational Quote From a Childhood Hero"

"Blah blah

blah blah blah blah blah blah blah blah blah blah blah blah blah blah blah blah blah blah.

Blah blah.

Blah bla-blah bla-blah,"

Blahed by Eros "Blah" Phanes.

Forward

An Introduction by Elisha Dukes

Ah. The forward. That part of the book where I brag about knowing the author, how greeeeeat the book was, how it impacted my life, and where I provide some authority and credibility for the author and tell you why you HAVE to read this *particular* book ... I'm only doing this because I'm a friend. And the publisher, which is probably the only reason this random deity let me ferret out the truth needed to blackmail him into keeping this. And I'm kinda embarrassed about the preface, which completely broke convention. I'm sorry about that boring mess. Blah blah blah. Blah. It's, well, kinda bland. And really similar to the epilogue, which is definitely an issue. However, I do think that if you enjoy slapstick humor and strange inside jokes for which you are not an insider, you may possibly want to read this book. Maybe not, it's up to you. You want to read it, do. You don't, don't. This book changed my life, by making me a prosperous publisher, (at least, I hope it has if you're reading this) and I hope it does the same for you.

Table of Contents:

Prologue

Eros stared down his menacing opponent. As his mind teetered at the brink of insanity, he shook his fist at his dastardly foe. He fought valiantly for hours, and many songs will be sung of his glory,[3] but each time he attacked his foe threw his own mind back at Eros, shattering his soul to its innermost depths. Eros, weak and tired, was barely able to defend himself as his enemy seemed to laugh at his futile attempts to master it.

"Empty scroll, you shalt not best me." Eros sat at his desk once more and hung his fingers above the scroll, pen ready to write. Yet he could not think of anything. His mind was a whirlpool of thoughts, and he kept grasping at empty straws.[4] Then he had a thought. Magic burritos,[5] lizards, and little pieces of paper all fighting a bottle of evil

[3] Most are "Pirate Pop", the music genre where pirates sing pop songs. Really. Look it up.

[4] This switch between two stupid metaphors is an accurate representation of Eros's brain state at the time.

[5] Specifically breakfast burritos.

hot sauce who rules his galactic empire with an iron cap. He was about to begin writing when the smart[6] part of his brain chimed in.

That's a terrible idea, dude. You know that.

"No, it's not," Eros said out loud to his brain. "It's a great idea. It's got it all: a basic plot, characters."

Does it have a theme, backstory, or even an ever so slightly sad part?

"We'll cross those hurdles when we get to them, brain."

Hmm... his brain responded. *How do you even plan on having them defeat the evil hot sauce? Is there even a climax?*

"Of course there's a climax. They defeat the hot sauce with an ancient magic that the heroes discover at the last minute."

But is there any lore or hints that suggest that that might happen? Any exposition between the characters that might set that up?

Eros sighed. "No, brain, there isn't."

Let's explore other options, then.

"Fine." Eros fought with the empty scroll and his brain until he had one brilliant idea that would change everything.

"Brain! Brain! I have an idea!"

---

[6] *cough* Annoying. *cough*

What?

"I can writ an autobiography!"

Did you just say 'writ'?

"Maybe! So?"

Brain thought about it for a second.

Okay. Go for it.

"And I'll write the whole thing in third person omniscient!"

Wait, what-

And so Eros began writing.

That One Time the Universe Got Made

Darkness. A void of nothing. It was as big as a house, or maybe a skyscraper, or maybe a flea. Too dark to tell. The darkness was all engulfing, everything and nothing all at once, though it emitted an almost lonely aura. Out of this nothing formed a consciousness. The consciousness glowed, shedding the first light on the universe.[7] The dim light revealed to itself that it took the form of endless turmoil, stretching forever and ever in a pit of- "CHAOS," it thought, and so it was called until the end of days. Chaos set his form and wandered the universe, endlessly searching for who knows what. He suddenly tripped on a rock, falling down into the endless void. How did he trip on a rock if the universe had not been created yet? How did he trip if he wasn't a malleable thing? I don't know, but when he did, the curiosity of what happened to him sparked the first being, Gaia, the earth. Gaia looked around at the darkness around her and said her first words.

[7] I mean, like, a few photons of light, but it was something.

"This is boring." Now, with the invention of language, a little piece of air got displaced in the cosmic equilibrium. Thus, a different amount of air was breathed in by Chaos, causing the god[8] to burp. That's when everything got interesting.

"HEY EVERYBODY!" shouted a tall Greek man with golden wings and hair. "HOW ARE YOU DOING!?" Erebus and Tartarus[9] materialized behind him as Gaia and Chaos came to investigate.

"Hello," said Gaia, "Who are you?"

"I AM EROS!" he yelled. "NICE TO MEET YOU!"

"Why are you yelling?[10]" Gaia asked.

"BECAUSE MY VOCAL CORDS ARE AD-justing." Eros settled down as Chaos scoffed and started to float away.

"You guys are loud. I'm out," Chaos said as he floated away.

"Okay, bye, Dad!" Eros waved at Chaos as he floated away. "What a great guy."

Nyx manifested near them as Eros hovered and looked around.

"What do we do now?" Gaia asked. Tartarus and Erebus appeared near them. Crickets would have chirped, but that wouldn't have made sense. Crickets hadn't been invented yet.

Nyx answered that quickly.

---

[8] Spirit? Titan? Force? Being?

[9] Notice how the others have names. This is because Eros, like any self-respecting deity, loves mystery.

[10] She said, inventing yelling.

"Umm? Let's just... uh... I don't know. What should we do?" wondered Nyx.

"We could ask Dad," Eros suggested, but Chaos had already left.

"Maybe we should make something to live on," Tartarus suggested. Everyone agreed with that.

"What should we make?" Erebus asked. Still no crickets.

"We could all, like, turn into things and just stand on each other's heads and stuff to make a landmass." Eros suggested.

"What's a landmass?" asked Gaia.

"What's a head?" asked the cricket, and everybody stared at it. Except, there were no crickets yet, and when everybody stared at the cricket, they were staring at nothing... Now that that's cleared up, he explained to them all the new words he made up and also the concept OF words which he ALSO made up and they all morphed into bunnies.

All the bunnies climbed on each other's heads and they were like a bunny multi-layered pie and they lived in a utopia called Bunny-Land for a billion years. But pretty soon they got super bored so the gods had a meeting about starting another world.

Two newcomers were invited to the meeting, the children of Nyx and Erebus, Aether and Hemera. You see, from the moment he was born, Eros knew he was the god of love and emotion.[11] While it took time for the others to cement their spots in the universe, he knew his true nature right from the start. The hard part was explaining it to them.

[11] He's really cool that way.

The Following Excerpt is a Word-by-Word Record of a Day in Bunny-Land:

Eros: No, no, no, you don't get it. *ahem* LOVE.

Nyx: Saying it twice doesn't help much, Eros.

Eros: You and I are friends, right?

Nyx: We're acquaintances.

Eros: That's actually really hurtful. Anyway, LOVE is like friendship, but higher up on the tier list.

Nyx: What's a tier list?

Eros: One thing at a time. Love is like, when you make something and you care for it and you just love it.

Nyx: Defining something with itself is stupid.

Eros: You're stupid.

Nyx: I could walk away right now.

Eros: Sorry, sorry. Maybe I should show you.

(Let the record show that Eros then grabbed a passing Erebus by his little bunny ears and pulled him over.)

Erebus: What's happening?

Eros: Oh, nothing. Do you want Erebus here to help?

Nyx: What's the difference?

Eros: It's easier, I guess. There's a far more interesting product, I guess. In fourteen billion years some kid will draw a family tree of us gods and it will look like a big mess of interconnecting lines with little names below them.

Erebus: Do I get a say in-

Eros: Quiet. Nyx?

Nyx: I guess I could use some help.

Eros: Okay!

Erebus: What happens now?

Eros: Oh, I just need some of your godly essences.

Nyx: You need our wha-

(Let the record show that Eros then reached into the bunnie's hearts and pulled out balls of ichor, smushing them together into a ball. The area flashed with light and two little bunnies appeared in front of them)

Aether: Goo

Hemera: Gaa

Nyx: EROS ARE YOU INSANE-what are those?

(Let the record show Eros bowed to Nyx and presented her with her babies.)

Eros: Your babies, madame.

Aether: Gao

Nyx: Awwww. They're adorable!

Erebus: Nice, dude. They are pretty cute.

Aether: Goo gaa

Hemera: Gaa goo

Nyx: Eros, thank you thank you thank you-

Hemera: WHAAAAAAAAAA!!!!!!!!

Erebus: What-What happened?

Hemera: WAAAAAAAAAAA!!!!!!!!

Aether: HWAAAAAAAAAA!!!!!!!!

Nyx: EROS, WHAT'S HAPPENING?

Eros: Gotta go!

Hemera and Aether: WHAAAAAAAAA!!!!!!!!!

Nyx: EROS!!!-

(Let the record show that Eros flew from the scene, leaving Nyx with two stinky baby bunnies and Erebus, who she really hadn't liked that much before then.)

END OF RECORD

"Here, here!" Tartarus banged his imaginary gavel on an imaginary podium as everyone took their seats. "We gather here today to dictate the starting of a new world, a world where we may make things." Scattered clapping.

"Yay," cheered Aether.

"Yes. Settle down." Tartarus banged his gavel some more. "The first thing we must do is dictate who will be what."

"I want to be the under-!" yelled Erebus.

"Wait your turn!" Tartarus interrupted.

Tartarus flipped through some papers and straightened his suit. He finally looked back to the others.

"Erebus."

Erebus stepped forward.

"I want to be the underworld!"

"No. As the judge, I choose MYSELF as the underworld." Tartarus decided.

"That's not fair."

"It is fair. I know because I'm the judge."

"Nuh-uh."

"Yuh-huh."

"Nuh-uh."

"Yuh-huh."

"FINE," Erebus grunted, "but I get to be the darkness."

"Nuh-uh," objected Tartarus. "Darkness comes WITH the underworld. Everybody knows that."

"Nuh-uh."

"Yuh-huh."

"Nuh-uh."

"Yuh-huh."

"Nuh-uh."

"Yuh-huh."

"Nuh-uh."

"Yuh-huh."

"Nuh-uh."

"Yuh-huh."

"Nuh-uh."

"Yuh-huh."

"Nuh-uh."

"Yuh-huh."

"Nuh-uh."

"Yuh-huh."

"Nuh-uh."

"Yuh-huh."

"Nuh-uh."

"Yuh-yuh."

"Nuh-uh."

"Yuh-huh."

"Nuh-uh."

"Yuh-huh."

"Nuh-uh."

"Yuh-huh."

"Nuh-uh."

"Yuh-huh."

"Nuh-uh."

"Yuh-huh."

"Nuh-uh."

"Yuh-huh."

"ALRIGHT!" Nyx butted in and stood up in front of Tartarus. "You can get the underworld!" She pointed at him. "And you get darkness!" She pointed at Erebus.

"B-but he'll just take the upper underworld anyway!" Tartarus stammered.

"Hey! Who's the judge here?" Nyx asked.

"I am," Tartarus replied.

"That's right!" She stomped off. Tartarus took a deep breath and banged his gavel, bringing Hemera in front of him.

"What do you want to be, Hemera?" He asked.

"This place is too dark. We need some light. I think I'll be day," she responded.

"Day? What's that?"

"Oh, just some light so we can see things better."

"But your father is darkness. Wouldn't that be offensive?"

"Eh, I'm hitting that rebellious phase," shrugged Hemera.

"I hereby declare you..." he was raising his gavel when Nyx shouted for them to stop.

"WAIT!" she ran up from where she had been muttering about how petty boys were and stuff. "You can't be day, Hemera. It's the ultimate insult to your father."

"I've made my decision, Mom."

"Fine. Then I'll be night."

"But Mom, night is the opposite of day. Why would you want that?"

"Because I'm your mother. Thus we must be polar opposites." She finished with a loud *hmph.* Tartarus banged his gavel and made the decision final as they walked away bickering.

"Next, Aether!" Tartarus shouted as Aether hurried to the stage. "What will you be, Aether?"

"I'd like to be with both my mother and sister." He thought for a second. "Maybe I can be the area between the outside and the world, where day and night take place. Like, a-ai-Aer?"

"Air? Sure." He banged his gavel and Aether shuffled away. "Gaia!" Gaia walked up. "What do you want to be?"

"Hmmm. Well, when we make new things they need someplace to live, right?"

"Right," Tartarus answered.

"And they can't live in the underworld because it's icky and dark in there, right?"

"That's hurtful, but right."

"And they can't live in the air because they wouldn't be able to move around, right?"

"Right."

"So we should make a place where they can live, right?"

"Right."

"So I think I should be that place!"

Tartarus thought about this for a second.

"Sounds good. What will it be called?" Tartarus replied.

Gaia also thought about that for a second.

"How about Earth?"

"Good enough," he banged his gavel for the last time. Where was Eros during all of this, you may ask? He was just standing around nearby, watching and eating popcorn.[12]

"Is it over yet?" he asked Tartarus when Gaia walked away.

"Yeah, it's over. Now we just need to have a bajillion meetings about how to arrange the planet. It'll be fun!" he responded.

"Ugh." Now, we won't bore you with most of the meetings, but we will tell what happened in the most important one.

[12] After all, who wouldn't want to know where that guy is at all times? He's just so incredibly great!

These are the Minutes of Meeting 127,463,286,853,536 on the Creation of the Universe:

Tartarus: Order, Order! I call this meeting on the setting of the parameters of the new world.

Gaia: Today we should talk about the fact that Aether keeps flying into space.

Eros: Why?

Gaia: So we can stop it from happening.

Eros: But it's hilarious.

Aether: That's what YOU think.

Nyx: What should we do? Aether keeps hitting me on the way out.

Gaia: He shouldn't be. I mean, he has control over air. He should be able to just swerve out of the way, right? Am I making any sense right now?

(Let the record show that all the eyes in the room pointed towards Aether.)

Aether: It's actually kinda funny when you think about it…

Nyx: I'll get you for that someday…!

Tartarus: Order, Order! We need to find a solution!

Eros: We could make a new god.

Erebus: I'm not doing that again.

Eros: Then who else?

Tartarus: Not me.

Aether: Not me.

Nyx: Not me.

Hemera: Not me.

Eros: Well SOMEBODY has to volunteer!

Gaia: I will.

(Let the record show that all eyes in the room pointed to Gaia.)

Gaia: Well, it can't be THAT hard to raise a kid!

Nyx: Oh. That's funny. Ha. Ha ha. Hahahahahahahahaha.

Eros: Are you sure about this, Gaia?

Gaia: Whatever.

Eros: Okay. One sky god coming right up.

Erebus: WAIT! Could you make TWO gods?

Eros: Why?

Erebus: Well, you may have noticed that my lips are a little parched.

(Let the record show that everyone started licking their lips.)

Nyx: I am also quite parched.

Tartarus: So am I.

Eros: Everyone is. Alright, a sky god and water god coming right up.

(Let the record show that Eros reached into Gaia's heart and pulled out two balls of godly essence. He smashed them together and suddenly two little gods appeared.)

Gaia: *gasp*

Eros: Here they are!

Gaia: LOOK-AT-THEM LOOK-AT-THEM LOOK-AT-THEM THEY'RE-SO-CUTE!!!!!!!!!

Uranus: Goo.

Pontus: GAA.

Eros: Another good deed by me.

Uranus: Wah-

Nyx: So it begins.

Uranus: Waaaaahhhhhh!!!!

Pontus: Goo-Goo Gaa-Gaaaaaaa? Waaaaahhhh!!!!!

Gaia: Eros? Eros! How do I get them to stop!?

Eros: Up-up and away!

(Let the record show that Eros once again flew away from a pair of crying babies.)

Gaia: There he goes.

Erebus: At least the babies are cute.

Aether: That one's kinda handsome.

(Let the record show that Aether pointed at Uranus. Gaia stared at the infant.)

Gaia: Yes. Handsome.

And the rest is history.

What's That Phanes!

"Hello, and welcome back to What's! That! Phanes!" The crowd cheered as Hecate ran through the crowd and stepped up to her podium. "I'm glad to see we've got a full crowd tonight!" The crowd roared again. "With the exception of Eris, of course, because we all remember what happened the last time she was invited to a party-" The doors burst open. A small but crazy-eyed child stood in the spotlight for just a second before she started winding up.

"Eris! No!!!" Hecate yelled. "Guards! Stop her!" Some small centaurs with black "SECURITY" spears started closing in on her, but it was too late.

"For the fairest!" yelled the girl[13] as she threw a glistening golden peach into the crowd.

"Not again!!!"

[13] And it was Eris, just for those people who are really bad with context clues.

Ten years later...

"Hello and welcome back to What's! That! Phanes!" The crowd cheered as Hecate walked in and stopped at her podium. "I'm glad to see we got everyone here... again! We also now have lockable doors! So that's a nice plus! Hopefully there won't be another *situation.* You guys are so petty." Hecate stared directly at Hera, Aphrodite, and Athena, who became incredibly interested in their shoes all of a sudden.

The three goddesses grunted in annoyance.

"Anyway, let's get down to the show! As you all know, this is a show about the first, the ones there at the beginning, the people who started people, primal beings!" The crowd erupted with applause. "Well, there's no use stalling, let's meet our contestants! Who's our first contestant?"

The loudspeakers blasted. "He's the son of Hermes, the god of nature, the guy who hides behind shepards and then scares the mutton out of them, Pan!"

The doors blasted open. Dryads danced through the aisles, with wreaths upon their brows and beautiful green togas, throwing beautiful bouquets into the crowd. They were followed by Pan, a tall satyr blowing his horn all around as green grass grew at his feet. Hecate clapped politely as he galloped up to the podium.

"Helloooooo Olympus!" Pan bleated.

The crowd roared. Naiads played music as smooth and flowing as the oceans they loved on intricate golden harps. Mountainous Oreads participated in fierce mock combat.

"Thank you! It's nice to see we have such a wonderful crowd tonight," Pan yelled. The music stopped as he started talking. They hung on Pan's every word like their lives depended on it[14] as he paused for dramatic silence. Pan smiled and looked at the captivated audience and the detailed set. "I've put together a great show, don't you think?"

"Actually, I put together the show," Hecate corrected.

"And I agreed to come. 80/20."

"I sent out a mass email. You were the first to respond."

"Because I'm so attentive."

"Because you're addicted to your phone."

"I'm the god of *nature*. I don't have a phone."

"Your screen time average is thirteen hours and thirty-seven minutes.[15]"

"How do you know that?"

"You posted a screenshot of it on FacePaw® with the caption: 'Spending the weekend on my phone' with the hashtags, '#ScreensRule, #NatureDrools, and #UnrelatedHashtagsBeLike'"

Pan stared at the amused Hecate angrily. "50/50 then." Pan gave her a quick death glare and turned to the crowd. He plastered a smile on his face and motioned for the A/V people to crank the music back up.

[14] Even though they couldn't die.

[15] But what she didn't know was that Pan... had another phone.

"Anyway, let's PARTY!" The spirits continued their activities as the crowd started getting up from their seats and dancing.

"Uh... Hecate?" A short dryad[16] with glasses walked up to Hecate. "We need to start the show soon." Drad stared out at the screaming masses of nymphs and gods. "Should I call security?"

Hecate just shook her head. "Nah. Pan's a rational guy, right? We're live, so he must be smart enough to not greatly impact our schedule."

Ten grueling hours later...

As the last Oread was escorted out and the last beach ball popped, everyone sat down in their seats. "FINALLY," muttered Hecate. "Who's our second contestant? *yawn*"

The crowd roared, but they were tired, so it was more of a 'ROOOOOOAR-zzzzzzzzz...'

The loudspeakers turned on and kind of whispered, "He's the son of Nyx, the end of life, the guy who causes your cells to stop working, its death himself, it's Thanatos-zzzzzzzzz..."

The doors opened yet again and a ghoulish carcass with deathly black wings bursting from its back jumped into the room. Thanatos cackled as the grass beneath his feet withered and died. A bunch of ghosts ran in after him, screaming death rock. Thanatos shook his head vigorously.

---

[16] His name was Drad.

"I love Olympus!" he screamed. "Am I right, guys!? Let's PAR-TEEEYYY!!!" He looked around at the sleeping crowd. "Guys! C'mon. This is the good part where they sing about how everyone dies one day and life is hopeless. It's kinda my mantra,"

Nothing but blaring snores from Hephaestus.[17]

"Alright. I guess I can use this. Just give one second," Thanatos pulled out his IrisPhone®.[18] He dialed a number and let it ring for a minute. Finally, someone picked up on the other end.

"Hello?" A very soothing voice that sounded like a bird tweeting in the forest, a waterfall gushing down, and a whale singing a ballad to its forever love at the same time came from the phone. It seemed to the caress the ears, like a nice pillow after a day in the spa-zzzzzzzzz.

•••

•••

•••

•••

[17] He really needs to see a doctor.

[18] Buy today! Who needs Hermes when you've got a top-of-the-line, rainbow, lightweight phone!? *Rights Reserved.*

•••

•••

•••

•••

•••

HUH!? Oh. Sorry. Fell asleep a little there.

Thanatos spoke into the phone. “This is Thanatos. Is this Hypnos? Brother, is that you?”

The voice spoke back, “Yeah. This is Hypnos. Ya know, they have caller ID now. You can see who’s calling before you even pick up. But never mind any of that. What’s up bro? I saw you in Hades a week ago, but we didn’t get the chance to talk. How’s the business? Still got that scythe?”

“The business is good. The scythe still freaks people out.[19] But we’re getting off track. You know that game show I’m on?”

---

[19] Its name is Jimmy, for the record.

"Oh yeah! The game show! I was just there for Hecate."

"What!? Hecate!?" Thanatos looked over and saw that Hecate was indeed asleep. She stirred for a second but didn't move from her spot on the podium.

"Weird how she sleeps standing up, right? Like a horse or an elephant."

"Ugh," murmured Thanatos, clearly offended. "You put my audience to sleep! We were going to have a death metal party!"

"Bro, nobody likes death metal. The Muses won't even inspire it."

"What do you mean? Everybody loves death metal!"

"Do they, bro? Do they?"

"Well... I... You..."

"Do they really?"

"That's not the point! I need you to wake my audience up. Make them feel well rested and all that, please? Bro to bro."

"...Okay. But you've got to help me with creating a way to sleep that completely prevents heart attacks."

"No way. I can do heartburn."

"Heart attacks."

"Triple bypass."

"Cardiac arrests."

"Deal," Thanatos closed his IrisPhone®. Suddenly everyone woke up with a jump and stared at Thanatos. He walked up to the set and stood at his podium, all without a word.

Hecate looked bewildered but quickly shook it off and went back into host mode. "Oooooo-kay then! Who's our third contestant?"

The loudspeakers blared louder than ever. "The son of Iapetus and Klymene, the man who shielded humanity from the terrible Titanomachy, the fire thief, it's Prometheus!"

Prometheus ran in from the doors as thousands of little human beings danced around him.

"Ugh," groaned Hecate. "Did you have to bring the humans? Seriously, they're kinda annoying."

"They followed me, lady," said Prometheus. He shooed them away as he stepped up to the podium.

"Fine. But they better not be back," muttered Hecate. "I prefer cats much more. Anyway, let's meet our guests!"

The loudspeaker blasted its sound all over the room. "In the curtain on the left, we present you... Eros!" The curtain turned, revealing an incredibly handsome man standing with birds flying all around him. He had two bright golden wings resting on his back and short gold hair.

"How are you doing?" Eros asked the crowd. All the birds flew away peacefully as he stepped forward.

"Eros, everyone-Oh, for all the darkness of Erebus!" As Hecate was talking, the humans had gotten onto the stage and were surrounding Eros with hugs and awe.

"Prometheus, get your humans out!" Hecate screamed.

"Nah, it's okay." Eros booped a cute little human on its cute little nose. "I like them."

"Ooooohhhkay then. Just keep them away, okay? They smell. Who's our next guest?"

She started introducing the other guests. Tartarus fell in and the boulders that followed him battered the stage. The room was covered in darkness as Erebus swooped in. Nyx flew in on her black-blue chariot and filled the room with stars. The air in the room grew tense as Aether materialized in. Gaia blossomed from a flower and Uranus stepped out of the sky, crashing into the skylight and spraying glass everywhere. Once the confusion was sorted out, Hemera stepped out from a sunspot and Pontus flooded the room.

"Pontus, everyone!" Hecate yelled to the crowd. "We've finally got all our guests here!" The crowd cheered. "So it's time to start! Our first game will be 'Who Is That?' where we put a primal being in a room, and you have to guess, Who. Is. That! Let's start," A darkened room with a figure in it materialized into the wall. The figure walked over to a chair and sat down. A very warped voice emitted from the figure.

"Hello. I am life and death and I destroy what gets in my way. All beings love me, but get trapped in me and you will die. Who am I?"

Pan dinged his bell.

"Yes, Pan?" Hecate asked.

"It's me. Pan," answered Pan.

"It can't be you, Pan."

"Why not?"

"Because it has to be one of the contestants."

"I could be a contestant in disguise."

"Are you?"

"No."

"Then do you have a real answer?"

"Yes."

"Then tell me what it is." There was an uncomfortable silence as everyone stared at a calm Pan.

"Moving on!" Hecate pressed a button and the voice started talking again.

"I am fast and restless and yet I lay on my bed all day. I am kind and calm yet always raging.[20] Who am I?" Thanatos dinged his bell.

"Yes, Thanatos?"

"Is it Pontus?" asked Thanatos.

"That is correct!" The bells dinged and a little screen on Thanatos's podium lit up. It flashed blue and displayed a screen that said: '200 POINTS'.

"What's that?" asked Prometheus as his screen turned blue as well.

---

[20] Raging because they have to put so much in the bank.

"Did I forget to mention that there are points in this game? My bad!" Hecate chuckled in a sly way.

Pan looked at his zero points and frowned. "I will destroy you both," he sneered in an unsettling way.

"Next!" screamed Hecate. Another figure appeared in the room and spoke.

"I am everywhere and yet I am nothing. Some call me Eros, but I go by other names. Who am I?"

Prometheus dinged his bell.

"Yes, Prometheus?" asked Hecate.

"Is it Eros?"

"Nope!"

"But they just said they were Eros!"

"And some people call me Magic Lady With Wands For Hands. Next hint!" yelled Hecate.

"I am what everything runs from but what they can never hide from. I am fear personified and I will hunt you forever. One day all will be gone and I will be there. Who am I?"

Prometheus dinged his bell. "Is it Erebus?" he asked.

"That is correct!" The screen lit up on Prometheus's podium displaying his new two hundred points. Pan sneered at him but reasserted his gaze to the room, more determined than ever. The next figure floated in.

"I am the puppet master, the one behind the curtain, the sustainer of life. I am unicorn-slayer,[21] the winged god, the first bird. I who makes the world work, the one behind it all, the king of the mind! Who am I?"

Prometheus dinged his bell.

"Is it Eros?"

"Yes it is." The points flashed onto his screen.

"All right! The points are Prometheus six hundred, others... zip! Anyway, next up, we'll be playing... What! Does! That! Mean?" announced Hecate. "In this segment, we'll be looking at passages and asking, 'What Does That Mean?' Here's our first one,"

A passage turned onto the screen.

[21] Long story

You also, Eros, primeval founder of fecund marriage, bend your bow, and the universe is no longer adrift. If all things come from you, friendly shepherd of life, draw one shot more and save all things. As fiery god, arm yourself against Typhon, and by your help let the fiery thunderbolts return to my hand. All-vanquisher, strike one with your fire, and may your charmed shot catch one whom Zeus did not defeat; and may he have madness from the mind-bewitching tune of Cadmus, as much as I had passion for Europa's embrace.

Thanatos dinged his bell.

"I think it's Zeus saying, 'Hey... uh... Eros? Typhon took my thunderbolts, think you could get them back? Maybe mess him up a little? Pretty sure he deserves it.'"

"Correct!" The points flashed on his screen. "Next!"

And there, all in their order, are the sources and ends of gloomy earth and misty Tartarus and the unfruitful sea and starry heaven, loathsome and dank, which even the gods abhor ... There stands the awful home of murky Nyx wrapped in dark clouds. In front of it the son of Iapetos stands immovably upholding the wide heaven upon his head and unwearying hands, where Nyx and Hemera draw near and greet one another as they pass the great threshold of bronze: and while the one is about to go down into the house, the other one comes out the door. And the house never holds them both within; but always one is without the house passing over the earth, while the other stays at home and waits until the time for her journeying come; and the one hold all-seeing light for them on earth, but the other holds in her arms Hypnos the brother of Thanatos, even evil Nyx, wrapped in a vaporous cloud. And there the children of dark Nyx have their dwellings, Hypnos and

Thanatos, awful gods. Glowing Helios never looks upon them with his beams, neither as he goes up into heaven nor as he comes down from heaven

Thanatos's bell dinged.

"Far away, there is a house near Atlas. It is the house of Nyx and Hemera, and they are never in the house at the same time. Me and Hypnos live there, but I don't think the author likes us very much." Then in a muttered voice he spoke again. "Gotta find that guy." He wrote something down on his IrisPhone®; *"Hesiod, Theogony 744 ff (trans. Evelyn-White) (Greek epic C8th or C7th B.C.), must destroy all copies of it."*

"Correct!" Hecate answered, not noticing anything. More points added into Thanatos's screen. "Next!"

To Nyx, Fumigation with Torches. Nyx, parent goddess, source of sweet repose from whom at first both Gods and men arose. Hear, blessed Aphrodite, decked with starry light, in sleep's deep silence dwelling ebon night! Dreams and soft ease attend thy dusky train, pleased with the lengthened gloom and feastful strain, dissolving anxious care, the friend of mirth, with darkling coursers riding round the earth. Goddess of phantoms and of shadowy play, whose drowsy power divides the natural day; by fate's decree you constantly send the light to deepest hell, remote from mortal sight; for dire necessity, which nought withstands, invests the world with adamantite bands. Be present, Goddess, to thy suppliant's prayer, desired by all, whom all alike revere, blessed, benevolent, with friendly aid dispel the fears of twilight's dreadful shade.

Pan dinged his bell. “Hey Nyx? Night is pretty great, but there are some babies out there who don’t like it or you. You should probably shut that down? Pretty please? With a cherry on top?”

“Correct!” Points finally illuminated Pan’s podium.

“Now for our next segment!” Hecate said cheerfully.

“Yay!” A random spirit in the audience yelled.

“Quiet, Simoeis,” Hecate scowled. “Anyway, with Pan having two hundred points, Thanatos with four hundred, and Prometheus in the lead with six hundred, we’re going to play Wheel! Of! Tartarus! In Wheel of Tartarus, contestants spin the wheel to decide what special challenge they will do, in Tartarus! Since Pan is currently in last place, he gets to spin the wheel!” A giant wheel rose out of the floor in front of Pan with all sorts of random things to do on it. Pan took a deep breath and spun the wheel.

Didididididididididi-di-di-di-di-di--di--di---di----di-----di. The wheel stopped on a red slot that said *Catch the fish.*

“What’s ‘*Catch the fish*?’” asked Pan.

“You’ll head to the biggest lake in Tartarus in just a few minutes! A bunch of Pontus’s favorite fish have gotten out, and you have to get as many as you can back to him!” Buckets popped out of the floor as Hecate spoke. “Gather the fish in a convenient bucket stored on your head and drop them in the corresponding pool to win a point. Whoever has the most points when time runs out wins!” When Hecate finished, the studio warped around everybody until they were transported to Tartarus.

“Wow,” gasped Thanatos.

Above them stood over a giant canyon of darkness and fire that seemed to stretch upwards forever. Before them stood a giant crater filled with water and fish, all jumping around and flopping everywhere. After the fish stood three giant pools, labeled PAN, PROMETHEUS, and THANATOS. Off to the side of the pools was a large pond with a giant golden fish flopping around in it. Thanatos looked at the pool.

I should get that fish. It's probably valuable. I should go grab it. Then he noticed the raging herd of hippocampi guarding it. While Thanatos was thinking, Prometheus clipped on his bucket-helmet, and the others followed.

"Ready to lose?" asked Pan, turning towards his fellow competitors. He turned away snickering. Before Pan could say any more quips, Prometheus turned towards Hecate.

"What's that?" he said, pointing at the fish.

"The fish? That's the golden fish. It is worth two hundred points and ends the game."

The hippocampi whinnied.

"Anyway, ready, set, GO!" A clock came down over the pools and started ticking down from ten minutes. Pan ran in, the Prometheus, then Thanatos, and soon they were all waist-deep in the crater grabbing at fish.

"They're too slippery!" shouted Prometheus as a fish slipped from his grasp.

"Try grabbing harder!" suggested Thanatos. No matter how they tried, though, the fish would always slip out from their hands. At seven minutes left, none of them had any fish in their bucket.

I'll have to try for the golden fish, thought Prometheus. He ran for the fish as Thanatos struggled to contain a grouper that he had almost caught.

Prometheus is making a move for the gold! thought Thanatos. He ran towards the fish too. When Thanatos reached the fish, Prometheus was already battling the hippocampi. A hippocampi charged at him but he dodged out of the way just in time. The hippocampi snarled and charged again. This time Prometheus grabbed its horn and jumped up, twirling around and landing on its back. It whinnied and ran forward, charging towards the wall.

Prometheus grabbed a rock and held tight, pulling its horn hard enough that the hippocampus flipped over, careening into the herd and knocking all but one into the crater. The last one whinnied and stampeded towards him while he was catching his breath.

"WATCH OUT!" warned Thanatos. Prometheus turned as the hippocampus ran towards him but didn't have time to react. Thanatos sped forwards, sliding onto the rough ground and grabbing its tail. He tried to fling it into the water, but it resisted and it slipped from Thanatos's hands.

Right as it was about to make Thanatos Casserole, Prometheus delivered a powerful jump-kick into its side. After a quick breather, both Prometheus and Thanatos stepped up to claim their prize. Their hands touched the giant fish at the same time.

"Hey, wait," stammered Thanatos. "This fish is mine."

"What!?" retorted Prometheus. "I beat all the hippocampi! It's MINE."

"And I stopped them from coming back!" quipped Thanatos. "Plus, you're already in first! Let ME win this one!" As Prometheus was thinking of a response, a loud *whooshing* sound distracted him. He turned to find a giant Mauna Loa rushing towards him.

"Why do these things always happen to me?" The fish smacked him directly in the face. It hurt a lot, but he shrugged it off. "HA! Do you think that can stop me!?" A whale shark started sailing towards them. "Oh, for all the darkness in Hades-"

Next to him, Thanatos was hit by a Grey Whale, only being able to mutter that it was technically a mammal, not a fish. The last thing that Prometheus saw was Pan walking by him.

* * *

Prometheus lapsed in and out of consciousness. He saw Pan waking up to the fish. He saw the fish cower in fear. He saw Pan reach for it as it cowered away from him. He saw it slap Pan across the face and him falling down.

'*Someone had better been recording that,*' He thought. He saw Thanatos crawling up from his spot but then falling back as a grouper hit him. Then Prometheus fell unconscious.

"Wake up, sleepy head," Prometheus woke up to see Pan slowly shaking him. "You've been asleep for the last couple minutes!" Prometheus stood up and hobbled around.

"Who threw a Mauna Loa at us?" Prometheus asked, his head throbbing. Pan snickered.

"That *was ME,* but-" Prometheus turned and sucker-punched Pan in the face. Pan turned, holding his red cheek and stumbling backwards. "That's not a very nice thing to do."

"Why would you do that!?" Prometheus fumed. Pan laughed again.

"Rules are rules. 'The ends justify the means.' You of all people know that! I got the fish and that's what matters," Prometheus muttered something that would definitely not be allowed in this autobiography, and woke Thanatos.

"What happened?" Thanatos stuttered as he rose to his feet. "Who did this?"

"Pan did. He stole the golden fish,"

"Pan! That little- I'll make you suffer for-" Before Thanatos could mutter anything more NC-17, Pan clicked his tongue against his mouth in that one way that everyone hates.

"Tsk-tsk," he warned. "I'd spend my time looking for fish," For the first time since he had been woken, Prometheus looked at the clock. The giant clock was counting down from 30 seconds.

"Oh no!" screamed Thanatos. "We gotta go!" he jumped straight into the water, but it was no use. He grabbed at fish and lunged towards sharks but there simply wasn't enough time. Prometheus sat at the side, watching as Thanatos ran around. The time counted down, and when it ran out, Pan had won. Hecate sighed as they returned to the room.

"Pan, you win this round. Here are your points," The points flashed on his screen.

"Yes! Woohoo!" Pan danced in his spot.

"Oh, shut your trap," Hecate flicked her wrist and a giant boulder flew towards him. Pan dodged it with ease but stopped celebrating.

"Rude," he muttered. The wheel popped up again in front of them.

"Thanatos, now YOU get to spin the wheel." Thanatos grabbed one of the rungs and pushed, sending the wheel into a fast spin. It spun for exactly thirty-nine seconds before it stopped at a spot that said; *The Bunny Maze.*

"You got *The Bunny Maze*! You'll be heading down into the labyrinth to find Eros's golden hare, with just an ancient, cryptic poem to guide you! You each have a panic button to get you out, but that won't get you any points!" The room around them again morphed into Tartarus, but this time there was an endless labyrinth in front of them. Large yellow birds flew in murmurations around them, and Eros himself was hovering around the top, surveying. A large block of stone pushed the three towards the maze and sealed the entrance. Thanatos slammed the full force of his body against the wall, but it was no use. They were stuck in there.

"I don't think it'll open," Prometheus said.

"Well, better get to work then," Thanatos said. He walked towards a giant parchment hanging on the wall.

"What does it say?" asked Prometheus. Thanatos squinted at it. The parchment was inscribed with crumbly old runes.

"I don't know. This is the most ancient writing I've ever seen,"

"Give me that." Thanatos handed it to him.

"How will you know what it says?"

Prometheus laughed.

"I invented literature. I'm sure I can read this," He sat there looking for a second, and finally turned to Thanatos. "My Proto-Ancient Old High Greek is a little rustic, but I think I got it," He began reading.

Here you are all trapped inside this ancient maze of stone.

And all the cold and darkness may shiver you to the bone.

But if you ever think of finding the hare who they call Carrot,

Follow Eros's child, like a triceratops or parrot.

"What?" asked Thanatos. "That's it?"

"That's all it says," answered Prometheus.

"Huh. I don't get it. We have to find the rabbit by following Eros's child, which could be a Parrot or Triceratops?"

"Me neither," Prometheus scratched his head. "What do you think, Pan?" He turned to where Pan had been standing when they got there, but there was no one there. He looked all around. There was just endless stone. "Hello?" The room echoed around him.

Pan was, in fact, five miles away, running aimlessly.

"I have to make it before those simpletons," he said to no one in particular. He turned left and encountered a huge Hyperborea walking around. "Oh. Good. A guide," The Hyporborea turned towards him, dragging a grant icicle behind him.

"Bow down before me, ice giant, and show me the way through this befoul maze," Pan commanded, frustrated.

The Hyperborae grunted as he got closer.

"I said, BOW, you Crete'n!" Closer. "Where. Is. The. Bunny!? You'll pay for this," Pan yelled back.

Closer.

As it was almost upon him, Pan opened his mouth once again."What are you doing, you big icy imbecile? Has your brain shrunk like a sun-soaked grape in Dionysus's great vineyards-"

A giant *splat* echoed through the maze as Prometheus and Thanatos walked through it.

"You wanna team up? We'll need it to beat that dirty cheater, Pan," asked Thanatos.

"Sure," answered Prometheus. And that was that. They walked around and around and around and around and around and around and around and around and around and around and around until Thanatos stopped walking.

"Ugh. We'll never get through this if we don't use the poem! We'll just have to figure it out ourselves," He sat down on the cold floor, and so did Prometheus. Prometheus looked up at the ceiling. It was a dark and hot night in Tartarus, but that was kind of how Tartarus worked. Even with the darkness, birds fluttered by. Prometheus watched them, and a wheel-made oil lamp turned on in his head.

"Thanatos, what do Triceratops and Parrots have in common?" Thanatos thought for a second.

"They look innocent but they could give you a world of hurt?"

"What? No!"

"They have cells whose nucleases have nuclear envelopes covering them? They consume organic material, are able to move, breath oxygen, they go through a ontogenetic phase whatever that means? They have a Notochord, a Dorsal Nerve Cord, Pharyngeal Slits, and an Anus?[22] They're bilaterally symmetrical, coelomic, triploblastic, and have segmented bodies? They are advanced chordates and have a cranium around their brain? Adults have vertebral columns instead of notochords? They have a high degree of cephalization? Their Epidermis is multi-layered? Their muscles come in three forms- striped, unscripted, and cardiac? They have well developed coeloms? They have full alimentary canals? They have hearts with three to four chambers? They have strong respiratory systems?"

"No, no, no, no, no, no, no, no, no, no, no, no, no, and no! Did you just read a chapter of a taxonomy book? They're both BIRDS! And birds' great ancestor is..." More thinking.

"Evil itself!"

"No! Eros! We need to follow the birds, and they'll take us to the bunny!" At this news, Thanatos jumped to his feet and ran towards the birds. The birds flew down the maze and were quickly followed by Prometheus and Thanatos.

The birds turned left, and so did Prometheus and Thanatos. The birds turned right, and so did they.

The birds kept going straight, they kept going straight.

The birds got confused and retraced their steps a little but got back onto the right track, and they-OK you get the idea.

[22] Alright, laugh it up.

After a few minutes, Prometheus turned right with Thanatos close behind, the birds all scattered. Laid before them was a huge room filled to the brim with carrots. Carrots were on the walls. Carrots piled on the floor. There were even carrots piled into the shape of a giant carrot. It was very lavishly decorated. Lots of variety. Orange carrots. Slightly less orange carrots. Mushy orange ones. Old orange-brown ones. Thanatos watched interestingly.

"I sense a theme," He muttered. Soon, a giant hopping sound reverberated through the room. Prometheus ducked behind a bunch of carrots while Thanatos ducked behind, well, more carrots. Carrots flew as a huge shimmering figure was cast into the light. Prometheus gasped as he saw a massive bunny made of glistening solid gold.

Squee squee squee it squeed. Prometheus slowly stood up and walked towards the bunny.

"Hi there," The bunny turned towards him rapidly. It stamped its feet and whimpered.

Mimimimimi it whimpered.

"It's okay. I'm a friend," The bunny whimpered some more as Prometheus put his hand on it's nose. It purred and sat on the ground with Prometheus rubbing it's ear.

"How'd you do that?" asked Thanatos.

"When your brother created animals, you get to know them well,"

"So, now what do we do?"

"I don't know we should-" As he was speaking, a large hole in the wall opened in the wall. A sign above it said: *Put Bunny Here.*

"And now we know," Thanatos laughed.

"Here. I'll let you," Prometheus chuckled.

"Really?" Thanatos gawked.

"Sure. You need the points. Here, I'll show you," He then showed Thanatos how to gracefully climb onto the bunny and gently ride it over to the hole. He was almost all the way there when a voice from just inside the maze echoed into the room.

"Stop!" Thanatos turned to see a dark figure, bruised and bloodied, walking up to him dragging a giant icicle.

"Pan?" Prometheus squinted at the beaten form of the nature god.

"Let me through!" He shoved Prometheus down as he walked up to Thanatos, who had already dismounted the bunny. "Now you listen. I'm capturing this bunny," he waved his icicle into the air.

"I had to fight some lowly ice giant that thought he was better than me just because he had a weapon and was sixteen times stronger than me, so I am getting these points!" He pointed the icicle at him.

"And you can't stop me," He then proceeded to hit the rabbit in the back with the icicle. The icicle shattered on impact, of course, because it hit solid gold, but still, the bunny screamed and ran into the cave. A gate closed around it as it went in and a loudspeaker boomed;

"YOU WIN!" The room morphed around them as they returned to their podiums. Hecate was standing at her podium, frowning.

"The points go to Pan," Then all the birds and obstacles came out of Tartarus and out the doors to go home.

As the last birds left, Eros dived through the hole in the spotlight and landed in the audience, and while coming into his spot, he smiled and turned, propelling his right wing into the back of Pan's head.

"Oops," he grinned. As he took his position, the wheel appeared again.

"Prometheus, you'll be spinning next," sighed Hecate. Prometheus pumped his fish into the air and enthusiastically spun the wheel. The wheel spun, and it eventually landed on a spot that said *Hide-and-Go-Erebus.*

"You'll be climbing out of Tartarus ro find Erebus, who has hidden himself somewhere dark deep in his realm!"

"Isn't Tartarus 1,578,000,000 miles deep?" Pan asked, worried.

"Do you have any plans?"

"Yes, actually. Big plans. I-"

"Cancel them all. Now go!" yelled Hecate. The room transformed around them until they were yet again standing in Tartarus. Before them was a giant cliff that seemed to stretch on for miles.[23] Rocks came tumbling down it and there were quite a few lava pits. Stretching up the rock wall were a trillion little handles for clipping rope into. Near the face of the cliff was a bunch of rope and three climbing suits. Everyone put on their climbing suits and started to get the rope.

"That's odd," said Thanatos.

"What?" asked Prometheus.

"There are four sets of rope," he replied.

[23] 1,578,000,000 miles. Weren't you listening?

"But there are only three people here."

"I guess someone will get some extra rope."

"I should get the rope. After all, it would be easier, and I need to preserve my energy to pound you both!" Pan laughed at the insult as Thanatos looked at Prometheus and Prometheus looked at Thanatos.

"Are you thinking what I'm thinking right now?" asked Thanatos.

"Oh yeah," answered Prometheus. "I am DEFINITELY thinking what you're thinking right now."

*   *   *

Once Pan was securely tied to the nearest rock,[24] Prometheus and Thanatos set out to climb the cliff. It was pretty tough. Every few seconds one of them would fall and have to climb back up, but they got used to it. At one point, Prometheus was executing a jump to a large handhold, and he missed and fell down. Thanatos helped him up and he made the jump along with Thanatos. They sat on a small outcropping, eating the lunches they had been given in their climbing suits. Thanatos looked up at the million miles to go.

"We still have a while to go," Prometheus chuckled.

"At least Pan isn't here. It's like all our troubles have been tied up with him," And then a giant rock landed three centimeters away from them.

[24] Which was not hard, as rocks were in abundance.

“Aaaahhhhhh!” screamed Thanatos. Huge boulders started raining down and Prometheus and Thanatos were thrown into the cliff wall. “What do we do!?” Prometheus tried to stay calm.

“We-*wheeze*-need to-*cough*-stay calm,” He looked around. “We need to get *there*,” He pointed to a cave a few hundred meters above them.

“How? We can’t go out there,” gasped Thanatos.

“Maybe we can,” He held up his hand, which was holding a brussel sprout sandwich.

“How will that help?”

“Tartarus hates brussel sprouts! He won’t let his boulders touch it!” He held the sandwich up and climbed back onto the path. Sure enough, the boulders swerved to avoid the sandwich and cleared a safe path. They made their way to the cave and ducked inside. Inside the cave, they sat at a small patch of dirt in front of a lava pool. Some boulders surrounded it, and it seemed to just be a normal cave, when Thanatos noticed something.

“What’s that?” He pointed to a large rock with a tiny little indentation in the middle. Prometheus ran his hand over it and realized what it was.

“It appears to be some sort of button. Should we push it? It could do something unimaginably horrible to us.” Thanatos thought about it.

“Nah. I have kind of a sixth sense about those kinds of things. Plus, what could it possibly be that would be so bad?” Prometheus looked around at the foreboding rock and the lava pit and heard the torrential screaming that was kind of the white noise of Tartarus.

"Are you serious right now?" Thanatos laughed.

"C'mon. Let's push it. The worst that could happen is us falling back to the bottom," He turned and pushed the button, which clicked into the rock. The ground began to shake as a large part of the rock wall slid open, revealing a nice, silver, great glass elevator playing some absolutely delightful music. Thanatos started walking to the elevator. "See? I told you we should've pressed it-"

BOOM!

A giant lava wave blasted Thanatos back onto the floor along with Prometheus. As he scrambled to his feet, a giant molten lava eagle flew from the pool and let out its treacherous call;

SKWEEEEEEEEE!!!! At this, three more eagles emerged from the lava. Prometheus shuttered.

"It had to be eagles. Why couldn't it have been snakes?" The eagles cawed and dive-bombed towards Thanatos, almost knocking him out of the cave. Prometheus ducked behind a rock with him, and they were able to hide from the malicious birds when they heard grunting noises coming from the entrance.

They turned as they saw a dirty and annoyed Pan struggle to the entrance. A boulder hit him straight on the head but he didn't move an inch.

"I. *Huff*. Am. *Whoof*. Going to. *Wheeze*. Flay you both alive," He then screamed and ran towards them. Before he could get to them, though, a blast of lava blew him back into the wall.

The eagle that hit him let out a call. Pan turned to the eagle.

"Well, alrighty then," He jumped out and ran towards the three eagles, fists flying, but they just blasted him back into the wall. He kept trying, but to no avail. Prometheus turned to Thanatos.

"*Psst. Let's go to the elevator,*" he whispered.

"*What about Pan?*" asked Thanatos.

"*He'll be fine. He's providing a distraction for us. Let's go,*" They hustled forward, not making a sound as they sneaked into a crevasse near them. The water in it was steaming, but it was impressive there was water in Tartarus at all.

"Time to go spelunking," Thanatos said. Prometheus giggled. Thanatos looked at him, concerned. "What is it?"

"Nothing. Nothing. It's just..." he started giggling again. "You said 'Spelunking'!" They both giggled while he and Thanatos shoved themselves into the crevice. They swam underwater and resurfaced in a room that barely had enough space for them. Even so, they wiggled through it, and eventually got out on the other side with the elevator. They began tiptoeing very quietly to the elevator.

"*Now remember,*" whispered Prometheus. "*Don't make a sound-*"

CRUNCH!

Everyone stopped what they were doing, including Pan, which is impressive considering he was right then mid-air, and looked down. Thanatos had stepped on a leaf. Pan looked at them. He looked at the leaf. Them. Leaf. Them. Leaf. Leaf. Leaf. Them. Them. Leaf. Them. Them. Them. Leaf. Leaf. Leaf. Leaf. Them. Them. Them. Them. Them. Them. Them. Them. Leaf. Leaf. Leaf. Them. Leaf. Leaf. Them. Them. Them. Leaf. Them.

"What are you doing?" he asked. Prometheus tugged his collar.

"We were... um...-RUN, THANATOS!" They ran for the elevator as Pan unfroze and sprinted for it too. Once they were both in, Thanatos started laying it on the "close door" button, but the door went as slow as ever.

"Why isn't it working!? I'm pressing the button!" he screamed.

"Don't you remember!? The 'close door' button does ABSOLUTELY NOTHING!" answered Prometheus. And so the doors closed slow as ever. Just before it closed Pan stuck his hoof in and the doors opened.

"You think you could stop me? I'll never be stopped!"

"Okay. Let's see if your face stops this rock." Prometheus threw a rock at Pan, hitting him right in the face.

He fell back.

"What was that!?" Pan ran for the elevator, but the door was already almost closed. Prometheus smiled and stuck his tongue out at Pan before they closed.

"Yes!" screamed Thanatos. "What now?"

"We wait, I guess," And they did wait.

Now, the elevator wasn't half bad. It had little handles to grab onto, and it had glass walls that you could look through to see all the rocks you were passing by. Every so often you could see a poor soul being tortured for eternity. It was fun. After almost 7.1772681[25] minutes of waiting, they reached the top. At the top was the gloomy

[25] Assuming the elevator was about ten million times faster than normal ones.

underworld, and it turns out *gloomy* was the only way to describe it. There were a few lost souls drifting around, but not much else. Thanatos sighed.

"Home sweet home. Well, no time to lose. We have to find Erebus. Then they set out to look. It was silently agreed that Thanatos would get the points, but they needed to find Erebus first. They searched for fifteen minutes with no avail, and they eventually sat down to think about it.

"What should we do?" asked Prometheus. "The elevator is making noise, which means Pan is coming up, and we'll never be able to find him in time!" He sighed.

"Wait," said Thanatos. "I just had an idea," He ran over to the nearest wall, while the elevator *dinged.* Prometheus backed toward Thanatos as he kept talking. "So the underworld is just Erebus, right?" The door began opening. "So if Erebus is the underworld, theeeen..." the door was almost halfway open. "We just need to notify him that we found him! So we just gotta..." the door was almost fully open now. "... *knock!*"

As Pan stepped out of the elevator, the dark voice of Erebos called out.**"YOU FOUND ME!"**

Thanatos pumped his fist into the air. "Yay! Yes! Back to the game show!" Thanatos stood there waiting for a minute. "Why am I not going back to the game show?"

"OH YEAH. I GUESS YOU'RE SUPPOSED TOO. BUT YOU KNOW WHAT? YOU'RE NOT."

Prometheus shivered.

"W-wa-wa-wawa-why?" he asked.

"BECAUSE... I'M BORED. WANT SOMETHING TO DO. IT GETS LONELY DOWN HERE SOMETIMES. ANYWAY, I WANT YOU GUYS TO FIGHT EACH OTHER. LAST TO FALL WINS. BYEEEEEEE"

"B-b-bu-bu-but- and he's not listening to us," stuttered Pan, who had left the elevator. He turned to the other two. "Well. A fight's a fight," He pulled out two daggers from his belt and swirled around, instantly wearing light mail armor. Prometheus spun around into a lightweight ninja suit, sporting a nunchuck. Thanatos grabbed a scythe and spun around, revealing a dark hood and cloak. The fight began when Prometheus jumped up against Pan, who blocked his attack by jumping to the side. Prometheus slid and grabbed his wrist, flipping him over to Thanatos, who tried to slash him but missed. This went on for a while, neither side gaining the upper hand. Then, Prometheus got the jump on Pan while he was fighting Thanatos and used his back as a jump board, knocking him to the ground.

"Yes!" screamed Thanatos. "In your face!"

Pan sat there grumpy and brushed the dirt off his hooves.

Prometheus walked up to Thanatos, smiling."We did it. Good job."

"Yeah. We did. We should be friends."

Prometheus chuckled."Maybe if you make humans immortal."

It was Thanatos's time to laugh. "Not in a quadrillion years."

"Then I guess I'll be seeing you later."

"I guess you will." And then Thanatos pushed Prometheus off the cliff. As he was falling, the place faded around them and they returned to the game show. Hecate was frantically pressing a button at her spot.

"Why won't it-stupid button doesn't-you're back!" She looked up at them and congratulated them for finishing the final game. "I don't know what Erebus was doing, setting you up to fight like that, but hey, it's good television. Anyway, the points go to you, Thanatos!" The points flashed on his screen as Thanatos beamed. A giant TV screen popped up above Hecate. A brown rope was shown with the word "Tie" on it. A giant rock dropped from the top of the screen. It hit the rope, breaking it in half. The rock fell out of the screen as the words on the rope read "Tie Breaker". The crowd clapped enthusiastically.

"It's the time for the ultimate Tie Breaker!" This question will make or break the competition!" announced Hecate. "Enough explaining, let's do it!" A giant podium rose from the ground in the middle of the room. It was studded with jewels and covered by a bunch of nice purple fabric. The fabric parted to show a giant golden scepter studded with blue and pink diamond. Shining at the top was a white black opal decorated the staff. Carved into the opal was a million different runes, possibly telling the story of the universe itself.

"Ooooooo," Prometheus oohed.

"Aaaaaahhh," Pan aaaahhed.

"They're gonna give you the Darwin Award for this foolishness," said Thanatos. Prometheus turned his head towards him.

"What?"

"Sorry. Force of habit. That's what I usually say when something surprising happens. Long story. Wooooow," wowed Thanatos.

"Wow indeed!" said Hecate. "This is the Scepter of the Universe."

Another round of oohs and aahs ensued.

"This signifies complete rule of the universe. I mean, Chaos could totally just take it, but he hasn't been seen since before the beginning of the universe. Get out your pencils and listen up!" The screen turned on and a voice echoed through the sound system.

"The question is... who has held the Scepter of the Universe? In the whole history of the universe? Who has held it?" Papers appeared before them and they started writing. Pan stroked his chin as the others wrote.

"And who was nex-ah yes, of course!" Pan, wrote down his thoughts. When a buzzer sounded, they set down their pencils.

"Now, before we finish, does anyone have any questions?" Zeus raised his hand. "Yes, Zeus?"

"Where did you get the scepter? I thought it was securely locked in my vault?"

"Oh. I can't tell you," There was a moment of silence. "Hestia. Anyhow, if there are no more questions, then we will begin reading the answers. Pan?" Pan straightened his papers and cleared his throat.

"Yes. I believe that the procession would be like this; Uranus, Kronos, Zeus, and me," He set down his paper and smiled. Hecate looked at him.

"Okay. Thanatos?"

"I think it went; Ouranos, Kronos, and Zeus,"

"Good. Prometheus?"

"My guess is that the Scepter of the Universe passed through; Eros, Nyx, Ouranos, Kronos, Zeus, and [redacted],[26]"

Zeus stood up from the crowd. "Wait, who?"

Prometheus looked at him. "Wouldn't you like to know."

Hecate whispered into her headset and then turned to the audience.

"The results are in. It's time to decide the winner! With a startling 100% correct our grand prize winner is, drum roll please..." a giant drum played.

Boom Boom Boom Boom Boom Boom Boom Boom Boom. The drum stopped as Hecate shouted;

"Prometheus!" The audience clapped as Prometheus walked up to her podium. He was handed a golden trophy and waved at the crowd.

"Thank you, thank you."

Hecate turned to him.

"And now for your real prize."

Eros flew over to them.

"Hey, Prometheus."

"Hey, Eros."

"How's the business?"

[26] Censored by the APPL (Association for the Protection of Prometheus's Liver.)

"Oh, you know how humans are, what with you controlling their every move. Actually, couldn't you have made them any nicer?"

"I work in mysterious ways, Titan."

"Alright, alright," Hecate continued. "Your grand prize is that you and Eros will be able to do WHATEVER YOU WANT with your competitors for the next! Six! Months!"

Pan and Thanatos came and bowed, Pan somewhat angrily. Prometheus looked at Eros.

"Really?"

"Really," Prometheus laughed.

"Nice," He turned to his servants. "Now, Thanatos, you come over here," Thanatos did as he was told. "Good. Now, Pan gets us all mango smoothies," Pan looked up at him.

"But-"

"Fresh from the blender, if you will." Prometheus commanded. Pan slouched off to get the smoothies. Thanatos smiled.

"This is gonna be a fun week![27]"

[27] You may have noticed this chapter doesn't have a lot of me in it. These are my memoirs, right? They should have me in them. Well, the truth is that writing is a hard thing to do. You know what an easy thing to do is? Write down the captions of a show while you're at a viewing party. And before you object, let me ask you this. Have you ever written an anthology of memoirs from your life? No? Then be quiet! - Author's Note.

A Normal Family Reunion

"Now that my bird-liquidizer is almost complete, I will rule the world!" shouted Κακός τύπος as his evil ray was hastily prepared by his minions. One of the minions ran up to him and saluted.

"Sir! The ray is ready to go, Sir!" Κακός let out a blood-curling cackle as he screamed:

"Fire when ready!"

The minion ran back to the ray and slammed his hand on a big red button. A giant blue ray of fire burst from the barrel of the ray, heading straight for a local murmuration of starlings. The birds tried to fly away, but there simply wasn't enough time. As the ray was just about to hit, a golden light streaked across the sky. It smacked into the fire and tumbled down, forcing it into itself. Henchmen screamed as the ray exploded violently, spraying dust and fire through the huge room. The gold thing sheltered itself by wrapping what appeared to be gold wings around itself. When it opened them, the henchman gasped as they saw its foreboding form. It was a giant man with golden wings jetting from his back and a sleeveless shirt that said ***Mondays, am I right?*** He turned to the henchman running up to him with a cold dead stare.

"Sir... Sir...!" the henchman gasped, "you are to leave these premises immediately!" The man turned to him.

"And what if I don't?" he said.

"You don't wanna know," the henchman replied.

"Try me." Immediately, a giant laser shot out from the wall and zoomed at the speed of light at the figure. Right before it reached them, though, the man flicked his wrist and a golden wing reflected the ray, sending it into the central control panel. The panel exploded in flames as minions ducked out of the way. The man started walking towards Κακός.

The evil scientist screamed at his minions: "What are you doing? Stop him!" The minions fired at him, but he just snapped his fingers and all the bullets fell to the ground. The man laughed.

"Alright." He sent feathers out that tickled the minions so much that they fell to the floor. "This has been fun." Bazookas fired at him but he grabbed the rockets with a million invisible hands and threw them towards control panels. "But I don't have the time." He grabbed Κακός by the neck and pulled him up to his eye line. "I am Eros, protector of birds. You have almost harmed many innocent starlings, and I cannot have that." Eros brought him to a ledge overlooking the smoldering ray. "And all great evil has a great punishment." Then he dropped him.

Κακός felt numb until two harpy eagles picked him up and carried him up into the sky. Eros flew up to him.

"Prepare yourself for the worst torture imaginable." The man *booped* Κακός on the nose. He instantly sprouted wings and feathers as Eros threw him into the backyard of a little suburb house a couple miles away. A little girl approached him as he shrunk into a tiny robin.

"Oh-my-gosh-mom-a-little-bird-you-know-how-much-I've-been-wanting-a-bird-and-this-is-the-perfect-opportunity-pleeeeeease!!!!!!!!"

Her mom examined Κακός.

"Okay, but YOU have to take care of it."

"OMG-I'm-take-such-good-care-of-it-and-I'm-gonna-sing-it-songs-and-play-wit h-it-and..." A primal squawk of agony emitted through the land as Eros flew out of the liar and dived through a sunroof into a Tesla Model S. He landed into the back seat and stretched his legs. His wings retracted as yawned and looked around. The car was white and grey on the inside and blue on the outside with T.V.s in the back and front showing a color play of *Oedipeus Rex*. A black-blue figure sat in front holding the steering wheel as it turned and slid through its hand.

"So you've returned. It only took you five hours." It frowned. Eros looked at it and crawled into the passenger seat.

"Nyx, I had to get my hair done for my cinematic entrance. Now let me turn on something GOOD." With a swipe of his fingers on the T.V., he turned on *Stupid and Stupider*. In the show, Stupid hit Stupider with a mallet and then Stupider hit HIMSELF with a mallet, so Stupid started dancing with a little baby emu until Stupider threw a boulder at him and it was really just the peak of comedy. Eros laughed and Nyx shook her head.

"I don't understand why you like that show. I don't even know why you like this CAR." She gestured around to the heated seats, cup holders, and little streaks of gray that just look SO cool. "A chariot would be much better." Eros scoffed.

"Nyx, the car is driving itself and could accelerate from zero to sixty miles an hour in less than a second. It changes lanes and parks itself and you've also gone four hundred miles without charging once. Plus, we have a family reunion. Gotta look good." Nyx looked at him.

"Why are you even here? Don't you have your own car?"

"Yeah, but Pan is using it to drive Prometheus and Thanatos to Orlando. After this reunion, we're going to Disney World."

Nyx frowned. "I wonder why. Pan hates roller coasters, bright lights, and fun."

The car pulled over into a gas station and Nyx filled the car up with electricity. They got back on the road again and arrived in Washburn, Wisconsin an hour later. Eros got out of the car and stretched his wings when they pulled over to turn off the super-autonomous autopilot. Nyx got out as well and waved as she greeted the sky.

"Hello, Hemera. See you at the reunion." The sky tilted into what almost looked like a nod as Eros walked into a local shop. He bought some gummy worms and started chewing on them as he walked down the street. When Nyx caught up to him, he handed her one.

"Try it. They're good." Nyx began chewing on it as Eros looked around. "Erebus said; *Once thee reacheth the lodging of meeting thee shouldst wend five miles east from the yond big tree with the purple ad'rn'd brancheth and thee shall reacheth the spoteth.*" Nyx looked at him, confused.

"He was wearing a monocle, and you know how he feels about monocles." Nyx cleared her throat as she ate the last bit of gummy worm.

"So, if we follow his directions from... here." She pointed at a tree with a branch painted purple, "We first walk the five miles..." They walked down a long road out of the town and into a forest area. The road thinned out as they walked until it was a simple dirt path. They stopped where the road abruptly ran into the side of the hill.

"That's weird," said Eros. "It just runs into the hill." He looked closely at the path and noticed that the tire tracks that lined the middle of the road stopped just before the road hit the slope of the hill. He scratched his chin and stepped onto the road. When he set his second foot on the dirt, the ground shook as a large portion of the road sank down into the ground a little bit. Nyx jumped up and ran down from the top of the hill she had been examining and looked down at Eros.

"What happened!?" Eros kicked some dirt out from his feet and looked up at Nyx.

"It appears to be a pressure plate of some kind." He looked at the size of the indention in the road and concluded; "I think we need the car." Nyx sighed and looked down the road.

"Fine. I'll go get it." She began walking away, but Eros shouted for her to wait. When she turned he held up his phone and tapped it. Several minutes of awkward silence later, Nyx looked at him. "Is something supposed to happen-" she was interrupted as the sound of squeaking tires pierced the air and a certain blue Tesla rolled up to her. Eros smiled and opened the car door for Nyx. She frowned as she sat in the passenger seat. "Still shoulda had the chariot."

They moved the car slowly onto the pressure plate and it dipped into the ground under their weight. A pole rose from the floor and opened, revealing a keyboard full of

Greek numerals. Eros reached out of his window and tapped in the password, [redacted],[28] and a door slid open in front of them. They drove in and the door closed behind them. The floor fell as they dove deeper into the hill. When the moving finally ceased, the door in front of them opened and they drove into a parking lot.

"Whoa," Eros said as he got out of the car. "Tartarus really went all out on this." He looked up at the gold-plated elevator and the peacocks running around in the spots of green grass hanging on the shaft. Nyx also got out of the car.

"What do you do for trillions of years? You learn carpeting." They walked up to the elevator and pressed the silver buttons for the top floor. Beethoven played. Eros was wearing a big giddy smile.

"I'm SO excited about the reunion! I've never been to one before, and I can't wait for all the exciting stuff!"

"Right..." said Nyx. "Exciting." They arrived, and were instantly greeted by their friends. It seemed everybody had come to the reunion. Hemera was sipping tea with Pontus as Gaia, Ouranos, Erebus, and Aether all were talking in a huddle while Tartarus was eating some chips in the kitchen. The first thing Eros noticed, though, was that everyone kept calling shoes "loafers".

"Odd." He thought. Everyone also kept calling tomatoes "To-MA-toes", even when Eros tried to correct them.

"Tom-A-to," he grumbled. He kept waiting for the exciting stuff to begin, but after an hour he sorta just sat down on a couch. While sitting down, he overheard Hemera and Nyx arguing about what the dessert would be.

---

[28] The passcode used by all immortals, and which was censored by the Commission to Protect Zeus From Cybercrime and Identity Theft.

Nyx started.

"We should get some chocolate soft-serve soon."

Hemera contested this.

"We should get vanilla soft-serve." At this point Eros overhead and whispered through his teeth.

"*Ice cream.*" Nyx continued talking.

"How about some frozen custard?"

"**Ice Cream**," Eros said in what was no longer a whisper. Hemera responded, not noticing Eros.

"We could get some orange sorbet?" Eros clutched his seat with such force that it ripped into his hands.

"SHERBERT." Nyx shook her head.

"You know what? We should just get some gelato and be done with this silly argument." Hemera agreed as Eros screamed as loud as he could;

"**ICE CREAM**!!!!!" He fell down onto the couch as Nyx and Hemera looked at him.

"What's wrong with you?" asked Nyx. "You need some ice cream."

*　　　　*　　　　*

After his outbreak, Eros settled down and moved into another room where he watched slapstick comedies and played in a box to his heart's content. He was watching

Stupid and Stupider for the hundred-and-forty-fourth time when he noticed Hemera had been watching the whole time.

"How can you watch this? It's so stupid and juvenile," she scoffed. Eros paused the movie and looked at her.

"You're stupid and juvenile." And that was that. After watching *Stupid and Stupider* sixty-five more times and making a fort with a kitchen, library, a bed *specifically* for jumping on, and an infinity pool out of a refrigerator box, Eros walked back into the main room. He talked for a while, and he even ate the gelato, which was DEFINITELY just ice cream, and he made sure to point that out several times. When it was nighttime, Nyx boarded her chariot and waved goodbye as everyone went to bed.

"Aaaaaaahhhhhhh," sighed Eros. "Rest." He piled as many pillows and stuffed animals as possible around him and laid down to sleep. He woke early in the morning and ate breakfast with Pontus as everybody got up. They talked for a while, telling each other where they were going after the reunion. When it was Eros's turn, he smiled and answered;

"I'm going to Disney World with friends." A couple of people laughed but Hemera sighed.

"Disney World is for children." And that's when Eros lost it. He screamed and kicked his foot into the table, sending it flying into the wall. He picked up a handful of strawberries and brought them down onto the floor. [29]

Eros turned to Hemera with a face full of rage. "THAT was out of line! I challenge you to a hasenpfeffer!"

"What's that?" She asked.

---

[29] It's a stress exercise.

"It's a challenge!" He answered. "Slob versus Snob!" Hemera turned her face away in disgust.

"I don't accept."

"What? Are you chicken?"

Eros smiled and put his hands on his hips and his wings into the wing pattern of a chicken. He cawed and pecked at the floor until Hemera resigned and agreed.

"Fine. What do we do now?"

Two hours later, they were outside on a table loaded with hot dogs. Eros turned to the crowd and made an announcement. "The first contest will be 'hot-dog eating'." First to eat one hundred hot dogs wins." He sat down and pulled up his plate.

"You're going down," Hemera said as she moved numerous forks into their numerous and incredibly specific places. Eros snapped on a baby bib and drank an entire bottle of soda, letting out a tremendous belch. He turned to Hemera.

"Sure I am." The bull horn went off and Eros grabbed a hot dog and ate it in three bites. He drank a bunch of water and ate another one. Hemera carefully cut a small piece of her hot dog.

"This is so exciting!" yelled Pontus. Eros threw three hot dogs into the air and flew up, catching them all in his mouth and landing back in his chair. Hemera was about to eat the piece of her hot dog when she realized that she, silly her, was using the oyster fork instead of the dinner fork. What an A-grade goofball!

"They're so evenly matched!" exclaimed Nyx. Eros stuffed a bunch of hotdogs into an empty water cup and ate it, cup and all. Hemera gently chewed and savored the flavors of the piece of hot dog. The crowd was full of exclamations of awe.

"Awesome!"

"Cool!"

"Mind-breaking!"

"Medically Impossible!"

Eros was literally eating hot dogs faster than light. Hemera began carving another piece as Eros reached for the last hot dog. He turned to his opponent.

"Ummm... Hemera?" She finished chewing and wiped her face with a napkin.

"Yes?" She looked up.

"Are you still eating your first hot dog?"

"Yes. I thought I might go on a brisk walk when I'm done."

"Oh. Okay." Eros looked at her and thought about something. Perhaps they both had different ways of living. Perhaps they could coexist. Perhaps, even, he had been eating a little TOO sloppily. He looked around at all his friends and the almost empty hot-dog plate and finally back at Hemera, still eating her hot-dog and he reached a conclusion.

"Nah." He threw the hot dog up into the air and opened his mouth so wide that it just fell into his open mouth. Cheers erupted from the crowd. "I win! I won!" Hemera scoffed and stood up.

"Fine."

"Woohoo!" Eros screamed as they moved to the next contest. It was a giant dusty ring with giant white borders. Everyone walked into the stands and Eros and Hemera walked into the ring. "Time for MMA/Sumo fighting!" The clothes on Hemera and Eros began expanding into giant puffy suits that they could bounce around in.

"What's this?" asked Hemera. Eros bounced around in his suit.

"Sumo suits." He bounced around playfully. Hemera stretched her legs and tested her new suit.

"You're dead."

Eros chuckled at the threat.

"I know you are, but what am I?"

It was an epic burn.

As they both did their stretching exercises, Pontus announced the rules.

"First to get out of the circle loses. You may use ANY. MEANS. NECESSARY. BEGIN!" The opponents started circling each other and as Hemera was shuffling around she tripped over a rock.

"Ow!" she groaned. Eros took the opportunity and pounced on her. They rolled around as Hemera struggled to get back up. She finally got up, and, harnessing her chi and bending herself into the shape of a crane, she leaped up and kicked Eros down. He groaned.

"You'll never get me out of this circle!" He jumped into the air and grabbed Hemera by the hand, throwing her up too.

"What are you doing?" she gasped, seeing them rise above the ground. "Now I can just fall away."

"Oh, you'll fall," Eros chuckled. "You'll fall hard."

"You asked for it." Hemera kicked Eros in the stomach, knocking the air out of his lungs. She took the opportunity to try and body-throw him out of the ring, but when she grabbed his legs he flipped his body back and smacked her in the face with his wings. She then pushed off him and took the opportunity to try and get to the ground, going into a pencil dive. Eros fell down too.

"Oh, no you don't." He caught up to Hemera and grabbed her, putting her into a headlock.

"You're going to use one of those samurai points of weakness to knock me unconscious, aren't you?" Hemera sighed.

"What made you think something like that?" Eros grinned, as he procured a small crowbar, which he just happened to have in his pocket, and knocked Hemara unconscious.

They landed on the ground and Eros threw her out of the ring, waking her. Pontus announced out of his megaphone the final verdict.

"Eros is the winner!" Cheers erupted from the crowd.

"Thank you! Thank you!" said Eros. "Let us go onto the final challenge."

"What now?" Hemera groaned. Eros smiled.

"A writing contest!" They walked into a dark damp room complete with stools corresponding with tables with typewriters on them. The tables were opposite from each other and each had a cup holder on them. Pontus again announced the rules.

"The rules are simple. Write something that the judges, Tartarus, Nyx, Erebus, and myself will judge. You will ALSO have to yell at some interns to get your drink,[30]

[30] Usually coffee, and even if they got your order right, you must say it is wrong.

since that is required by ancient law. Begin!" They sat down and each began typing rapidly on their typewriters.

"My book is going to be an instant classic!" Hemera smirked.

"Sure it will." Halfway through the writing, Eros looked over at his intern and drank his soda pop. He then proceeded to yell at them that the pop was half a degree off from being perfect and that they were a terrible intern and that the next time he saw them he'd flay them alive and that they were fired. The intern ran away as he went back to writing.

"Check that off the list."

Hemera screamed at her intern and had just gotten back to writing when the bullhorn went off.

"Quittin' time!" Pontus yelled as the bullhorn echoed through the room. "Present your writings!" Hemera went first. She gave her book to the Pontus, who opened it to the first page and began reading.

A Manuscript

on the

Histories

of the

Life

and

Times

of

Hemera

Vol. 1

What I Did Last Sunday

A normal day. Nothing peculiar happened.

At all.

Nothing.

I sat on the couch.

Due to the Pauli Exclusion Principle, my electrons did not fall through the couch.

That's good.

Very good.

I thought about the store.

At the store you buy such things as toiletries.

Toiletries are things like soap and shampoo.

Soap and shampoo help clean you.

Soap and shampoo are good things for you to own.

I like soap.

I also like shampoo.

I started reading a book.

It had paper.

I started on page one.

Then I went to page two.

Then three.

Then..."

Pontus stopped and looked at Hemera. "This goes on?"

She nodded. "For over a thousand pages."

Pontus looked down at the book with a face full of dread.

"I think we've seen enough here." He set down Hemera's book and picked up Eros's book.

"SEE GERALD TELEPORT

"LOOK, THEODOSIA

"LOOK, LOOK,

"SEE GERALD

"SEE GERALD TELEPORT

"TELEPORT, GERALD, TELEPORT

"THEODOSIA SEES GERALD TELEPORT

"THE END!"

Pontus looked up from the book with his mouth hanging open. He set the book down and sat down, winded. He looked around, and with a tear of joy trickling down his cheek said, "That... that was... that was the best book ever written.[31]" A quick meeting with the judges confirmed this; Eros had won the final event.

"Whoooooooo!!!!!!!!" Eros gloated as he accepted the trophy. "I win!!!!!!" He started running around in a circle with his trophy.

"Fine. What do you win?" grumbled Hemera. This stopped Eros in his tracks.

"Heh heh heh. Wouldn't you like to know."

[31] Besides this one, right?

"I would. What is it?"

"Nothing."

"Really? Nothing?"

"I didn't think about winning anything but your pride."

"Oh, good." Hemera began to walk away but Eros called her back with a smile on his face.

"But since you mentioned it..."

Three Days Later...

Eros, Prometheus, and Thanatos screamed in joy as they went down a big dip in Space Mountain. "Whoooaaaa!!!!!!!" screamed Eros as the ride skidded to a stop and they got off.

"Let's go again!" said Thanatos.

"I would, but I'm thirsty. Drinks!" Prometheus snapped his fingers to a tired satyr standing by them. He went up to them and gave them smoothies, which they drank. Eros looked around.

"Where's the entertainment?" Eros snapped his fingers and Hemera came out, doing improvised dancing with a stick.

"At least it's **good** dancing," she muttered. Eros laughed.

"Now sing the *Stupid and Stupider* song!"

Hemera fell into despair.

"Nooooooooooooooooooooooooooo!!!"

Eros Overuses Shapeshifting

Eros walked aimlessly. “What a great day,” he thought. He walked some more. Walk. Walk. Walk. Walk. Walk. Walk. Walk. He passed some minor gods looking up at the sky with adoration and fear plastered on their faces.

“What’s that in the sky?”

“It’s a bird.” One said.

“It’s a plane.” Another commented.

“It’s a fire-breathing demon!” gasped a third.

"And it's getting closer!" The first panicked.

"RUN!!!" Everyone started screaming and running for their lives.

"No, it's a bird," Eros responded. A yellow goldfinch landed on his held-out finger.

"Oh." The second god sighed. "That's no fun."

"Bye," said the third one. They walked away. Eros continued walking aimlessly. He whistled a jolly tune until his IrisPhone® rang.

Pho-pho, pho-pho, pha-pho-pho-pho, pho-pho-fe-fe-faa. Pho-pho, pho-pho, pha-pho-pho-pho, pho-pho-fe-fe-faa. He clicked the screen and put it to his ear.

"Hello?"

Hey. It's Tartarus.

"Oh. Hey. How are you?"

Not so good. The titans fashioned a megaphone out of rock. Now they yell even louder than before, and they usually yell pretty loud.

"Sorry. Why are you calling me?"

Right. You know Kampe, right?

"The jailer of the Hecatoncheires and cyclops. I thought she was dead."

That doesn't really matter in the underworld. I put her in a cell but she stole a fork from the cafeteria and dug a hole in me.

"You have a cafeteria?"

Maybe you would notice if you EVER VISITED. Not the point, not the point. She dug a hole and stood at the rim looking out into Chaos. Then Gyges walked by.

"Good ol' Gyges."

Indeed. He walked by and, noticing the hole, came into the cell to grab her. However, before he could do so, Kampe jumped into the hole.

"Oh no. A beast of doom and destruction fell and disintegrated into Chaos. My regards."

Don't interrupt. Now, when she jumped out-

"I won't interrupt anymore."

Good. Now if you would just listen to what I'm saying-

"I have learned my lesson about interrupting."

When she jumped in-

"I am truly sorry."

Hmm. When Kampe jumped out, a Stygian bird caught her and they soared away.

"So why can't you locate her?"

I have. She posted twenty pictures of her location on FacePaw®.[32] *But we need an amulet to get into her hideout. Kampe made it out of bronze and split it into six pieces, giving each type of animal's ruling party a piece.*

"Let me guess. Did she use the vertebrate types, fish, bird, mammal, reptile, amphibian, and then simplify the invertebrates into 'bugs'?"

[32] *@TheRealKampe*

Yep.

"I hate it when they do that. Can't we just go to their headquarters and demand the amulets?"

Unfortunately, Kampe planned for that. The first place she went was to Hecate's cave, demanding the secret to keeping away gods. I found Hecate blubbering and shaking, saying she was forced to give her the spell. Now the animals have a protective barrier around them that will let no gods in.

"Can we turn into animals and infiltrate their ranks?"

That's why I'm asking the master of shape-shifting. Can you do it?

"Couldn't you just use your unimaginable power to blast her hole open? Any one of us could do that, in fact."

I don't have anything going on. After a hundred billion years or so, you start looking for opportunities for fun. Can you do it?

"Maybe. A dramach or sixty million might change my mind."

Fine. But be quick. I've got a 'scared straight' thing next week with some local demons. They're getting too proud ruling the fields of punishment and whipping people all day.

"Yeah, that can do something to a person."

Yeah. Tartarus out.

Eros was left standing there and thinking when Tartarus hung up.

"Only one thing to do now." He was about to jump into the air when a small boy with glasses ran up to him.

"WAIT!" he yelled. Eros waited as he ran up, catching his breath when he got there. "Your adventure that is supposed to represent the whole animal kingdom only has the Arthropoda and Chordata phyla of the animal kingdom. There are 38 different ones that are also animals!" Eros thought about this.

"Well, those guys, those worms, and coral, and mud dragons... they're boring. The more everyday animals are much more entertaining to read about." The boy lowered his head.

"Oh. But what about the ones that aren't bilateral? Those could be interesting." Eros shuttered at the sight of a non-bilateral coral animal right next to him.

"Those guys are *freaks*. Now, if you don't mind, I have a cool cinematic shot to do." He jumped high off the ground, leaving a cloud of dust and a sizable crater behind. As he gained in altitude, Eros began to grow feathers all over his body, wrapping his wings around him as he began to slow in speed. He relaxed and fell into a free fall, spreading his wings mere inches off the ground and soaring into the air.

"Did you get that!?" he screamed at the muses, who had been theatrically filming the whole thing.

"Yep! It looks great!" said Euterpe, muse of music. "Perfectly fabuloooouuuussssss!!!!!!"

"Okay. The singing can stop." Melpomene, muse of tragedy said.

"I thought it was great!" giggled Thalia, muse of comedy. "You're always a Debbie Downer, anyway, Melpomene."

"I prefer the term 'Negative Nancy'," retorted Melpomene. As they argued, Eros glided away. He soared through the sky, letting out a loud *caw!* As he dove through a cloud and felt the cold water on his face.

"What a beautiful day." He glided along. "Absolutely perfect." He soared through another cloud. He looked around for any imperfections. Anything at all. Aaaaanything at all. Anything. At all. Anything at all. "Something better happen before I have an anxiety attack." And something did.

"Stop!" Two giant eagles flew up to him. "State your name and purpose!"

"What is going on?" asked Eros.

"Troublemakers! Some birds have taken possession of a storm cloud and are using it as a warship," they replied in union. "State your name and purpose!"

"My name is Eros! I am... selling some rocks to local birds!" he answered. "Top business leads me here!"

"Oh." Guard #1 said, disappointed that Eros had a legitimate job and he couldn't detain him. He never got to detain anyone. It just wasn't fair.

"Where are your rocks, then?" Guard #2 asked.

"Well the thing is, I'm more on, like a recon mission. Gotta find more rocks."

"Okay. Are you sure that you have a real job?"

"Yeah."

"And you would tell us if you didn't so we could detain you?"

"Definitely."

"Good luck." The eagles flew away and Eros continued flying through the sky. After a bit more flying and fifty-three and a half more security checkpoints, he saw it.

"Whoa." It was a huge cumulonimbus cloud that stretched as far as Eros could see. Birds flocked around it and dived through it as it floated in the air. Below the cloud was a large island where the birds had anchored the cloud to the ground with magic chains. The island was almost concealed by an entrancing mist around it and was well hidden from any outside onlookers. A patrol was placed around the cloud, and when they saw him they went to meet Eros.

"Who are you?" they asked.

"I am Eros. I have come to scout for rocks. It's rock season and I work on commission, so you know how it is.."

"Hmm. How do we know you're not a spy? Birdonia will not stand against oppressors as the war for freedom has just begun. All hail Birdonia!"

"Birdonia! Birdonia!" chanted the others.

"I am no spy. As astute as you are, though, how could you possibly let trade into your glorious state while snuffing out all the spies at the same time?" Eros asked.

"If you wish to pass, you shall swear on Eros's wing. No decent bird would break that oath." Eros's eyes perked up.

"Yeah. Yeah. I swear on Eros's wing"

"Alright. You may pass. All hail Birdonia!"

"Birdonia! Birdonia!" Eros flew away from them, diving through a hole in the cloud and flying down to the island, landing in a bustling market.

"This looks normal." He looked around at the place and it looked like a normal trade hub. The ground was covered in sticks from the bushes and small trees of the island. Small nests were to the side of the path, with birds in them carrying goods to be traded. It was perfectly normal. "They must have some kind of valuables I can trade for the amulet." He eavesdropped on one of the trades to find out what it was.

"Hey, Sammy." A small but fast bird said. "I got you some grubs." She pulled some grubs out of her feathers and put them in a little hole in front of Sammy.

"So few?" Sammy asked. "I expected more from you, Samantha."

"Quality, not quantity." Samantha responded. "I got these from the other side of the island. By the good holes. And they've never been frozen. They are fresh from my feathers. A good meal is guaranteed."

Sammy laughed.

"You always have the best, Samantha. I'll give you five grapes for it."

"Really? Only five? Would, be, a, shame, if, I, took, my, business... *elsewhere*." With each word, she took out another grub from her feathers.

"Well, I have been working very hard. Fine. I'll give you a rat."

"NOW we're talking! Is it from the northern plains?"

"Dream on. It's from the south plains."

"Hmm." Samantha quickly settled down. "Okay. I'll take it."

"Coming right up." He flicked his head into the air and began jamming it up into the sky, making a gross sound until a rat finally jetted out of his mouth. "Here you are." It landed with a *plop* at Samantha's feet.

"Thanks, Sammy." Samantha said, "*I hear the king only eats rats from the northern plains.*" she murmured.

"Rats from the northern plains, ehh? I better get some of those rats." Eros flew off to get some of those rats. As he flew, he noticed a beautiful green area of rolling grass, dotted with small holes and crevices perfect for rats. But when he dived down to the edge of it, he was startled to see that a giant rock wall encircled it. He walked down to some huge bronze gates locked on the other side, with a mop[33] slid into some holes on each door on the other side. A small plover boy was playing with some rocks when Eros flew up to the mop and tried to grab it. He quickly sprang to his feet[34] and blocked the entrance.

"No, no, sir! You can't go in there!" they yelled, worried. Eros scoffed.

"Why not?"

"Because that's the northern plains! They belong to the king! Birds who trespass get be-winged!"

"Hmm. I can risk it."

"No, they'd catch you before you moved a claw!"

"There's NO way in?" The little bird seemed taken aback by the question and immediately got defensive.

"No! Of course not! I mean, no. Of course not."

"NONE at all?"

---

[33] Birds don't have much upper body strength, okay? A mop slid into some holes on each door on the other side is like Fort Knox to them. They even have a saying; "You want to break into ________? Well, why don't we just break into a door that's blocked by a mop, which was slid into some holes on each side of the doors?" The other bird would then be devastated, and they would run away in embarrassment, filled with terrible shame.

[34] An expression which doesn't pair well with birds.

"Well... there is one. But it's waaaaay too risky!"

"Really. Perhaps I can make it worth your while." He turned away and channeled some of his power into his claw. It formed and morphed into a diamond prism, with speckles of platinum and rose quartz. He turned around and plopped it at the feet of the snowy plover.

"Whoa." He stared at the gem as it twinkled in the sunlight. "Follow me." They walked around the wall to the back. Somebody had wedged a small drift board in between some rocks and a small tunnel was open.

"Where does it lead?"

"An old rat-hole. But I must warn you, the rats are very sneaky. You'll never find them."

"Got it. Sneaky rats. Anything else?"

"The tunnel is too small. You couldn't possibly squeeze in."

"Hmm. Well-hey look over there!" The plover boy turned and Eros shrank, becoming about the size of a robin. He turned back around.

"I didn't see anything-hey I could swear you were bigger a few seconds ago." He looked at the newly-smaller Eros. "Now you're like, perfectly sized. Huh." Eros hopped up to the hole and turned back to the plover.

"Thanks."

"You're welcome." He flew away and Eros walked into the hole.

"Alright." He trotted down the tunnel. It winded left and right and right and left, going from hole to hole as it went along. Eros could see light as he was walking along when a rock rolled out from a side path and blocked his way. A giant spider crept in front of him, flexing its many legs as it got closer and towered over Eros.

Whooooo daaaaares? Its eyes looked at Eros and licked its lips.

"I am Eros, and I have come to get some rats from the northern plains."

Thissssss is myyyyyy path. None shall crossssss. She hissed in Eros's face. *For I am Ungoliant, bird-eating spider!* She raised her legs in the air, laughing maniacally, although spiders can't laugh, so it sounded like someone letting the air out of a balloon, mixed with coughing.

"Ungoliant? Isn't that from Tolkien?" Ungoliant turned to look at him.

What? No. She scooted her copy of the *Quenta Silmarillion* out of the way.

"And doesn't the bird-eating spider live in southern Africa? This is the middle of the Atlantic." A bead of sweat rolled down Ungoliant's cheek.

It doesn't matter! What matters is I'm about to eat you!

"You can keep telling yourself that, but I have to go."

Mwa ha ha! You'll never leave alive!

"Aww. That's too bad-what's that over there?" Ungoliant turned to look.

I don't see anything-hey where'd you go!? Eros had turned into a Bee Hummingbird and was making a run for the rock.

"Bzz," he buzzed. Ungoliant's eyes darted around, looking for him. Finally, she spotted him nearly to the rock.

There you are! She raised her leg and smashed it against the ground, nearly crushing Eros.

"Bzzzz!!!" Eros was going for a small crevice he could use to bypass the rock and get in.

You're not getting away from me! She punched the rock, causing the crevice to start to collapse in on itself. Eros jumped in to try and get through before it closed when Ungoliant jumped at him, her mouth open and ready to swallow him whole.

"Bzzzzzzzz!!!!!!!!!!" Eros was almost in Ungoliant's mouth when he slipped through, causing her to land on her face.

Nooooo!!!!!! Ungoliant screamed as Eros flew away. He looked around and realized he was in a small, dirty hole in the ground. Dirt and rocks lined the walls and sunlight peaked in from some leaves covering the ceiling. A small nest of sticks was laid out in front of him.

"This is kinda peaceful," Eros noted as he stood on a long root protruding from the rock. Just then, the rock blocking the hole began to be taken. A muffled hiss of anger emitted from the other side. "Time to go." Eros quickly buzzed away.

Above the leaves, the ground opened into the flourishing plain Eros had seen on his way over. Eros flew over the holes and peeked in, but each time one of them was occupied, there would be a little blur of fur and the rat would be off and running down the plain.

If there were multiple rats in a hole, and even if they were mostly sleeping, one would give off a *squeak* and they would all bolt into different directions.

"I need some way to trap them." Eros thought, and he thought and he thought and he thought and he thought thought thought. And he thought some more until *ding!*

he figured it out. "I'll bait them with a doll, but I'll cover it with honey and they'll get stuck! I'm a genius!"[35] Eros quickly sewed up a giant life-sized doll of an apple pie, which is kind of hard to do when you're a hummingbird the size of a quarter. He then smeared honey all over the plush and hid behind some bushes. Sure enough, it didn't take long for a small mischief[36] of rats to notice it.

Squeak squeak! (Looketh at that beautiful pie, Ecthelion!) squeaked one rat.

Mmmph squick! (I do say it is a beautiful sight, Glorfindel!) squeaked Ecthelion.

Cheep chip! (Silence! I, your king Fingolfin, demand that we go and eat it!) squeaked a very kingly rat.

Hess hiss! (For Gondolin!) hissed Glorfindel.

Hiss! Hiss! (Gondolin! Gondolin!) chanted Ecthelion. The three and their friends ran for the pie, jumping on it and realizing too late it was sticky.

Chirp chirp! (What is this foul contraption!?) yelled Fingolfin. *Hiss squeak!* (Release us!).

"I'm afraid I can't do that," said Eros, flying up to the pie.

Squeak chirp! (A Balrog! We are surely doomed!) screeched a rat pup, nearly fainting.

---

[35] Any affiliation to persons or events or that one time that Ananse did the exact same thing that one time in African folklore is purely coincidental. All rights reserved.

[36] Which is the correct term for a group of rats, and not a pack, plague, colony, murder, or a swarm. So be quiet.

Hiss! Mmmph! (Never! Let me have a go at him!) said Glorfindel. He tried to wiggle out from his trap but was unsuccessful. Eros pulled out a sack from his wing and put the pie in it.

Squeak squeak! (Quiet, fool! This Balrog has wings!) screeched Fingolfin. (Balrogs having wings is totally not canonical in any way and was only popularized by Peter Jackson's "Lord of the Rings: The Fellowship of the Rings!*)*

Squick! (No! They would never make such a terrible misinterpretation!) yelled Glorfindel.

Squeak! (Really!) yelled Fingolfin. *Squeak!* (A more accurate interpretation would be a man of pure darkness, surrounded by flames, holding two flaming whips! On another point, all three balrogs have died by some sort of fall!)

Squeak! (Not Durin's Bane! He fell to the depths of Moria with Gandalf and survived!)

Squick! (Yes, he did! First of all they landed in water, which extinguished the Balrog's flames for a time!)

Squeak? (Wouldn't the balrog's huge body have splashed through the water, creating a wave and drowning Gandalf?)

Squeak! (The Balrog was the size of a man!)

Squick!? (WHAT!?)

Squeak! (Yes! Anyway, Gandalf and Durin's Bane fought up to the peak of Zirakzigil for three straight days! Finally, Gandalf pushed him off the peak, so he fell and died, by way of fall!)

Squick! (How did Gandalf gain the power to do that!? He was but a low-level Maiar!)

Squeak! (I could tell you for several hours how!)

Squick! (Do it, then!)

Squeak! (First of all...)

"Guys, I'd love to debate this all day, but I have places to be," interrupted Eros. He began closing the sack.

Squeeeeeaaakkk!!!! (Noooo!!!! Gondolin!!!!) yelled Ecthelion as the sack closed.

Eros flew to the king with the sack in his wing. The king resided in a large tower that sprouted out of the side of the island. It was only accessible by a small window at the top that led into a huge throne room. Eros tried to fly in stealthily, but he was caught by guards. They grabbed him by the wings and brought him before the king.

"Who dares approach me without invitation?" The king was a bright gold eagle covered in jewelry; he wore a solid platinum crown and around his neck was a piece of solid bronze.

That must be the amulet, thought Eros.

"Answer me, peasant," ordered the king.

"I am but a humble tradesman. I have come to make a trade with you."

"HA!" laughed the king. "What could you possibly have of value?"

"Oh, just all of your favorite rats." He pulled the pie out and showed the king.

"What? How did you get those?"

Eros laughed.

"Not important. What is important is my reward."

The king nodded his head.

"Yes! Anything! Ask and you shall receive!"

"I want your amulet."

The king froze and thought about his offer. Then he smiled slyly.

"Of course."

Eros shrugged and began to remove the rats from the pie. They walked around sickly but slowly gathered into a large group.

"And now for my payment."

At this, the king cackled.

"Guards, leave us." The guards flew out the window, leaving just the king and Eros.

"Umm… are you getting to the reward-giving part?"

"No, you insolent fool. You will never get my precious amulet." He poked his wing at Eros's chest, which wasn't easy because, again, he was roughly the size of a quarter. "It was given to me by the great Kampe, and I plan on having it forever." They backed up to the window. "I'll throw you in the sea and your foolish hummingbird heart won't be able to take it."

"I see one flaw in your plan, though," answered Eros.

"Oh, yes?" laughed the king. "What's that?"

"My foolish hummingbird heart beats at 1,260 beats per minute." He ran forward, grabbed the amulet, and flew out the window before the king could react. Eros startled flying away as the king staggered back.

"You'll never get away! I'm faster than you!" He was about to leap after him when he heard the pitter-patter of tiny feet behind him. He turned to see rats armed with some twigs and pebbles.

Squeak squeak! (Attack! For Gondolin!) yelled Fingolfin.

Squeak squeak! (Kill the Balrog!) added Ecthelion.

The rats arrayed themselves into an arrow shape and attacked, hitting his feet and back. They then divided into halves and the rats in the back formed a tower, climbing onto the king's face and body.

"What? Nooooo!!!" screamed the king as Eros flew away.

* * *

After safely depositing the amulet in a safe at his house, Eros dived into the Pacific Ocean and hit the water with a *splash!* He grew golden flippers and dorsal fins as he sank into the water. When he finally hit the ocean floor, he had grown into a shimmering, fully-grown dolphin. Eros checked out his new features, satisfied.

"Alright! I'm a fish!" he exclaimed, proud. As soon as he said that, a small fish with glasses swam up to him.

"Actually, dolphins are mammals."

"Quiet." Eros swam away and explored the beautiful sandplain he was in. He looked up and could see the sun shining in through the beautiful blue water. "I could stay here for hours," he said. The small fish swam up again.

"Actually, you'll have to go up every eight to ten minutes. You know, to get air. As you are a mammal."

"I said quiet!" Eros swam around for a bit until he saw another dolphin on the horizon. Or, not the horizon. He saw another dolphin, like, six hundred and fifty feet ahead of him.

"Hello!" said the dolphin when it got closer.

"Hello! I am a dolphin!" said Eros, definitely a dolphin.

"Me too! Being a dolphin is the greatest!" They high-flippered.

"Well, fellow dolphin, my name is Eros," chirped Eros.

"My name is Bobobobobobob. But you can call me Bob."

"Great. Take me to your ruler."

"Oooh. Are you doing an alien impression? I wanna play!" Bob stuck his flippers in the air and started moving like a robot, even though they were playing aliens. "Bleep blorp bleep blorp." Eros sighed. They played 'aliens'[37] for another couple of minutes until Eros stopped.

"Alright. Seriously. I need to talk to the ruler of all fish." Bob settled down.

[37] *cough* Robots *cough*

"You mean Queen Queenfish? Her palace is right over there." Eros turned his head to the left and sure enough, a glittering coral palace was right there, with lush anemone fields and fish all over.

"How did I not notice that before?" Eros wondered.

"Literary magic."

"Ah, of course. Can you take me there?"

"Sure!" Bob swam to the palace and Eros followed him. When they reached the palace, they were stopped by two guards. They were large catfish and they carried long staffs of coral with threatening anemones on top. They thrust their make-shift spears at the dolphins and stopped them.

One of the guards hit his spear on the ground.

"Security check!" They overwhelmed the dolphins and quickly patted them down. One grabbed a donut from on top of Eros's blowhole.

"What's this!?" he screamed in Eros's lower jaw, which received sound.[38]

"It's a doughnut. With sprinkles."

"Did you say it's a dough-BOMB with POISON sprinkles!?"

"No."

"Good. Have a nice day." The guards patted down Bob and gave them each 'I was successfully frisked by guard #1,236,738,438 and guard #1,236,738,439' stickers. They then let them through and the dolphins were in the palace. The two immediately swam

[38] Look it up if you don't believe it. I dare you.

into the throne room and saw the queen, a regal fish with another bronze shard tied around her head. She stared down regally[39] at them. Bob nudged Eros's fin.

"Bow." Eros bowed, which was awkward because he pretty much leaned forward and hit his head on the floor.

"Thank you," said the Queen. "What message do you bring?"

"My queen, I only ask for your goodwill," answered Eros. "I have been sent by Delphin, god of dolphins, to receive a boon."

"A boon. I do remember owing Delphin a dollar or something.[40]"

"Yes. Delphin asks for the amulet you wear on your neck." The queenfish looked at Eros with surprise on her face.

"This? This was given to me by that *beast* Kampe. I would give it gladly, but I'm afraid that Delphin should probably ask for something else."

"What is it?" Eros asked.

"If I gave this away Kampe would scale, gut, and filet me. Delphin will just have to ask for something else."

"Our lord Delphin explicitly asked for the amulet."

" I have spoken my answer. Run back to Delphin and tell him to ask for something else. I am the richest fish in the ocean. I can surely give him a dollar back.

---

[39] Did I mention she was quite regal?

[40] That was true. Delphin never let anything go. Whenever Eros met him, he was all; "That one dolphin owes me a favor" and "That queenfish owes me a dollar that she STILL hasn't paid. It's shameful."

And don't even think about stealing it. My security system is the most secure in the whole ocean. Delphin will have to come ask for himself."

"We shall ask him."

"Good. Now I'm going to put this into my safe. Goodbye!" She swam off with a final glimpse back at the two dolphins. Eros turned to Bob.

"C'mon. Let's go."

"Where are we going?" asked Bob.

"To break into the Queenfish's safe."

"But that's bad. That's her personal security system. We shouldn't intrude."

"As dolphins, we must obey the will of our Lord Delphin. Now come on."

"Fine. But if we get arrested, I'm pinning it all on you."

* * *

They crept into the safe room, which was a long dark rectangle covered in security cameras. At the end was a big bank safe with a keypad next to it. Bob frowned.

"This feels like stealing," he thought out loud.

"It's not stealing. It's borrowing," Eros assured.

"Really? Are we giving what we take back when we're done with it?"

"No."

"Do we have permission?"

"Yes."

"Then why is the security on?"

"Well... I guess we technically don't have 'permission'. I mean, it's not like we're bandits or cat burglars."

"Then why did we put hats on our dorsal fins so our prints wouldn't be 'traceable if cops investigated'?"

"Because it's more fun this way. C'mon, we gotta disable the security cameras."

"Hmm..." They set to work. Bob distracted the cameras by dancing around as Eros made a small EMP out of paper clips and lint. When he finished he quickly swam up to Bob.

"The EMP is ready." Bob looked a little worried at the news.

"A EMP? Will that hurt anyone?"

"Nah. This is just a very short-range EMP. It shouldn't hurt anyone."

"Oh. That's goo-"

"Unless I made a *very* simple mistake. Then it could cause mass destruction in Main and the Iberian peninsula," Eros added. Bob shook with worry.

"Well, at least it's not a weapon of mass destruction-"

"I guess that's why they call it a weapon of mass destruction," Eros interrupted. "But I would never make such a *simple*, so *very* simple mistake..."

"I guess I trust you-"

"...a so *incredibly* simple mistake." Bob sighed.

"I guess you're right."

"Of course I'm right."

Eros clicked the EMP on and all the electronics in the room went down. They swam forward and just as they were about to get right in front of the safe, they found a bunch of silvery-invisible tripwires blocking the way.

"Rats. Tripwires," Eros observed. He was observant like that.

Bob looked confused. "Shouldn't the EMP have deactivated any traps?"

"The EMP only targets things that were on at the time. Anything off-" He tested one wire by prodding it with his fin and spikes shot out of the floor, impaling anything that was there. "-still works." He thought about the problem for a second.

"I guess if we very carefully swam through-" Eros was interrupted by the sound of Bob jumping through the water, spinning and twirling until he'd landed at the end. Eros stared at Bob. Bob stared at Eros.

"I do gymnastics on the weekends."

"I can see that." Bob hit a button on the side of the wall. The button snapped all the wires back into the wall. Eros swam up to the safe, their final obstacle. To the bottom left of the huge door was a small wooden keyboard with 10 numbers on it. It was entirely automated by pulleys and gears, so the EMP didn't take it down. Bob swam up to the keyboard and examined the numbers.

"If we put in use modern cryptology onto the birthday theorem of '09, we should be able to-"

"Swim away, please," interrupted Eros. Nothing happened as Bob swam away, puzzled.

"Why did you have me-"

"Cover your ears." Bob covered his ears and Eros placed a small box next to the safe and opened it, revealing a silvery substance inside. He swam away quickly.

"What's in the box?" Bob asked.

"Pure sodium-"

A loud BANG! shook the room and the front of the safe was blasted open. They turned to see a raging flame destroying all evidence of the cause. "-and Greek Fire." They swam into the safe and started looking for the amulet.

"What's so special about this amulet anyway?" Bob asked.

"Oh, it's...a family heirloom. For Delphin." Eros found the amulet and put it on top of his blowhole.

"Okay. I trust you completely." They swam out of the vault and left the palace, finally meeting back out in the sand plain.

"Well, I gotta go," Eros said. "I have other things to do."

"Aww, so soon? But I just met you!" Bob responded, bummed.

"Sorry. But here. Thanks for the help." He pulled out five giant pears he had taken nonchalantly from the vault and gave them to Bob. Then Eros swam to the surface and left Bob examined his newfound riches. Eros only heard him mutter one thing before he was out of earshot.

"Still feels like stealing."

*   *   *

After depositing the fragment in his safe, Eros wondered how he should locate the amphibian headquarters. He only knew one amphibian, Sal the Salamander, but Eros guessed that calling him was a start. He called him.

Pho-pho, pho-pho, pha-pho-pho-pho, pho-pho-fe-fe-faa. Pho-pho, pho-pho, pha-pho-pho-pho, pho-pho-fe-fe-faa.

After a few seconds, someone finally picked up.

"Hello?"

Hello.

"This is Eros."

Oh, hey man. How's the business?

"You know how it is. How's the small body of water?"

It's great. Flies are bountiful.

"Good. Now, no reason, but do you know who is the federal leader of all amphibians? Again, no reason."

Why, the all-knowing axolotl of course. In Mexico City.

"Thanks. See you later."

Wait a minute. I've yet to tell the story of what happened last Tuesday.

"I really have to go."

It was a beautiful day. The flowers were blooming. The sun was shining. The feast of FrögFešt was just hours away. But it was all about to change. Evil-Sal, the terrible doppelgänger of myself was plotting-

"I really have to go."

-evil. In a great flash of darkness he- A shrill voice interrupted Sal's story on his side of the call.

SAL! What are you doing with the emergency phone?

Mom, I'm talking to my FRIENDs!

You don't have any friends! Except for that weird 'Eros' guy.

He's the second most powerful being in the universe[41]*, MOM!*

Excuses, excuses! Come. Maybe he can watch soap operas with me. The phone moved to a room where the TV was blaring.

"That's my cue to leave."

Sal's voice came screaming to the phone. *NO, EROS YOU GOTTA HELP ME-*

Eros hung up. "I guess I'm going to Mexico City." He quickly swam a couple thousand miles to the mainland, then hitched a cab to a small parking lot in a Mexico City Park. Eros walked up to the canal and stood in front of it.

"Here we go." Eros jumped super high into the air and in midair became a beautiful axolotl. He fell down and, staring straight at the water, was caught in a net.

[41] The first is the all-knowing axolotl, of course.

"What a cool axolotl." A Mexican man tapped Eros on the head. Eros fumed with rage because that was exactly what Eros did when he found an axolotl. Another man walked up to him.

"Where'd you find it?"

"It just dropped out of the air! Weird, right?"

"Weird. Load it in the truck." Man #1 walked to a large, white, unmarked truck and opened the back, revealing that it was filled with water tanks. Eros was dumped into a small aquarium and Man #2 closed the doors. A dim light flickered on and off overhead and Eros could see more axolotls in their own tanks. Music blared in the front of the car but Eros could still hear the men talking.

"Where are we taking this batch?" Man #2 asked.

"The usual. To the veterinarian and then the animal rescue place for them to be freed in the wild." There was a long silence. Then Man #1 burst out laughing and so did Man #2.

"Good one."

"Yeah. We're actually taking them to daycare. No sand fighting today."

"'*Sand fighting*'?" thought Eros. "'*DAYCARE*'?' I gotta get out of here!" He swam around his aquarium, scrutinizing every inch of it. It was a small space, packed with junk. A thin layer of sand covered the bottom, and the sides were covered in muck and algae. An empty soda can was lying in the far right corner. Eros shivered. "Why is it so cold in here? It's 80 degrees outside!"

"Axolotls are supposed to live in water at 59 to 65 degrees."

"What? Who said that?"

"I did." A regal blue axolotl walked out from the shadows

"How come I didn't notice you before?"

"The shadow line is really dark. Look." He stepped back into the shadows and he disappeared. "I'm gone." He stepped back into the light. "And I'm back." He kept stepping back and forth. He stepped into the shadows. "Gone." He stepped out of the shadows. "Here again." In. "Where'd I go?" Out. "Here I am." You get the gist. After about an hour of that Eros finally stopped him.

"Okay. How do you know that?"

"I used to be the royal knowledge man. My name is Gill. I used to brag that I knew all the information in the world and had once visited the..." suspenseful music played, "...local library. Then it was discovered that I only knew the facts I knew because I once had a couple dinners with the all-knowing axolotl when I opened a restaurant and she came."

"So you were fired?" Gill laughed. His gills bounced around his face as he shook his head.

"No. They just arranged more dinners. The queen is pretty hard to talk to and I make just the BEST bug soup. Anyway, while I was swimming to the local bug pocket, I was captured by those men. I've been here for weeks, avoiding being caught. I've almost been sent to daycare a few times. I thought I would try for the sand fights next time. Daycare is the worst torture there is."

"Don't you want to get out of here?"

"Sure, but it's impossible. We need water to breathe."

"I thought we were amphibians."

"We are."

"Then aren't we supposed to be able to breathe air, then?"

"Nope. We live our whole lives underwater." There was a long pause. Eros looked around and noticed a large metal pipe that administered all the water to the aquariums. The power box for the pipe was stuck on the wall with duct tape and the main pipe ran right above his tank. He looked at Gill.

"Say...just hypothetically, if someone broke the main pipe, the truck would flood with water, right." Gill looked at him questionably.

"That's not very hypothetical. Besides, it's made of metal. You could never break it."

"Well, even if it's highly improbable that it will happen, if I truly *believe* I can, then I can do it."

"You weigh less than a tenth of a kilogram."

"I still *believe*."

"It's your funeral." Eros swam to the top and surveyed the pipe. It was loosely constructed and badly designed, with small pieces of tape holding it together.

"Hmmm." He found a spot near the middle of the tank and aligned himself to hit a large piece of tape. He then harnessed some of his godly power and jumped out of the water, spinning his gills so fast that they turned into a saw, cutting into the pipe and letting a huge gush of water pour out of the pipe. Eros surfed the wave back into the aquarium on a pebble and Gill frowned watching him.

"Lucky shot." The water filled the aquariums to their brinks and the truck began to flood. Murmurs of confusion erupted from the other axolotls.

What's going on?

Did we fall back in the river?

Did the river fall back onto US? The water began to slosh around, attracting the attention of the men in the front.

"What's going on?" asked Man #1.

"Is that water sloshing!?" exclaimed Man #2

"It is! The water pipe broke!" The truck careened into the break-down lane as the back doors of the truck flung open, splashing water all over the road they were on.

"Aaaah!" Man #1 screamed.

"C'mon! C'mon!" They ran to the back as all the axolotls frantically tried to swim outside. A section of the Mexico City canal was right by the road, and if they just swam into the drainage ditch, they would be free to go.

"Oh my gosh, the axolotls are-look at those cars hydroplaning!" Both of the men laughed as cars passing them swerved around dangerously.

"Now!" yelled Eros as they swam for the canal. The men diverted their attention from the ensuing wreckage just in time to freak out.

"Get them!" shouted Man #1, AKA Captain Obvious. Man #2 grabbed at an axolotl but it slipped through his hands.

"They're too slippery!" noted Captain Obvious's sidekick, Already Assumed Andrew. The axolotls quickly swam across the moist ground and headed down the small hill leading to the canal. The men screamed in frustration as the entire truck of axolotls escaped as they could only watch. When they reached a small atoll, Gill swam up to Eros.

"Nice work."

"Now that we're free, can you take me to the royal palace?" Eros asked him.

"I suppose." They swam deep underwater to a huge stone palace immersed in seaweed. After a number of security checks, they were about to walk into the throne room, a large, glistening room filled with gems when a man wearing a yellow and red uniform abruptly stopped them.

"Where are *you* going?" Eros looked at him in confusion as Gill sighed.

"*The one day that he persists. The one day.*"

"Who are you?" asked Eros.

"I'm the royal customs enforcer. There are traditions to be upheld and *I* am the one to uphold them."

"So you're *still* doing this, Gary?"

"Do not use my mortal name during work, *Gill*," Gary answered accusingly. "Where have *you* been the last few weeks?"

"Trapped in a highly-illegal endangered species trade. What about you? Still living in your grandmother's basement?"

"Not the point. Now, before you are to enter the throne room, we must perform some short activities to ensure you are ready."

"If we must." They then began an elaborate set of customs including dressing in fancy clothes, taking a four-hour class on proper etiquette, and being taught and tested on the entire history of amphibians. After their 50th test on desert rain frogs, Gary decided they were ready to go in.

"I hereby decree that you are ready to go in, no matter how much of a personal *annoyance* I may have."

"Finally!" Eros sighed as he ruffled up his clothes and randomly laid a leaf on top of his head. "Sure was *cool* when *y'all* amphibians blinked into existence 30 years ago!"

"No! Everything you just did was complete... *sputter* just complete... GARBAGE compared to what I just taught you!

"Oh, give it a rest, Gary," interrupted Gill. "You had the most obsolete job in the government when I was kidnapped and you have the most obsolete job in the government now. Nobody cares." Gary tried to look calm and collected but it was clear the insult had mentally destroyed him.

"I'm going to pretend not to be hurt by that. Of course, bill 16AC: B//6; 'The April Fools Bill' of April 1st, 1739 prohibits hiding feelings, so I *will* be hurt by it." He started choking up. "*That... was the MEANEST thing I have EVER, and...*"

"Oh, can you just get on with it?" scoffed Eros.

"Fine. You may enter."

"Finally." The doors opened to reveal a beautiful court filled with elite amphibians dancing around. There was a large air pocket and a small beach above the area where the court members of other[42] species could breathe. Atop a golden throne sat a huge pink axolotl with a very aged but wise face.

"Who are you?" she asked.

---

[42] lesser

"I am Eros, my lady, and this is Gill."

"Ah, Gill," she responded. "I was wondering when you would be back."

Before Gill could say anything, Eros decided to break up the conversation. "If you don't mind, I would like to skip the pleasantries and just get to my reason for being here."

"If you wish."

"I would like your bronze amulet."

"The one I received from Kampe? Certainly. If you can answer me this riddle."

"Anything."

"*Don't,*" whispered Gill. "*The all-knowing axolotl's riddles are notoriously hard.*"

"Trust me. I've got this." Eros turned back to the giant axolotl. "Administer the riddle, please."

"As you wish. You have been stranded on an alien planet. The only way off is to please the three local rulers: Arr, Eff, and Tee. You must give them each a precious amulet that corresponds to each lord. The problem is that you don't know which is which. To figure this out, you can ask three yes or no questions to any one lord. A plaque placed by you tells you that Tee's answers are always true, while Eff's answers are always false. Arr's answers are random. Just to add to this, you know that the words 'Ulu' and 'Ozo' mean 'yes' and 'no', but you don't know which corresponds to the other. What questions do you ask to ensure you get off the planet safely?"

"*See? I told you it was hard.*" Eros thought about the riddle for a bit. He pondered it deeply, wrote down a few things, watched several Ted-Ed videos on ViewTube, and finally answered.

"I got it. Ask the alien in the middle; 'If I asked whether the overlord on my left is Arr, would you answer 'Ozo'?' If you are questioning Arr, the answer is meaningless, if you are asking one of the others, they will reply both in the same way. Through selective reasoning, you can deduce that the alien on the right is not Arr if the aliens answer 'Ozo' and that the alien on the left is not Arr if they answer 'Ulu'. Now you go to the lord you have determined isn't Arr and ask them; 'If I asked you 'are you Eff?' Would you answer 'Ozo'?' If they say 'Ozo', they are Eff. If they say 'Ulu', they are Tee. Then ask the newly named alien 'If I asked you 'Is the center alien Arr' would you answer 'Ozo'?' By their answer you can tell if the center alien is Arr or not. Give them each the correct amulet and leave. There." Gill stared at him in amazement.

"*How did you do that?*" Gill asked

Eros smiled.

"It's a really easy logic puzzle." The all-knowing axolotl interrupted them.

"Correct. You may have the amulet." They gave Eros the amulet.

"Thanks." He quickly said goodbye to Gill and swam away. There was silence in the court.

"It wasn't *that* easy a logic puzzle." Gill frowned.

*   *   *

After securing that amulet, Eros headed to the Amazon Rainforest. A while ago, he went to a lizard convention because those simpletons had been throwing around accusations that dinosaurs were reptiles! They were birds! Eros's domain! Dinosaurs were HIS! Anyway, Eros was yelling at some idiot snakes when he saw a map of their stupid lizard kingdom. The Amazon Rainforest was its capital and, when he was later kicked out for punching a snake in the head, Eros swore that he would head right there and show those guys what's what. Of course, that had been six years ago, but there had been a Stupid and Stupider marathon and he forgot. As Eros fell through the sky, he changed into a small gold dart frog and dropped onto a tree. He climbed down and started across the swampy murk of the rainforest ground. He was jumping around in the mud when he heard the hissing of a snake behind him.

"Who's there!?" He whipped around to find a large green snake looking him over.

"I am Sylvessssster. Whooo are youuuu?"

"I'm Eros."

"Well, Eros. This is myyyyyyyy swamp! I do not like tressssspasssers!"

"I'm just leaving."

"I do not like tressssspasssers who lie! You are with them! You simpleton!"

"Did you just say *simpleton* without slurring your words? Do you snakes just do that "s" thing to impress people?"

"Noooooooooo! Whyyyyyyy would we do thhhhhhattttt? If we diiiiiid, everyone elsssssssse would have to be stupid idiotssssss, though!"

"There! You did it again! With *stupid*!"

Sylvester began sweating profoundly.

"Letsssssssss talk about sssssssomething elssse!"

There was a short silence as a puddle formed from Sylvester's nervous sweat.

"'Them'?"

"Yes, you scuuuuum! Them! They built their little hovel by the big log to the east. Right on my land!"

"Who?"

"Those idiot snakes! Foooools! Rebelssss waiting to be crushed! They say ussss, friends! They wrrrrong. They..." Sylvester smiled, "...*dead* wrong."

"So what does this have to do with me?" Sylvester stared at him evilly.

"They want me to guard their base. Let in friends, keep out enemies, they say. No way in but my swamp, no. Not a single sssspot!"

"So..."

"So, I must not let them use me, no. Cannot let them win. This is still my land! Mine! So I must do what I choose. And I choose the taaaassssstiest snacks!" He snapped his teeth and Eros ducked out of the way just in time.

"Wait! I'm poisonous!" Sylvester stared at him and hissed in anger.

"Hmmmm. It appears you are. I shall not eat you, but I say you should get out of my swamp."

"Alright. I'm going." He began to jump away slowly as Sylvester watched him. When he had gotten about fifty feet away, he started frantically running east.

"Hey! Sssssstop that!" Sylvester yelled as Eros booked it away from him.

"No!" Eros replied. He escaped by the skin of his gums and frantically ran for about fifteen minutes before reaching a very large pit. The pit had a large dead log laying across the top like a bridge, and hundreds of snakes patrolled the area. Eros slowly jumped towards the center, hiding under leaves and sneakily evading snake surveillance. When he finally reached the center, Eros saw a pile of logs with a giant elegant boa constrictor, who was engaged in a heated debate with a small blue snake.

"My Queen, with all due respect, constricting your prey is less fun because you have to spend more energy just to get your prey to die, not to mention the dirt, and other icky stuff on the creature's body, which you get all over yourself when you strangle it," said the blue snake.

"Thomas, you must be the most frog-brained... IMBECILE to not know how great it feels to just STRANGLE the life out of your prey! It really adds a bit of gratitude to your kill," answered the Queen.

"But, my lady, when you bite and swallow your food, the juices of the meal are squeezed out and you can taste every single delicious part of it!" retorted Thomas, who obviously felt very strongly about his argument.

"Ugh! I can't even talk to you, Thomas. You are obviously biased for your... foolish way of eating. Leave me." Thomas slithered away, muttering something as he crawled out of the pit and out into the rainforest.

"Hello?" Eros asked as he jumped into the small clearing around the queen.

"What? Who's there?" The queen swerved her head around frantically.

"Me." The queen traced the sound until she saw Eros.

"There!" She quickly slithered over and angrily grabbed Eros in her long tail. "Who are you!?"

"I'm just a passing traveler. My name's Bronzy."

"No passing traveler would come here!" She narrowed her eyes at him. "You want something." Eros laughed nervously.

"You got me. I'm a local... bronze-buyer. I was wondering if you, say... would have any large pieces of bronze?"

"Hmm. But you're a frog." Eros pretended to look offended.

"You got a problem with that?"

"I just don't know how you hold the bronze."

"I have my ways."

"Like, a wagon or something? It would have to be pretty small, manufactured in one of the big frog settlements. But that's not the point. How come I've never heard of you?"

"I'm new to the bronze market. Just started last week."

"Hmm. What was your name again?"

"Eros?"

"You said your name was Bronzy." Eros stared at her, and a little sweat trickled down his cheek.

This is not going well, he thought.

"What do you *really* want?" The queen asked.

"Oh, nothing. Just... oh, you wouldn't want to know," stuttered Eros.

"What? What is it?"

"It's just... the gods said..."

"The gods? What did they say?"

"Oh, you know those gods. Always bad-mouthing subordinates."

"Did the gods say something bad about me? Did they slander my name? That sounds just like them."

"Well, they said that that bronze piece of yours..."

"Yes?"

"...the one you got from Kampe..."

"What about it?"

"...was a sort of..."

"A sort of filler that covers the page with short but monotonous conversation?"

"...was a sort of emotional security thing. Like a blanket." The queen screamed with terrible anger.

"That is such a jerk move! They're just jealous that I don't have those gross, meaty legs of theirs! Nothing impedes me from just sliding anywhere I want!"

"Okay...well I told them that you would never have something as lame as that."

"Smart frog."

"But they didn't believe me."

"Jerks."

"So I told them that I'd come to your land and personally show them that you weren't a wimp like they said you were."

"They said I was a wimp?"

"Not the point. The point is here I am." The queen stared at Eros skeptically.

"I suppose you want me to give you the amulet now."

"It's the only way to prove those stupid gods wrong." The queen sighed and began to scrape leaves off of a pile until she revealed a large piece of bronze. She picked it up in her mouth and began to give it to Eros when a small little snake stopped her.

"My queen! The gods have sent a message. They want to do an intervention with Iris about her emotional-support rainbow. As a person who they believe to be above those sorts of things, they want you to come." The queen scoffed.

"Really?" she scoffed sadly. "I'm sure they said it sarcastically."

"Actually, they said it completely seriously. Like this." The little snake changed his tenure to make a super serious voice. The queen frowned and glanced at Eros.

"Are you sure?"

"Absolutely!" The little snake slithered away as the queen took their full attention to Eros.

"Well, well, well, well, well, well, well... trying to trick me, eh? I thought it was weird that you tried to trick me and, upon the reveal of the trick, revealed that you were actually part of something completely different. This new trick, you see, didn't coincide with the need to come up with the first trick, so it was all very confusing. Although...am I rambling?"

"A little."

"Oh. Sorry."

"It's okay."

"Thanks. A lot of snakes around here don't have good enough manners to say anything-that's not the point! The point is that you tricked me, and that is a... uh... a bad... a bad thing!" Eros stared at the queen's angered face and intimidating stature and tried to muffle a giggle.

"Nice wordplay."

"Silence! You want my bronze, do you?" The queen had a slick smile on her face. "You may have my bronze if..."

"Yes?"

"IF..."

"What is it?"

"IF..."

"Oh, Just get on with it. We've been talking for three pages!"

"If you can survive my impossible challenge!" The queen laughed maniacally and looked for a reaction on Eros's face. There was none.

"Which is... ?" He stared at his right wrist as if there was a watch, even though there wasn't, in that devastating way that sarcastic people do. "I've got places to be. Chop chop."

"Silence!"

"You already said that."

"Oh. Umm... let there be quiet! I challenge you to spend... one day in Antarctica!"

GASP gasped a snake nearby.

"Also," *GASP* gasped another snake.

"A third," *GASP* gasped a third.

"Another" *GASP* "-okay that's enough." Everyone stared at Eros, expecting a reaction of horror.

"Is that it?" Eros said, not miffed. Another row of gasping began but the queen stopped them.

"What do you mean; 'Is that it?' It's the most terrifying challenge of all time!'" All the snakes murmured in agreement.

"Why's that? You all scared of a little cold?" The queen frowned.

"Hah. You have no idea what that means!" She laughed cruelly. "Your body will freeze like a popsicle in a freezer!"

"But a popsicle is already frozen."

"Grrrrr. You won't be such a wise guy when you freeze like a popsicle in... all-seasons room on a nice summer day!"

"But then it would melt because of the heat. Unless, of course, the room had an AC unit or walls to keep the heat out. But, however, if that were true, it would then not be considered a *proper* all-seasons room. Though-"

"Begone! I shall banish you to Antarctica for THREE days! May you go and freeze into ice! MWA HA HA!"

"Fine, I'm leaving." He hopped away from the queen as her and her court laughed at him. When he got near the water, a large sea turtle jumped out. It had a green hexagon pattern on its shell and a little yellow sign on top of it that said 'TAXI'.

"Turtle Taxi. Heading straight to Antarctica." Eros stared in confusion.

"This day couldn't get any weirder." The turtle rolled his eyes at him.

"Haters gonna hate. Are you getting in or not?"

"I didn't call a taxi." The turtle sighed and opened a scroll hidden beneath his shell with his mouth.

"*By order of the queen may this frog be escorted to Antarctica in this taxi here...*you get the idea."

"Um... okay." He hopped onto the turtle's shell and it shot out into the ocean. So fast, in fact, that Eros had to grab onto the sign to keep from being flung black into the spray. He climbed up the shell until he was able to sit on the front of the sign. The turtle turned its head to Eros.

"So, you've been banished, eh?"

"Yup. Pay attention to the water." The turtle swerved, nearly hitting a rock.

"Pshaw. I'm a professional." He pushed off the water, flying an inch into the air and avoiding a ball of flaming knives.

"Why are there balls of flaming knives out here?" The turtle seemed to notice it for the first time.

"Oh. We must be near a cluster." He jumped over several more balls of flaming cutlery and landed in the water near a small tropical island. As the turtle sped along, crocodiles bit their trail.

"Careful!" Eros cautioned as a crocodile bit the water where they had just been a yoctosecond ago.

"I am, I am."

"But how are they even here? This isn't their native habitat!"

"This isn't my native habitat, but you don't see me getting all whiny about it."

"Oh, fine." Eros leaned against the sign and tried to relax as best he could for a while. After about an hour of squatting there, he looked around and noticed small icebergs floating around in the water. They were floating directly towards a large white glacier that towered over everything else in sight.

"We're here." Eros yawned.

"Where-?"

"Antarctica. The Ross ice shelf, to be specific. Thank you for using Turtle Taxis."

"Is there anything *interesting* I need to know?"

"Oh. Umm...the Antarctic continent is actually a huge archipelago of islands that are connected by millions of years of ice and snow collecting to form packed ice! Isn't that just *incredibly* trivial?"

"I guess, but do you know any laws or customs I should know?"

"Well, the UN has decreed that the Antarctic continent is a common ground for humanity, but countries still establish awkward territories that may cause some international strife should oil be found in Antarctica, as mining is strictly prohibited under the treaty-"

"Are there any *animal* rulers in the area?" The turtle looked at Eros with some skepticism.

"Just the penguins," he said. "Steer clear of Emperors Penguins. He pulled over to an ice beach. "Now, this water is too cold for my blood. I gotta watch out for killer whales, so get out quick."

"Alright, alright. I'm going." He hopped off the turtle's shell and it sped away as Eros bounced away into the snow.

"This should be easy." He hopped around and slid across the ice. It began to snow as he moved inland.

"Uh oh. Better find shelter." He looked around until he noticed a small icy hole in the side of the glacier.

"There." He began moving towards the cave.

"This isn't so hard." He hopped along. About two minutes after he got there, Eros got to the tip of the cave. He was happy to get out of the storm, but as he moved farther into the cave, he noticed he was going slower than usual, his feet were moving slowly and each of his breaths were deep and long.

"What's happening?" He tried to think about everything he knew about frogs. *They took part in metamorphosis, they puff air into a flap into their neck, or was that bullfrogs? Umm... they're cold-blooded!* He tried to warm himself by rubbing his hands together, but frog joints don't really work that way and he ended up just rubbing his arms all over the snow. "Stupid ligaments." As he almost slowed to a stop, he noticed a huge black and white figure approaching him. As he blacked out, he murmured with his last breath; "At least I'll be mildly tasty..." His eyes shut and he lost consciousness.

*   *   *

Eros drifted through the yawning chasm that was his mind. He attempted to flail around and propel himself forward, but he was unsuccessful. Then a chilling laughter echoed through his astral form, and it got closer and closer until the voice was almost upon him. Right then, Eros woke up abruptly in a little cave. He could only see an engulfing blackness all around him, but he could smell the cold and feel the snow melting around him. He could hear the wind rushing outside of the entrance and the water dripping from the roof of the cave. The darkness above him was warm but it felt like it was falling right into him. Something was sitting on him. He screamed at the top of his lungs but it sounded sort of like a zebra with vocal issues. The thing that was sitting on him squealed with surprise and stood up.

"Ah! You're up!" The dark thing had a large white belly and a long beak. Once Eros's vision cleared, he realized that he was staring at a large penguin. Eros tried to stand up.

"Where-where am I-ohhh!" He fell down with a splitting headache.

"Careful." The penguin moved a little snow onto Eros's forehead.

"Who-?"

"My name is," *the penguin made an indecipherable collection of chirps from its long beak* "but you can call me Jim."

"Well, Jim." Eros rubbed his head. "I'm Eros. What happened to me?"

"Well. I found you lying in the snow an hour or ten ago." Eros was shocked by how long he'd been out.

"Oh. Did I pass out?"

"Yeah. Sure, you also had a stroke, causing total brain death. Also, your heart stopped for thirty minutes. And your bones turned to jelly. During all this, you were in a terribly deep coma. But I guess you could say you 'passed out'" Eros was shocked.

"Ten hours of that? How did I survive?"

"Plot armor." Jim picked Eros up with his beak and nestled him in his wing. "That should keep you nice and warm." He started waddling towards the mouth of the cave.

"Where are we going now?" Eros yawned.

"Outside. The Emperor's penguins are very specific about work times."

"Huh." Eros looked around. The sun was shining in the middle of the sky. "Why is the sun up? It was up when I got here ten hours ago." Jim scoffed.

"It's always up. And if it's not up, it's down. Six months a year up, six months a year down."

"Oh." Jim waddled to a large area filled with penguins. As he moved towards the center he passed some other penguins coming back from the later-twelve-hours-of-the-day shift.

"Hey, Jim," said one tired penguin.

"Hey, Jerry."

"Looking spiffy, Jim."

"Right back at you, Jerry." After Jerry left Jim quickly sat down on a small collection of white eggs about the size of the palm of a human[43] hand. He remained motionless and silent for a couple of minutes.

"Ummm... What happens now?"

"Now we sit and warm the eggs." More silence followed.

"For how long?"

"Oh, twelve hours or so." A few penguins moved into more comfortable positions and continued sitting.

"Why so long?"

"Warming the eggs is important. They need to be nice and cozy or else they'll freeze."

"But I thought that females stayed with the eggs."

"The females are off getting food for a while."

"So they just left you to watch the eggs?"

"Well, not exactly-"

"They ditched you."

"No, they...yeah. They pretty much did," Jim sighed.

"I'm going to sleep," Eros yawned, nuzzling into Jim's wing and falling asleep. After about two hours, he woke to a loud chirping. A bunch of tall penguins were waddling towards them, and all the penguins that they passed dropped to their flippers

[43] But who cares about *humans,* right?

with deep bows. Between four of the bulkiest penguins was waddling a very regal penguin wearing a little ice cube on his head. Jim kneeled down to his wing and whispered into Eros's ear.

"That's the Emperor. He's Antarctica's leader." Eros whispered back into his ear.

"Is he an Emperor penguin?"

"Yeah. How did you know?"

"Just a hunch."

"Well, he's very powerful. So hush up." They waited until the penguins passed them. Jim watched as they disappeared over the horizon. Then he turned back to Eros. "Okay. They're gone."

"What's with the ice cube on his head?"

"Some penguins from South Africa sold him it. They said it was a beautiful crown. He assumes he's just insane and that it IS a beautiful crown and not an ice cube."

"So, like, the EXACT plot of the Emperor's New Clothes?"

"Yeah.[44]" Eros fell back to sleep. He woke hours later as Jim walked back to the cave.

Did I sleep through the day? he thought. *Just two hours left to go. This should be a piece of cake.* Jim waddled back to his cave and laid Eros down on his side.

[44] Three months later, when the eggs began hatching, a nestling would point out the Emperor's foolish mistake. In a way, it was a silent and profound comment on how children can act out against authority when adults cannot, but in every other way, it was just funny how the Emperor ran off screaming in embarrassment.

"So. Where are you from? How did you come to Antarctica, Eros?"

"Well, it's kinda a long story." He pulled a small but compact filmstrip from his ... pocket... and shined it at the wall of the cave. A picture of a strong-robed man surrounded by brilliant light appeared. "In the beginning, Eru Ilúvatar created the unnumbered Ainur using the Flame Imperishable. The strongest of the numbers was Melkor-oops." Eros took out the film strip. "That's for TolkienCon. Where is it-" He looked around in his 'pocket'. "Must have left it at home. I'll just tell you. It all started yesterday when my friend Tartarus called me..."

Several Minutes Later...

After the story was fully told, Jim dropped to the ground and groveled. "I'm not worthy... I'm not worthy..." Eros rolled his eyes.

"Oh, don't grovel. I hate it when they grovel. *I'm not worthy... I am too inadequate... I should be shoved into a small hole for one to two hours...* Ugh.

"But, Lord Eros, I am not eligible for such a great adventure like yours. You must forgive me."

"Ah, it's fine. I wasn't eligible for that painting contest, but I still entered."

"Did you win it?"

"No, I got second to last. But I sabotaged another painter's painting and THEY got last!"

"Oh. Well, if you truly don't want me to grovel, can I ask a question?"

"Is it pointing out any inadequacies?"

"Well, you *could* interpret it as-" Eros grew the size of his frog body until it scraped the roof of the cave.

"YOU DARE JUDGE ME!? YOU SHALL BE PUNISHED!!" Jim cowered in fear.

"R-re-really?" Eros returned to his regular size.

"No. Ask me anything."

"If only lizards were allowed in the lizard realm, why was an amphibian frog allowed in it? They would be blocked by the spell."

"I guess they weren't very observant."

"But you wanted to become a lizard and you became a frog."

"I didn't say I was very observant."

"Well, I assume you'll be going back in a few hours."

"Yeah."

"And I know what you're going to say, but I need no gifts. I'm happy with my life the way it is."

"Okay. I'll send the super-yacht somewhere else then." Jim perked up at the sound of that.

"Well, I didn't say that." Eros laughed and settled down into a deep sleep.

Hours Later...

Eros woke up with Jim nudging him with his flipper. "Sir, wake up!" Eros opened his eyes and stretched his arms in the air.

"What?" he yawned.

"There's a turtle outside."

"A turtle?" Eros's brain slowed down in the cold, so he couldn't really remember.

"A turtle. Has a little sign on top of it. Yellow and wood. Says 'TAXI'"

'TAXI'? Where had he heard that before? And a turtle... OH YEAH! "I know him. He's my ride outta here."

"Oh. So I suppose you're leaving now."

"Yeah." Eros tried to pat Jim on the back, but he wasn't tall enough so he ended up just patting him on his left knee. "Watch out for a huge gold boat with your name on it. Like, literally *inscribed* with your name."

"Okay." Eros hopped away and jumped on the turtle's back.

"How was Antarctica? I'm surprised you're still alive."

"I had some help from a friend," Eros replied. He told the turtle a modified version of what happened.

"So, what happened with the Emperor Penguins?"

"What? Nothing."

"But when you left I told you to watch out for Emperor Penguins."

"Yeah."

"And you saw the Emperor Penguins during your adventure."

"True."

"So, what happened?"

"Nothing."

"Nothing at all?"

"Nothing at all." The Turtle scowled and looked directly through the fourth wall.

"Well, that's just lazy writing."

*　　　*　　　*

After getting back to the rainforest and retrieving the amulet from an honor-bound-yet-still-reluctant queen and putting it in his safe, Eros flew to the European Mediterranean coast.

"Stretching 3,700 miles across, Portugal, Spain, and Italy, the Argentine ant's supercolony is the largest collective of non-warring colonies in the world."

"The number of ant colonies number in the thousands, containing an approximate one hundred thousandth of the ant population, about one quadrillion individual ants.

"Because of the large size, there are hundreds of queens that all work together. Though, unknown to humans, there is a super-queen that rules them all who is quite revered among insects."

Eros put down his fact book as he reached his destination at [redacted], which can only be described as [redacted], filled with [redacted]. He quickly transformed into a red worker ant and fell to the right of a small anthill next to a large green leaf that had blown off a tree. Ants were actively ripping pieces of it and bringing them underground. Eros shrugged.[45]

"When in Rome." He grabbed a piece and shuffled towards the mound of dirt. When Eros was almost inside he was abruptly stopped by a big strong ant. Eros stared up at his threatening form. He was half a millimeter taller than Eros! The ant frowned at him.

"I haven't seen *you* around here lately."

"There's a lot of ants coming through here. Maybe you forgot me."

"I never forget a face."

"But our faces all look the same."

"I never forget an incredibly small incremental number of differences in a head, antenna, eyes, legs, petiole, mesosoma, and gaster."

"But, dude, there's probably about 800 to 1,000 ants coming through here every day." The ant looked skeptical.

"If you want in, tell me the secret passcode."

---

[45] This paragraph was censored by Ants United.

"Okay." Eros racked his knowledge of everything, forever for the passcode. "Got it."

"[redacted][46]"

The ant frowned and reluctantly allowed him in.

"You better stay out of trouble or you'll get coming for you," he said as Eros scurried down the tunnel. It got very dark and chilly quickly but Eros was surprised at what minuscule details he noticed around him. He could feel the dust floating in the dead air and the surface impurities on the walls. He could hear ants scurrying around and talking, eating food, and talking some more. Eros quietly listened in on two ants crouching in the corner, whispering about everyone that crawled by.

"Oh my gosh, Ant #9528! Ant #5239 just passed by! Did you know that he found a Dorito near here but didn't tell anybody?!"

Ant #9528 gasped.

"No! Way!"

"Yes! Way!"

"Ant #9328, you must be lying! Not sweet, innocent #5239!"

"It's true! I heard they punished him by-" As Ant #9528 described how the rations of that greedy doofus #5239 had been withheld for, *gasp*, twelve hours, Eros could sense a big bulky ant creeping up behind him. The two ants seemed completely

[46] Censored by ANT Standards Institute Corporation, or ANSI Corp.

oblivious about them and they started to gossip about a new ant who had come as an emissary from a fief about three miles from the hill.

As Ant #9528 told how there was not a lot of rain there, and it caused the ants there to be; "like, really hot all the time,"[47] although, it was apparently; "a dry heat." The ant jumped out and made the two jump up in surprise.

"#9528! #9328! Get to work!" he yelled as the two scrambled to head down the main tunnel. He wiggled his feelers around and sensed Eros standing nearby. "You! Get up and get to work!"

Eros shuffled down the tunnels, listening to any ants coming through holes in the walls. As they came from different branches of the tunnel, he could sense compartments, rooms with baby ants, and storage for the winter filled to the brim with food. He passed a particularly large room filled with big bulky ants like the guard out front. On the walls hung rose thorns fashioned on little pieces of wood and pieces of leaves layered together into tough, bulky shields. Each of the hundred-or-so ants had little pieces of cotton on their abdomens with 'POLICE' in Portuguese on them. The back wall of the room was covered in a huge half-eaten cool ranch Dorito, which, written in brail across a tiny piece of tape, was "EVIDÊNCIA".[48] Eros reached the end of the tunnel and a huge, long hall led straight to the queen's area. Ants streamlined away from the middle and marched through servant's tunnels on either side. Right where the line broke was a small ant handing blades of grass to everybody who came by. Eros tried to walk quietly past the ant, but they noticed him before he could get very far.

"Here." They forced the grass blade into Eros's jaw so that it hung above his head in a surprisingly convenient way.

---

[47] Both meanings. 'Nuff said.

[48] Which is "EVIDENCE" in Portuguese, of course. See? This book is consistent sometimes... punk.

"Wait, I need to-" The ant didn't skip a beat, handing another blade of grass to the next ant in line. They waved their leg at Eros, shooing him away.

"Move along, sir. You're holding up the line." Eros sighed and shuffled to the left, entering a narrow tunnel packed with ants. The tunnel moved up and down, left and right in a long winding tunnel that eventually led to a big open depression in the ground filled with eggs.

The ants from his tunnel and the one on the opposite side converged into an area covered with a big green leaf. The ants laid the grass onto the leaf, folding them in an elaborate origami pattern and a queen towering above the eggs greedily ate them, pooping an egg out every few bites of grass, replacing an egg that would have just been taken away to a different room. It could be considered beautiful by someone who thinks that things that aren't beautiful in any way are beautiful.

Eros silently walked towards the queen, surveying her crown made of the tip of a banana peel and the little piece of glass that adorned her brow. He could not see the amulet. As he was laying down his grass piece, the queen stared at him acutely. Eros tensed at her piercing stare.

"Um... don't mind me." He continued to fold the grass while simultaneously searching for the amulet. He couldn't see it inlaid on any walls or ceilings.

While he looked around, the queen continued to watch him. Suddenly she stomped her leg on the floor, signaling all the other ants to stop. Eros looked up at her and immediately started folding the grass much faster.

Almost done, he thought. *Gotta find the amulet.* The queen shifted in her position and something shined from the dirt under her, bright enough to reach Eros's weak, tiny eyes. Eros gasped as a revelation smacked his brain like a cement truck.

The amulet is under her! he thought. As Eros finished folding the grass and presented it to the queen, she knocked it out of his arms.[49]

"Who are you?" she hissed. Eros recoiled as her face jutted towards his.

"Me!?" He acted shocked and completely oblivious to anything that might be going on. "I'm just a wittle worker ant!" Eros put on his saddest puppy dog eyes and hoped for the best. The queen was unaffected.

"Do you think I am an idiot?" The queen's eyes bored into Eros's skull.

"... No?" Eros asked questionably. She frowned.

"You say that with skepticism."

"Well... the number of neurons in your brain are in the low hundred thousands, so..."

"I am smart enough to sense when I am in the presence of such immense power, **simpleton**." Eros gave up his act as security ants ran up to him and circled him with spears. "Did Olympus send you?"

"Look, we can do this the easy way or the hard way. Dying would probably really suck for you, so I hope we can work this out," Eros threatened.

The queen laughed maniacally.

"You have no leverage over me! What does Olympus want with me anyway!? I have done nothing wrong!"

"Oh, really? See, what I thought was that you enslave literally a quadrillion, that's fifteen zeroes, ants as your mindless servants that bring you food and spend their entire

[49] Forearms? Legs? Mandibles?

lives under your rule. So, huh, what could the gods be mad at you about?" The queen was shocked by this targeted accusation.

"But I lay eggs!"

"Yeah, but I heard that you only laid eggs last December because you wanted a feast for Christmas morning." The Queen's face quickly turned from a look of surprise to scorn and anger.

"This insolence will not stand! Guards, seize him!" Eros shrugged.

"Hmm. I guess the bad way is always fun." A guard reached Eros, but he grabbed their arm and flipped it on its back.

"Seize him!" yelled the queen. Eros swiped his left hind leg at the ants rushing at him. They tripped and staggered, giving Eros time to run towards the queen. He jumped up and kicked at the queen's face, but she dodged him and he ran into a wall. The queen immediately looked up at the ceiling.

"What are you looking at?" asked Eros while simultaneously fending off thirty-six other ants.

"Rocks falling from the ceiling. When the kung-fu person misses, it usually turns out that rocks fall from the ceiling and crush the opponent."

"Nope. Just haven't practiced in a while." He jumped from the wave of ants and jumped at the queen, not missing his mark as his foot connected with the queen's face in a spectacular slo-mo *POW!* with a yellow striped background. He grabbed at the amulet and picked it up above his head.

"What do you want with Kampe's amulet, you disgusting Lilliputan!?"[50] Eros ran to the left side of the room.

"Oh,-there's-really-no-reason-I-just-need-to-borrow-it-for-a-second-I-don't-really-have-any-time-to-talk-right-now-byeeeeeeeee!!!!"

"No matter! Smush him!" Eros escaped down a corridor by stepping on the ant's faces as they ran after him.

"Sorry. I beg your pardon. I'll pay for any injuries," he said as he gave them all bloody noses.[51]

"You'll never find the way out!" The queen yelled as Eros escaped from her guards. "This is a labyrinth!"

"Okay," Eros murmured to himself, all the while escaping from over three thousand guards. "I just need to retrace my steps." He ran left as guards trailed right behind them. "Good thing I have a map." He pulled out a children's playsheet from 'Ivring's Insect Emporium'.

"Okay, if I turn right at Danny Dung Beetle, but stay away from Sally Spider, I should be able to..." Eros was looking around for Stippy the Stick Insect when the ground collapsed from under him and his body cascaded into a tiny little hole. He tumbled around until he dropped to a small circular depression filled with spider webs. Light shined in from the top, and none of the ants running after him seemed to notice his fall.

[50] Referring to the small people in Gulliver's Travels. If you got that, you're an over-cultured snob. If not, you're a culture-less pig. It's a Catch-22. Also, If you got that reference, you're an over-cultured snob. If not, you're a culture-less pig. So HAH.

[51] Or whatever you call their smelling glands.

"Hmm. What a convenient plot point." He slowly crept through the depression towards the top. Right as he started grabbing the dirt at the top, webs spit across the opening and covered it.

Whispering noises, whispered a thousand tiny voices. *Creepy whispering voices. Whisper whisper whisper.* Eros tried to find the source of the voices but everywhere he looked they were concealed by the shadow.

"Who's there?" asked Eros.

Nobody, replied the voices.

"Then who's talking?"

Nobody.

"Then who said THAT?" There was a long pause.

Okay, somebody might be talking. But we'll never tell you who we and our spider leader are.

"So you guys are spiders?" Eros began forming a plan in his head.

... Maybe. But you'll learn nothing more about us and our brownstone at 2946 Spider Street, Spider-Island, 47.74830° S, 179.02095° E.

"Oh, that's a terrible shame, because I have something VERY important to tell them. It's just a TERRIBLE shame, if you don't mind me repeating myself."

There is nothing possibly important enough to-

"Your leader might win 30 million dollars!"

HA! You think that would...really?

"They may have already won."

Sweet! She's right through here. The webs parted on the left side and a passageway opened to a large bird-eating spider. *We present our leader, having just come from an island in the middle of the Atlantic three short hours ago, Ungoliant!* Ungoliant turned and locked eyes with Eros. He backed away as Ungoliant crawled towards him.

"This is not good," he muttered to himself.

Why have you woken me? hissed Ungoliant at her subjects.

Leader! This ant says you may have already won 30 million dollars! Ecstatic cheers erupted sporadically from the unseen spiders. Ungoliant sighed.

I told you guys to not fall for those stupid scams. We don't even use human money anyway.

Oh. Sorry.

"I guess I should leave now." Eros started itching back to a hole in the webs covering the ceiling.

You're not leaving. Ungoliant grabbed Eros with her hairy leg and brought him up to her eye level. *Trying to scam my subjects, eh? Who are you?*

"I work for PowerLarvae. I was in the area so I dropped by." Eros struggled to escape the bird-eater's iron grip.

Your voice sounds familiar, yet I cannot put my leg on it. Have you had the pleasure of meeting me before?

"No, I can't say I have."

Hmm. No matter. You shall die for your offense anyway.

"Death! That seems a little extreme! Couldn't you just let me go with a stern warning?"

HA! You have tried to steal from us and it will not stand! Any last requests?

"Yeah. If you are Ungoliant, then may you die by the flaming whips of the terrible Insect Balrogs!" He let out a guttural cry that shook the earth around him. Three miles away, seven monsters of fire erupted from a local campfire. The fly-sized demons screamed and flashed their whips as they hit the cool ground. They were just about to run towards Eros's location when a Portuguese man sitting with his friend around the flame noticed them.

"*Algumas brasas saíram da chama,* (Some embers got out of the flame,)" said the one on the left.

"*Eu vou esmagá-los.* (I'll stomp them out.)" The one on the right got up and walked towards the Balrogs. They screeched as he stomped them out with his boot. Back at the depression, Eros repeatedly called for the Balrogs to come but they didn't answer.

Your beasts are not coming to defend you. It would be best to just give up now and surrender to a painful death.

"Umm... they're coming." He called them again and waited for something to happen. As they waited, Eros shifted in nervousness, exposing the amulet to Ungoliant's many blood-red eyes.

What do you have here? An amulet, eh? I thought this belonged to the queen. Eros tried to make up an excuse, but Ungoliant stopped him. *I don't need your excuses. This amulet will gain me much respect in the queen's court, I imagine.*

"You'll have to pry it off my dead abdomen."

That's the plan. Any last words?

"Just four. But you wouldn't want to hear them."

Educate me.

"Your shoes are untied."

My shoes aren't- When Ungoliant looked down at her feet, Eros kicked her in one of her eyes and wiggled out of her hands.

"Ha ha!" She ordered the spiders to grab him but it was too late. As he ran into the light, heard Ungoliant scream in rage.

That's the third time this week you've been tricked that way, my lady, one of the spiders mumbled. Eros snickered as he quickly ran out of sight.

*   *   *

Eros took a quick nap at home when he dropped off the amulet and then headed down to Earth to meet the mammal leader, a cat famous for its ferocity and wisdom. He dropped down into the suburbs of a big city near a river. As Eros fell through the air, he blurred into a golden-orange Aegean cat, stretching his body like a parachute and sticking his feet out at the last second, landing with a hard *thump* in the grass.

"Eight lives left," Eros mumbled as he staggered toward the front driveway. The door for the two-car garage in front of a large but modest house was closed, but Eros couldn't open the front door in his current form, so he butted his head into the wood. The sound resonated through the walls, and Eros's already heightened hearing was expanded by his godly powers, painting a 3D image of what was inside the garage. There was a micro-car to the right side, but three cats sat in suspense on the left, watching the door for any intruders. "*Meow?* (Hello?)" Eros resorted to making use of his power as an omniglot,[52] as cats were against any use of the Common Language in their species. They said it was 'stupid' and 'below them'. A cat inside meowed back

"*Mrrr!* (State your name and purpose!)"

"*Purr meow!* (My name is Eros and I come from Mykonos. I've come here to speak with your queen.)"

"*Meow meow.* (Why?)"

"*Grrrrreow.* (I wish to discuss the trade of long strings on sticks and little wind-up mousies.)"

---

[52] The power to know every language in the omniverse. This book was translated by Eros Industries. Except when it makes us look cool and consistent with the context. Then we totally have different languages.

"*Meowwww.* (Do you have an appointment with her majesty?)"

"*Meow.* (No.)"

"*Meow.* (Then you may not see the queen.)"

"*Purrr.* (Are you sure? I bet you guards don't have many super-fun toys.)"

"*Mew. (Are you trying to bribe me?)*"

"*Meow.* (I can get you guys some mazes with little balls with catnip inside them that you need to use your brain to get them out of the holes faster than you can say 'I want some mazes with little balls with catnip inside them that you need to use your brain to get them out of the holes.')"

"*Meow. Meow Meow.* (Well, we only get balls with broken bells and mousies that have already been torn to shreds. One time we got a really fancy toy, though. It was a really realistic-looking mousie that could climb walls and stick to the ceiling that ran around randomly, but only when its motion detector sensed cats, of course. It had a long tail that was partly a string that swirled around behind it. With a sonar system that detected cats all around and moved away from them, it was pretty hard to catch it, but if you caught it it played a nice victory tune that really just made you feel pleasant. It even gave you delicious treats! If you think it couldn't get better, you'd be wrong because its nose shined a red laser into a tiny dot that flies around the room, while, the whole time, it squealed like a real mouse for hyper-realism!)" Eros could hear the cat sighing in happiness just at remembering the toy.

"*Meow.* (Sounds like a fun time.)"

"*Growl.* (It would have been. But it turned out it was just a prank. It was really expensive, as I mentioned before, but while the queen got her money from tapping into part of the funds from a crowdfunding campaign to raise money for the next quarter's toy budget, the person who lives here paid for our toy with her hard-earned money, so we can't use it.)"

"*Meow.* (Wow. Must be sad. I could help you with your toy problems. I just need to come in.)"

"*Grr.* (Hmm. Alright. You can come on in.)" The garage door opened with a loud BRRRRR and Eros could see the cats inside the room. The two in the back tensed as Eros stepped onto the cold garage floor, but showed no indication of attacking. The guard cat Eros was talking to took its paw off the garage opener, scooped it into its mouth, and began walking deeper into the garage.

"*Mew.* (I guess I'll follow.)" The door had been left ajar and one of the guards arched over to it, bowed his head, and butted it into the door, causing it to slowly open. The cat and Eros walked inside and another cat closed the door with a similar gesture. The guard cat set the garage door opener on the ground, closed the door, and walked away while another cat picked it up without a single word from either.

Cats meowed as Eros walked into the living room. It was a nice place, with a comfy couch and a big TV, but you couldn't really tell because it was overflowing with cats. Sitting in the middle of the couch watching soap opera, was a large lump of blankets and fur that was, under further inspection, a person. Eros searched his vast memory for identification for them, which sometimes was difficult considering it included all of time and also everything that *could* have happened or did due to every decision ever, so Eros had a little trouble finding the person in a little under a Planck Time.

"*Mew meow, (Evelyn Abernathy,)*" he thought. What a person. At five, Eros had placed the routine ambitions of being an astronaut and the president and a firefighter all at the same time in her brain. When she was nine, she decided she wanted to be a lawyer, and after graduating valedictorian in high school, she went to Harvard, getting her Masters in Law and a nice job. Unfortunately for her though, Eros had just been to a cat show outside of time and space that was also in Cleveland, and he sent out a wave of cat-loving, hitting her pretty harder than the others. A 23 year old Evelyn was driving to work when she saw a cat on the side of the street meowing for help, setting her fate forever. By the time she was 30, all the stray cats in the state had moved into her house and the cat government,[53] which had until then been operating out of a quaint home in Springfield, Oregon, moved its capital to her house. They also moved their Capitol, making the ten feet around it Capitol floor. In the Capitol, which is spelled with a capital C, capital ideas like outlawing capital offenses and subsequent capital punishments, but also orchestrating better capital, by capitalizing the capital market, were laid out in the Capitol area.[54]

---

[53] The government of the cats, which is the watchcat of all mammal states, is in its simplest an anarchy led by a queen. In its most complicated form the queen threatens to scratch everyone if they don't concede to her decisions. A recent significant event in the nation was them officially condemning the play *Cats!*, banning it by law and branding all the cats in the production the enemy of the state. They also have waged war against the dual Rodentia and Rattus Prime clans, with no end in sight as peace talks usually fall apart on the principle of killing rat citizens for sport being wrong. The rats prepared dignified and thought-through presentations with graphs and ethical dilemmas, and the cats killed the rats for sport, so you can imagine it was quite controversial.

[54] Capitol Capital

(See Next Page)

"Arrrriairar!!" The cat lady screamed as something sad happened on her show. Jessica had just said a bunch of mean stuff about Sidney, and get this, even though she was RIGHT behind her and even WORSE, Jessica was talking to Anthony, who she KNEW Sidney liked and Anthony secretly liked Sidney even though...[55] The cat swished its tail at the lady and continued walking past.

"*Grrr.* (Ignore her. She is a meer proxy in our great design.)" The cat led Eros down some champagne colored stairs to a small landing. Two cats guarded a door on the left.

"*Meow.* (Who goes there?)" The one on the left meowed.

"*Mew.* (Let us in, Maud. This cat must see the queen.)"

Capital Capital!

[55] ...he acted like he liked Katy, who liked him back but was so embarrassed about it that she pretended to like Darren, who DID like Katy so they went out and it was really awkward for Katy and Anthony could totally go out with Sidney but he didn't because he thought she had a boyfriend because Sidney was so lonely she made him up and it was just totally pathetic, but also kinda sad.

"*Growl Meow Mew Mew Mew.* (Not so fast, Solembum. You may be the lieutenant of the garage from sucking up to Angela, but Scoobus and Oaken will have our tails if you endanger the queen.)"

"*Meow.* (Nonsense. This one comes to ask for better toys for the us guards in the garage, which we've been very underfunded for of late.)"

"*Grrr.* (Fine. But he better not try anything.)" Maud stepped aside as Eros and Solembum walked into the basement. Cats patrolled everywhere and there was a clear outlined path watched by many sentinels. They turned to the right, but Eros could see that on the left there was a huge Alaskan King bed with a few pillows and fluffy blankets, but most significantly there was a large assembly of cats sitting around yelling at each other.

That must be the Capitol,[56] thought Eros. The cats continued yelling at each other until they were out of earshot. They walked deeper into the ground until they came to a huge cat door enshrined with statues of clay and catnip growing in pots. A large group of cats guarded the door watchfully and one of the guards yelled at the two when they got close.

"*Meow!* (Who goeth there!? Stop! Do not move another whisker or we will cut off your tails!)"

"*Mew!* (Keep your fur on, Telvido. Maud let us in.)" Solembum responded to the guard.

"*Meow.* (How do I know you're not another cat in a Solembum suit?)," Telvido angrily accused me.

[56] The Capitol, which holds the C.A.T.S. (C.A.T.S. Are Terribly Smart), is merely a figurehead. Anything too boring for the Queen to handle is passed through there, but other than it the guard system is the only other thing not entirely engulfed in anarchy.

"*Grrr.* (How do I know that you're not another cat in a Telvido suit?)"

"*Rrrr.* (Hmmm. Well played. Fine. You may enter. But you'll be sorry for not respecting my power.)"

"*Mew.* (Sure I will.)"

"*Meow!* (You'll see! You'll all see!)" Solembum started walking forward and looked back at Eros.

"*Meow!* (Keep moving.)" Eros did as he was told and walked quickly away from the rambling feline.

"*Grr.* (What's his deal?)," Eros asked. Solembum chuckled at the question.

"*Meow.* (Telvido? He tried to foment an insurrection about two or three years ago, but he didn't print enough flyers and it failed.)"

"*Mew.* (So they gave him a job?)"

"*Meow.* (The queen values ambition. But he has anger issues, and the official statement didn't say we have to respect him, so...)"

"*Mew.* (Ah.)" They slid under the cat door and stepped into a gigantic throne room. Eros gasped at the stunning architecture and royal prestige that filled the huge[57] room.

The walls were covered in picture frames showing off splattered red dots with the caption TROPHY KILLS.

[57] I mean, proportionally.

There was a huge litter box filled with the finest litter that said ROYAL CHAMBERS, though it was purely ceremonial, as Eros noticed some terrible-smelling dress shoes a few feet away.

He also noticed over a hundred scratching posts lining the walls, but they too were ceremonial as there was a small futon nearby that was almost ripped to shreds.

Cat toys with bells and mousies lay scattered across the carpet more frequently as Eros and Solembum approached; soon they could see a novelty fluffy throne sitting on four roller wheels.

The throne was flipped around so that they couldn't see anyone who might be sitting in it. Two black-and-white cats guarded the throne from atop two cat towers, squatting in a pouncing position ready to attack anybody who got too near.

"*Hiss!* (Stop!)," hissed the left one. Solembum and Eros stopped in their tracks as the cats jumped down and glared threateningly at them. Eros glanced at Solembum, who seemed uncharacteristically shaky.

"*Mew.* (Who are they?)," Eros asked. Solembum shifted nervously at the question and answered in a whisper.

"*Meow.* (Scoobus and Oaken. The heads of the guard. The one on the left is Scoobus and the right one is Oaken. They're about five years old and the most terrifying cats you'll ever meet. They are bodyguards to the queen and are renowned for their ferocity. They also love tummy rubs. Needless to say, be very careful.)"

"*Mew!* (Silence!)," Oaken hissed. Scoobus inspected the two felines with an unnerving caution.

"*Grr!* (State your name and business!)," growled Scoobus.

"*Meow.* (I am Solembum and I am escorting this cat to meet the queen.)," replied Solembum. Scoobus raised an eyebrow at him, although he didn't raise it very high as he didn't have the proper facial muscles.[58]

"*Growl.* (We know who you are, Solembum. Who's your associate here?)," Scoobus growled with a frown.

"*Meow.* (I am Eros, and I come from Mykonos to advocate that you should give the guards in the garage more toys. I've got a four-pronged sales pitch for why the queen should consider-)," Eros reasoned.

"*Meow.* (Nonsense. They already have enough toys.)," interrupted Oaken. Solembum sighed at the blatant ignorance.

"*Mew-* (Actually, we have no truly *fun* toy-)"

"GROWL! (SILENCE, SOLEMBUM.)," Oaken yelled, interrupting the interruption to the interruption.

"*Meow.* (The queen is very busy right now.)," Scoobus replied in a cool but menacing tone.

"*Meow.* (Really?)," asked Eros with an even more menacing tone.

"*Meow.* (Really.)"

"*Meow.* (Really?)"

"*Meow.* (Really.)

"*Meow.* (Really?)"

[58] Or eyebrows.

"*Meow.* (Really-okay this is getting ridiculous. The queen is more busy right now than she has been in a long time. She's off in Egypt officiating a dedication to Bastet, so she can't come back here for a while.)"

"*Meow.* (Really? Then why aren't you there guarding her?)" Solembum inquired.

Scoobus shifted nervously. He was about to answer when Oaken interjected himself into the conversation.

"*Meow.* (We don't like the heat.)"

"*Mew.* (Oh. The heat.)"

"*Meow.* (Yes. It makes us very uncomfortable, the heat.)" Oaken nodded, and Scoobus followed suit.

"*Mew.* (So you were guarding an empty room, then?)" Solembum asked.

Oaken looked at Scoobus.

"*Meow.* (Yep.)," Oaken answered.

"*Meow.* (Lotta valuable stuff in this room.)," Scoobus added.

"*Meow.* (All those scratching posts.)," Eros *also* added[59].

"*Mew.* (Yep.)," Oaken replied.

"*Meow.* (The really fine litter.)"

"*Mew.* (True.)"

"*Meow.* (Especially all those toys.)"

[59] There are only *so many* applicable verbs, okay?

"*Meow.* (Yup.)"

"*Mew.* (Like that expensive robot mousie. I heard that was super fun.)" Eros added.

Oaken seemed startled by the statement.

"*Meow.* (Who told you about the mousie?)"

"*Mew.* (Nobody. I just *happened* to know that it looked really realistic, can climb walls and stick to ceilings, that it runs around randomly, only if there are cats in the room sensed by a motion and sonar system of course, with a long string tail that swirls around behind it. Even though it tried to avoid cats, if you caught it, it would pay a nice tune and give you treats. I know its nose shines a red laser that flies all over the room and that it squeaks for a nice realism! But most important of all, I know it's activated by a MOTION SENSOR!)" Eros started running in a circle as everyone else watched questionably.

"*Meow.* (You already mentioned the motion sensor.)," Scoobus corrected.

"*Mew.* (No matter. Just one second. It'll happen.)" Eros started running in a slightly bigger circle.

A Few Minutes Later...

After a few minutes and a hundred slightly bigger circles, when Eros was running the entire circumference of the room, he heard a small squeaking from the corner of the room.

"*Mew!* (Yes!)," he yelled as all the cats in the room watched, beginning to realize his trick. As the little mousie ran around on the floor around Eros, Scoobus and Oaken seemed to simultaneously completely understand his plot.

"*Meow!* (Catch it!)," Oaken yelled to Scoobus. They chased after it, but the mousie evaded them every time they got close. Eros ran around too, trying to force the mousie to move towards the throne. Solembum slowly backed away from the seemingly-insane cats, eventually breaking for the door and leaving, screaming;

"*Meow!!!!* (Get-us-good-toys, okay-see-you-later-bye!!!)" No one seemed to notice when Solembum frantically slammed the door shut, as the mousie was getting closer and closer to the throne. Unfortunately, Oaken had gotten up on a high ledge and was going to ambush the mousie when Scoobus and Eros chased it through.

Eros tried to steer it in another direction, but that only made Scoobus run faster, and when the mousie was in position Oaken jumped. Fortunately for Eros, though, as Oaken's paws left the platform he knocked a small ball of twine, and as he was about to land a direct hit, the twine ball hit the ground, allowing the mousie to sense it and swerve away, as Oaken landed with a *thump* on his feet, not skipping a beat as he immediately ran after the mousie.

"Meow! (No!)," Scoobus yelled as the mousie moved in front of the throne. It barely moved a centimeter when a small but fast brown cat pounced on it. The mousie played a victory tune and dispensed treats as the cat scooped them into her mouth and sat back down on the throne, which spun around as the cat menacingly laid down the mousie next to her, letting it instantly zip away.

"*Growl.* (Scoobus, Oaken. Back to your posts.)," growled the queen. The guards quickly did as they were told and jumped back into their posts. The queen then put her attention on Eros. "*Meow.* (You discovered my charade, eh? I was taking a nap, so this must be important. What do you need?)" Eros smiled nervously.

"*Meow.* (Your highness, I am Eros. I come from Mykonos. I have come here to advocate for some better, more fun toys for the cats in the garage. They don't have very many of them, and that mousie they have was bought using the human's hard-earned money, so they can't use it.)" The queen looked at him suspiciously.

"*Mew.* (Do not lie to me.)"

"*Me-* (I'm not-)"

"*Meow.* (I don't have to be the all-knowing axolotl to know that somebody who can trick my two best guards isn't a simple activist. How would your fake identity have even heard about a *specific* shortage of toys in a *specific* guard to a queen whose base is *specifically* kept confidential? You're an Aegean cat. What are the chances you heard all this from the *specific* place where your landrace originated, Mykonos, which is all the way in Greece? I would believe they are very small.)" Eros frowned. She was good. Time for plan B.

"*Mrow.* (Okay. You got me. I've been sent by Hades to get the amulets that Kampe distributed to every animal type. This is the last one I gotta do, so maybe you could just give it to me?)" Eros looked at her with his cutest kitty-cat eyes.

"*Meow.* (No! Not until you complete my.........ummmmm..................riddle!)"

"*Mew.* (Somebody already gave me a riddle.)"

"*Meow.* (Really?)"

"*Mew.* (Yeah. The all-knowing axolotl gave me it. I've also had a Herculean challenge to complete, but I've mostly just been stealing them in various ways)" The queen thought about this for a second.

"*Meow.* (I don't care! You must solve my impossible riddle now.)"

"*Meow.* (What's the riddle?)"

"*Mrow.* (TBD.)"

"*Meow.* (It can't be TBD if it needs to happen right now.)"

"*Meow.* (Fine. You have been stranded on an alien planet. The only way off is to please the three local rulers: Arr, Eff, and Tee. You must give them each a precious amulet that corresponds to each lord. The problem is that you don't know which is which. To figure this out, you can ask three yes or no questions to any one lord. A plaque placed by you tells you that Tee's answers are always true, while Eff's answers are always false. Arr's answers are random. Just to add to this, you know that the words 'Ulu' and 'Ozo' mean 'yes' and 'no', but you don't know which corresponds to the other. What questions do you ask to ensure you get off the planet safely?)" Eros smiled when he heard the riddle.

"*Meow.* (Ask the alien in the middle; 'If I asked whether the overlord on my left is Arr, would you answer 'Ozo'?' If you are questioning Arr, the answer is meaningless, if you are asking one of the others, they will reply both in the same way. Through selective reasoning, you can deduce that the alien on the right is not Arr if the aliens answer 'Ozo' and that the alien on the left is not Arr if they answer 'Ulu'. Now you go to the lord you have determined isn't Arr and ask them; 'If I asked you 'are you Eff?' Would you answer 'Ozo'?' If they say 'Ozo', they are Eff. If they say 'Ulu', they are Tee. Then ask the newly named alien 'If I asked you 'Is the center alien Arr' would you answer 'Ozo'?' By their answer you can tell if the center alien is Arr or not. Give them each the correct amulet and leave.)" The queen's jaw dropped in astoundment as he easily answered the self-acclaimed hardest logic puzzle in the world.

"*Mew.* (How did you solve that so quickly?)," asked the queen, clearly puzzled and, though Eros would never say it to her face, gobsmacked.

"*Meow.* (That's the same riddle the all-knowing axolotl gave me.)"

"*Mrow.* (Oh. Then you will need a new riddle...Wednesday, Tom and Joe went out for dinner. They ate lots of food and when they were done they paid for it. Tom and Joe didn't pay for it. Who did?)" Eros pondered the riddle.

"*Meow.* (Wednesday paid for it.)" The queen frowned at Eros *again* figuring out a puzzle she thought was pretty hard.

"*Meow!* (Next riddle!)"

"*Mrow.* (You said there was only one riddle.)"

"*Meow.* (I changed my mind. A cat is at a carnival and he goes to a booth where another cat says 'If I write your exact weight on a piece of paper then you must give me $50. If I don't do that I will give you the $50.' The cat sees no scale so he thinks he'll just say that the man is wrong, no matter what he writes. After a few minutes, the cat walks away $50 dollars poorer. How did the man win?)" Eros didn't even hesitate to answer.

"*Mew.* (The man wrote 'your exact weight' on the paper.)" The queen looked very frustrated.

"*Meow*-(There are three light switches that turn on a lightbulb upstairs. You don't know which one turns on the light, and the elevator, the only way to get up, only goes up. It cannot go down, so you can only use it once before it gets stuck up there. How can you determine which switch turns on the light while only going up onc-?)"

"*Meow.* (Turn on the first switch for ten minutes, then turn it off and flip the second switch. Then go upstairs, and check the light. If it's on, the second switch is the one. If it's not, then touch it. If it's hot, it's the first switch and if it's cold it's the third switch.)"

"*Meow.* (Humph. It seems you've exhausted my riddle supply. How *interesting*.)," said the queen, layering a pan extra *umph* on the 'interesting'.

"*Mew... meow?* (So...do I get the amulet now?)" The queen smiled as something popped into her 30-gram brain.

"*Meow.* (Not yet. You must pass one final test.)"

"*Mew?* (Then you will give me the amulet?)"

"*Meow.* (Yes.)"

"*Meow?* (Cat's honor?)" The queen shuddered at the thought of swearing the highest promise in cat society.

"*...mew.* (...cat's honor.)," answered the queen. "*Mew,* (Nobody else heard me,)" murmured the queen to herself, "*Meow.* (I can pretend I never said it.)" Eros heard her despite her attempt to be quiet

"*Mew.* (Scoobus and Oaken are witnesses. You guys heard that, right?)" Eros smiled at the guards.

"*Meow.* (I heard it.)," Oaken replied despite the queen's glare. Everyone looked at Scoobus, awaiting his reply.

"*Me...ow.* (I...heard it too.)" The queen sighed.

"*Meow.* (Fine. You'll never finish my task anyway.)"

"*Mrow.* (What is it then? This dialogue can't drag on for any more pages.)"

"*Meow.* (Don't rush me. I'm thinking.)"

"*Meow.* (You haven't figured it out yet? Wow.)"

"*Grrr.* (Writer's block happens, okay?)" The queen became increasingly frustrated as she failed to think of anything. Right as Eros thought she was going to give up and hand over the amulet, she smiled and whispered something to Scoobus. He in turn whispered to Oaken, and they both retreated through a back door.

"*Meow?* (So? What'll it be?)," Eros asked smugly. The queen chuckled.

"*Meow.* (Oh. It's pretty complicated so you better settle in. Long ago, our ancient cat ancestors found a powerful energy core. They knew they could power their magical food robots if they could just take it and harness it.)"

"*Meow.* (They had magical food robots who required powerful energy cores to power in the distant past?)," interrupted Eros.

"...*Meow.* (...yes. They were given to them by time travelers.)"

"*Meow?* (Really? Time travelers?)" She started getting nervous as Eros stared intensely at the queen with eyes as wide as a barn owl .

"*Meow.* (Yes. Now be quiet. So the cat ancestors tried to take the core, but the magic guardian, ummmmmm, Zalbazar the Mighty. So Zabarabarabarabar the Strong said it was for forbidden them to take the power core and the cats are all; 'we want that core and you won't stop-')"

"*Meow.* (Wait a minute. You said his name was Zalbazar the Mighty, not Zabarabarabarabar the Strong. Your story is ever-changing, oh wise one.)," Eros corrected, laying on the fancy words for extra shame.

"*Meow.* (Silence. As I was saying, Zazazazazz the Powerful told them to stop but the cats defeated him in a super clever and satisfying way.)" The queen suddenly stopped talking as if the story was over. There was a short pause as each of them waited for the other to speak.

"*Meow?* (Is that the whole thing? How did they defeat the guardian? How does this all tie into my challenge? Your story is full of holes.)," Eros said, interrupting the silence.

"*Mew.* (The ancient ancestors didn't leave very detailed records. It's mostly a bunch of paw prints and ink blots. One cat got the mutation of opposable thumbs though, and, while he was called a loveless freak for all his life and rightfully so, he wrote down the records that we still use today.)"

"*Meow.* (Great. Then tell me my challenge.)," Eros insisted.

"*Mew.* (Well, it's a very difficult challenge. You should probably just leave.)"

"*Meow.* (I can handle it. Tell me.)"

"*Meow.* (Are you sure? It's *really* hard.)"

"*Meow.* (Stop stalling. Just lay it on me.)"

"*Meow!* (Okay. I'll tell you. Your challenge is-OH MY GOODNESS WHAT IS THAT!?)" She stared expectantly at the door the guards had disappeared through. "*Meooooooooow!* (*ahem* I said 'OH MY GOODNESS WHAT IS THAT!?')" Just as Eros expected nothing to happen, the door opened up to reveal Scoobus and Oaken dressed in the worst costumes he had ever seen. Their backs were covered in foil, with empty toilet paper rolls sticking out sporadically. They even had a milk jug cap on each of their right eyes like monocles.

"*MEOW.* (WE ARE FROM THE FUTURE. CEASE IMMEDIATELY.)," Future Scoobus yelled in a robotic tone.

"*Meow.* (Oh no! Not cats from the future. I guess we should cease what we are doing until further instruction!)," the Queen screamed with her fakest scared voice.

"*MEW.* (YES. WE COME TO TELL YOU THAT YOU SHOULD NOT GIVE THIS CAT ANY CHALLENGES, NO MATTER HOW AWESOME THEY MIGHT BE.)," Future Oaken turned towards Eros. "*MEOW.* (IN FACT, YOU SHOULD JUST LEAVE, MYSTERIOUS ONE. FOR THE GOOD OF THE FUTURE.)" The Queen shook her head sadly.

"*Meow.* (Oh, that's terrible! But if the future is riding on it and these totally real time-travelers say so, then I guess you should go. It's a real shame, but that's how it is.) The three stared expectantly at Eros.

"*Meow?* (Seriously? You think you're going to get rid of me that easily? No offense, but this is kinda pathetic. You didn't even have black lights or anything sparkly, and when Scoobus moves his aluminum foil kinda slides off.)"

"*MEW!* (NO! THAT DOESN'T HAPPEN. MY FUR LOOKS LIKE ALUMINUM FOIL ALL THE TIME!)," Scoobus said, backing up defensively and causing his aluminum foil to start sliding off. The queen sighed as she noticed how stupid her guards looked.

"*Meow.* (Fine. Despite what you may have thought, these cats are not from the future.)," She waited for a surprised gasp that never came. "*Meow.* (You may not be surprised but you still have no leverage against me! I can have you forcibly removed now, and there's nothing you can do about it!)"

"*Meow.* (Really?)"

"*Meow.* (Really.)"

"*Meow.* (Really?)"

"*Meow.* (Really.)"

"*Meow.* (Really?)"

"*Meow.* (Really-we're not starting this again. Just tell me what in the world you're talking about?)"

"*Meow.* (I'm just talking about a picture of you and your guards wearing idiotic costumes that I just took and that can be posted onto Snapcat™, The-Twitter Bird-Is-Dead-I-Killed-It™,[60] and FacePaw® in less than a minute.)" He held up his Iris-Phone to show the queen a very, very embarrassing photo of the queen and her guards.

"*Meow.* (You wouldn't dare post that.)"

"*Meow.* (Wouldn't I?)" He typed in the commands to share simultaneously to all three sites. He raised his finger towards the 'yes' option on the 'Are you sure?' prompt. "*Meow.* (Just cave. It's not so hard.)" The queen shuffled nervously.

"*Meow.* (No.)" Eros inched his claw closer to the button. "*Meow.* (I won't give in.)" Super close. "*Meow.* (Never.)"

Right as Eros was going to hit the button, the queen caved like a 30-mile sinkhole would if 60,000 tons of Osmium[61] suddenly appeared on top of it. "*Meow!* (Fine! I'll cave!

[60] The forum where you post all your best, most gory, most incredibly splendorific kills for everyone to look at in awe.

[61] The densest metal naturally occurring. Pick up a book, people!

Just don't post that!)" The queen had Scoobus bring Eros the amulet as he set the phone down. "*Meow.* (Now leave. You've caused enough trouble already.)"

"*Mew.* (Okay. I'll leave. But first, *click*.)" The sound of Eros pressing the button and posting the picture reverberated through the room.

The queen screamed in rage as Eros quickly evaded the guards and ran through the house and out the front door, laughing the whole way.

*   *   *

When Eros reached the spot between space and outside of time that was his house, he ran inside and opened his safe with a 82,492,864,384,384,734,567,676,437,647,364,776 combination lock that was totally unique and in no way 1, 2, 3, 4, 5, 6, 7, 8, 9, 10, 11, 12, etc.

Anyway, after thirty minutes, or maybe ten seconds, or maybe six years,[62] Eros's safe clicked and the door swung open to reveal tons of Cheetos and Cheese Puffs shaped like former presidents, but most prominent, encrusted in a glimmering gem display hung on the back wall, were the five pieces of the amulet. They had been placed into a near perfect circle, and Eros could see where the last piece would fit.

"Alright. This is it." He laid the amulets in the correct places and set the last one down. When nothing happened, Eros started to rearrange them. Suddenly, when Eros had flipped them all over, they all started shaking uncontrollably.

Then, with a great *BANG!*, the bug fragment snapped into the mammal part, which then snapped into the reptile piece. Then that part started moving towards the

[62] It was outside of time.

collective amphibian, bird, and fish piece and welded together magically, which was accompanied by a giant energy shockwave that dissipated through the walls.

When the dust cleared, and Eros got all the frightened dust bunnies out of his hair, a bronze medallion dazzled his eyes, shining like the rising sun of the brightest morning on the first day, but also like the setting sun on the last day, before the blackest night engulfs all of existence and even time itself withers and dies. Eros sighed as he put the shining amulet in his pocket.

"Well, no use putting it off." He squatted down and jumped up through the ceiling, rising above his palace and the several other holes he had created. He soared over the space time continuum, personified as a raging river that is everywhere and nowhere and runs through all existence.

Eros calls it the 'Space Stream'. After soaring past the Karman Line and entering the inner atmosphere, he finally landed on the ground in a cool pose, like the one the Scarlet Spider uses,[63] on a tiny little remote island over a hundred miles off the Greek mainland.

When he looked up, all menacing-like, and surveyed his surroundings, Eros saw that he had landed on a beach, in front of a forested rocky area with a small game trail leading deep into the trees. Eros started walking through the trail. It started to get less and less maintained, as if the game stopped walking there, almost as if they were afraid of something. Eros began stepping over more roots and branches as he delved deeper into the forest. He could see a huge outcropping of a cave up ahead on the trail, but when he got close giant wooden gates slammed shut a centimeter from his face.

[63] And which her sister made fun of.

“Stop and exit the premises! This is a restricted area,” an ominous voice warned. Eros searched for its source and found it in a small humanoid being with snakes for arms and a single snake for a head.

“I need to get through. I have a package for Tartarusdaughter, first name Kampe? Kampe Tartarusdaughter? I’ve got some beautiful new torture devices she ordered a couple weeks ago. Tartarus has 9G, so it took us Amazonians at Amazon awhile to convert it down to 5G, but here it is.” The sentinel narrowed his eyes at him, which was hard because snakes don’t have eyelids or the facial muscles that allow things to narrow their eyes.

“I thought the Amazons were an all women clan.”

GASP Eros gasped. “This is the 21st century! Get with the times, dude!” He put on his best offended face.

“Sorry, I just assumed-”

“Oh, you just assumed, huh? You just *assumed* that a boy couldn’t be in the Amazons, did you. You seem to be *assuming* a lot of things right now.” The snake thing started getting nervous as Eros more heavily accused it.

“Look, you seem like a nice guy-”

“*Guy*, is it? You just assumed I was male?”

“I’m sorry, I heard your protest and I was like, ‘he must be-’”

“*He*? You didn’t even ask for my pronouns and you just assumed? You’re making some very dangerous assumptions today.”

“Fine. What are your pronouns-”

"Did you seriously just say that? I can't believe this! You better let me through here or I'll have a few hundred thousand people with signs here within the twelve-hour period!"

"Fine, fine. Head on through with your stupid package."

Eros smugly walked in as they opened the gate.

"Oh, and while you're being offended by everything, you called me 'dude' earlier. That insinuates a pronoun, you know."

"Actually, it can be used as a gender neutral term if you use it in the right context, WHICH. I. DID." Eros quickly responded.

"Rats."

Eros smiled as he heard the watcher's frustration. He was really good at seeming offended. He had invented the emotion, after all. He had invented all the emotions, but he was still really good at them. He could even get offended by people being offended that he was offended that they were offended because of him being offended by them; ('I'm sorry, you're offended that I'm offended and you are offended by my offense, which I am offended by? I take great offense from that!).

When Eros finally reached it, he stood before the giant outcropping and looked for the spot to put the amulet. It was completely covered in rock, so he thought there might be no opening, but as he looked it over he noticed a small circular indentation where he could possibly put the amulet. He smiled and started walking towards it, but as he was walking, a root decided it wanted to be best friends forever with Eros's sneakers, and he unexpectedly tripped.

THUMP. Eros hit the ground and his whole body glitched. Suddenly he was a monster with a terrible red snake for a head, gold wings with a shorter wingspan than usual, and a belt made of screaming bull heads that breathed white fire. It examined its surroundings cautiously.

"Hmm. Interesting." Eros glitched back.

"Oops. Gotta be more careful around this area." He sat up and clicked the amulet into the little indentation.

With a *click*, the amulet stuck into the rock and the wall exploded with a great flash of light. When Eros opened his eyes, the whole front cave wall was gone, like somebody had simply walked up, cut it out, and taken it away to lands unknown. Eros gazed into the great pit of darkness that undoubtedly contained a monster capable of torturing the Hecatoncheires and Elder Cyclopes.

What could possibly go wrong, he thought, and in he went. The cave was dark, but Eros grabbed the water from the moist ground and formed it into a floating ball. He then created some bioluminescent shrimp from thin air,[64] and put them in the water, so that the sphere glowed brilliantly. As he walked deeper into the hole, Eros tripped a couple times. Each time the monster glitched back, examining the location with a smile. Then Eros would glitch back.

He reached the end of the cave after about an hour of walking and looked around. The rock was burnt and scratched at, and a small military cot was sprawled out in the back. A monster with hair made of snakes, a long, spiky tail dripping in poison, and a flaming whip sheathed on her belt was passed out on it. Kampe's snake hair hissed at Eros, but not enough to wake her up. Eros grabbed a big rock and walked towards Kampe as the snakes tried to get him to go away.

Hiss hiss hiss, they hissed, *hiss hiss hiss.*

[64] As one does

Eros was about to knock Kampe out when a tiny pebble, one who had heard about all the rock and roots who had become B.F.F.s with Eros's sneaker's and was like, "I want to be B.F.F.s too!", hugged him, causing Eros to trip and fall, hitting the ground with a *BANG!* that promptly woke Kampe up at the worst possible time.

"What? What is it? I wasn't sleeping," Kampe yawned. She got out of her cot and looked at Eros drearily.

"Kampe, by order of the gods, you are to immediately return to Tartarus and get into your cell-" Eros couldn't even finish his proclamation before he was blasted with a wave of fire that left him buried sixty feet under collapsed rock. He glitched again. The monster was watching, seeming pleased with the situation. They flashed a smile at Kampe.

Eros glitched back.

"Ouch." He stumbled up to Kampe, who was watching him with a face full of fire, limitless rage, and unbridled power.

"Leave me be, spirit. Who are you?"

"I'm Eros Phanes. I gotta take you back to Tartarus now. Sorry." A look of fear and a little smugness filled Kampe's face at the realization that gods had sent such a renowned deity.

"I do not care! You can die, can't you?!"

"Under incredibly extreme circumstances, yes. But I'll be back within the week." Kampe contemplated that last part for a minute.

"No matter." She blasted him with fire again. This time, Eros stepped back and held his ground. He glitched again, and the monster sent back the fire with a ferocious wave of power. Kampe barely had time to shield herself before she was buried in an ocean of power. Eros glitched back, and the power stopped abruptly. Kampe looked at him with increasing disdain but a hint of curiosity.

"What is this vile trick, demon?" Kampe screeched.

Eros seemed confused.

"What? My shoes? They have no laces or velcro because they're slip-ins. You just slip the foot in. Really they're quite-"

"Not that, you buffoon. The monster glitching through you."

"Oh, that. That's Phanes. Back to the slip-ins. I really think they make putting on your shoes more efficient, becau-"

"Quiet about the slip-ins. Who is Phanes?"

"An alter from my Dissociative Identity Disorder."

"Which is..."

"An alternate personality created by the entropy of my mind. He is god of entropy and can take over when Entropy overwhelms my mind. The physical appearance just embodies my mindset at the time."

"You're insane."

"Medically. So, now, when something unexpected happens to me or I experience a large amount of pain, my other self, Phanes, comes out."

"Is he nice?"

"He's Entropy itself. What do you think? He can destroy anyone, in Mario Krt and real life."

Kampe laughed nervously.

"How do you play Mario Krt if there are two of you?"

"There are... others."

"Well, if this Phanes is coming, I shall destroy him too."

"Bad idea." Kampe unleashed a barrage of fire as Eros transitioned into Phanes. Phanes flicked his wrist, and the fires shot into the right wall.

"That was a mistake," Phanes said, smiling. Kampe charged at him writhing terrible fury. He smiled.

One Hour Later...

Eros dragged a bruised and bloody Kampe across the dark cold floor of a huge pit. He winced as he threw her down at the feet of Tartarus. "Got her."

"Are you okay?" asked Tartarus, seeing his cuts, burns, and a ruffled up left wing.

"Yeah. I'm fine."

"What did you do to her?"

"No idea."

The bruised heap of Kampe moaned.

Tartarus stared at her.

"Which one?"

"Phanes."

"Cool. You want to help me imprison her? We can gloat to her smugly."

"That sounds nice."

Then they walked out into the lantern set.[65]

[65] Helios thinks Tartarus is icky and gross, so he won't go down there. Instead the local daimons use lanterns and just pretend they're the sun.

Eros and the Giant Evil Space Dragon of Darkness

A beautiful forest. Huge trees covered the land below and prairies opened up like islands in the sea of green. Birds sang songs of heroes and villains and of redemption and victory, filling the land with a beautiful tune. Squirrels gleefully run around, digging bountiful caches of acorns in preparation for winter.

Pitched near a spring letting pure water flow from the depths of Gaia, was a tall black tent that reflected the dark, star-speckled sky.

Ah, that tent.

The mortal Elysium that was the forest could not have had a more beautiful thing.

Woven by Arachne, the tent was a spacious four-room paradise. It was arranged in a shape like a plus sign, with the entrance opening into the common area. This room had blankets on the floor, several board games stacked in the corner, and even a radio, which was solar-powered and connected to every radio frequency in the universe, scientific and otherwise.

To the left was the sleeping room, which had a humble cot and sleeping bag. Not so humbly, the ceiling was open to allow stargazing,[66] but it could also be covered as well. There was an alarm that woke you up in accordance with your sleeping patterns, and it did so by playing the sound of the forest.

Straight from the entrance was the preparation room. It was virtually an armory for nature, complete with seventeen different sunglasses and too many hats to count. There were a lot of bird calls, fish calls, bug calls, and beaver calls. If you can name it, there was a call for it.[67]

Finally, to the right of the entrance, there was the gallery room. Because when you carefully compile, label, and put into displays funny-looking leaves, twigs, and really soft moss, they take up a lot of space.[68]

Also, the tent could fly, turn invisible, smush into a black singularity for easy transportation, turn back into a tent and pitch itself, and in case you wanted information, every thread in the tent is thoroughly and magically programmed with the Amazon Iris® A.I.

Now I shall describe the entire history of the tent, who has bought it, and how it came to this forest.

Now, in the year 4,313 B.C. In a small town in Lydia, the seamstress Arachne

---

[66] With a magical spell that keeps the cold from entering the threshold. By the way, the whole place had perfectly adjustable heating.

[67] They all said "Property of Pan Lyterios." I wonder how those got there on the definitely rightfully owned calls.

[68] 'Nuff said.

sewed-

"Hey!"

A large gold hawk unzipped the door to the tent and stepped out, holding some marshmallow pokers and a brown camping chair that had the face of a cartoon bear on the back support, causing the watcher to infer that the chair was just an anthropomorphic bear chair. Trust me, it was a pretty hilarious gaf to all who saw the chair.

Trust me.

"Hey, you!" The hawk stared directly through the fourth wall as he squawked angrily.

Wait. Who is he talking to?

"I'm talking to YOU, Narrator!"

Is he talking to me?

"No, I'm talking to a DIFFERENT omniscient narrator," the hawk said sarcastically. "Yes, I'm talking to you!"

What is it?

"You were supposed to profile me, not the tent!"

Sorry, sorry. My mistake.

"It's okay, I guess," the hawk suddenly began growing. His feathers retreated into his back. His claws turned into feet with sneakers and socks inscribed with dinosaurs riding rocket ships layered on them. His beak retreated into his face to reveal his perfect teeth and sea-blue eyes.

"I'd like to keep my secrets secret, anyway," Eros said. He walked with his stuff down a short game path, which was blossoming with grass and fresh deer prints. As the trail snaked down a gentle hill, Eros could see a plume of smoke rising from an opening in the green. He could smell ambrosia kabobs roasting and hear nectar cups being clinked together in blind merriment.

Eros entered the circle of light and sat down with his chair a few feet from the fire.

Now, who's in attendance? he thought.

Of course, Hestia was sitting in the center of the fire on a small, fire-proof stool, kindling the flames and stopping them from spreading. She warmed the flames to a nice warmth, cold enough to not burn anyone who touched it, but warm enough to banish the cool breeze from penetrating the circle.

Hestia laughed delightfully as a tiny wisp of air swooped through the fire, making the tips of the blaze tickle her cheeks. With a simple swoop of her hand, she sent the wind out of the fire, and all was peaceful once again.

Across the fire, Hebe, cupbearer to the gods and goddess of eternal youth, sat on a gold throne, holding a golden apple in her left hand, and a cup of nectar in her right.

Hercules stood to the left of Hebe, his hand on her shoulder as they both watched the fire.

Scampering around behind them were the Olympians, who were struggling to fill their cups with nectar from a small fountain. They kept tripping, mostly over each other, and dropping their drinks.

"Get me another drink!" Hebe yelled.

"Yes, Daughter," Zeus answered, running off to the fountain to try[69] to successfully fill a small cup.

"And peel me a grape while you're at it!" Hebe yelled as Zeus tripped over Hera, who tripped over Hephaestus, who tripped over Poseidon, who tripped over Artemis, who tripped over Apollo...

"Don't you think you're being a little hard on them?" Hercules asked, watching the pile of gods grow progressively larger and larger. "They look pretty confused about doing these simple tasks."

"I've been carrying their cups for thousands of years. I think that they can handle it one day," Hercules nodded as Poseidon handed her a cup that was one-sixteenth filled with nectar.

"My lady, your nectar," Hebe looked at the cup and the measly amount of nectar, then back at Poseidon.

"This is barely filled."

"Yes, but it is very hard to scrape the very top of a fountain with a cup and get much nectar."

"Then just scoop the cup in deeper," Poseidon gasped in surprise as Hebe poured the cup out on the ground.

"But it might get on my hands!"

"Who cares if it gets on your hands?"

"I do! I don't like touching liquids. They just feel so..." Poseidon struggled to find

[69] For the 678th time.

the right word. "...wet."

Hebe sighed. "You've got to be kidding me," Poseidon frowned at what he thought was just blatant insensitivity to one of his greatest, most terrifying, terrible fears.

"I'll have you know my condition is quite real," Poseidon corrected. "I have Hydrophobia."

"You're the lord of the ocean, which is the biggest body of liquid in the world. You having a fear of water-"

"*Liquids.*"

"You having a fear of liquids is like me having Apeirophobia, the fear of eternal life."

"I'll assure you my phobia is very real and very intense. I do not appreciate you making fun of me for something that I have absolutely no control over. It's simply rude, to be honest."

"And I have Fictusphobiaphobia, the fear of fake phobias. Now get to work, or you'll have extra liquid in your cup tomorrow."

Poseidon hurried away and a half an hour later, after many tears and gallons upon gallons of nectar spilled, everyone was sitting down with full cups of nectar and some smoked ambrosia.

"So now that you're all sitting down-" Eros began, but was cut off by all the men jumping ten feet into the air in surprise.

The woman kept still, having noticed Eros an hour ago like normal people.[70]

The boys landed back on the ground with a synchronous *THUMP!* and looked around for what scared them.

Zeus was the first to spot Eros and was enraged that he had made such a fool of himself in front of his family.

"I'll teach you to hide in plain sight!" Zeus yelled as he hurled a lightning bolt at Eros.

The bolt shot through the air for exactly 3.6 seconds, accelerating at 1,046,700,000,000 Gs per millisecond, trapping air molecules in front of it, which created a thin plasma coating.[71] The bolt shot across the fire and was half a foot from Eros's face when he held up his right hand. The bolt stopped in midair and fell to his feet, where it burned a hole in the Earth forty feet deep.

Zeus quickly found his seat.

Once the bright shine of the lightning bolt finally dimmed to a glow, Eros started

[70] A guide to Olympians;
Girls rule (exception: Hera and Aphrodite)
Boys drool (exception: Hephaestus)

[71] The lightning bolt would be going at 90 percent the speed of light at the exact point that it would explosively make contact with Eros's face. This is not accounting for plasma drag, but the timing of this is not fast enough to substantially slow it. Though, fusion may slow the bolt down due to air molecules not being able to get away. The rapid breaking apart of atoms would also cause an expanding wave of x-ray and gamma radiation soaring through the campsite at the speed of light, which would either kill or simply obliterate the area. This is pretty fast, though the bolt could be accelerated to 99.9 percent of the speed of light by entangling certain electromagnetic fields, causing them to explode violently, accelerating the bolt to inhuman levels.

again.

"Now that that burst of rage has cooled, I'd like to formally announce my attendance here."

Hebe cleared her throat obnoxiously loud and all the other gods quickly followed Zeus's example.

"So, Lord Eros, I'm happy that you got my invitation. We were hoping you would come," Hebe said.

"You sent me 4,596 separate invitations over the course of eight hours, each one more desperate and pleading than the last."

"Well, as I said, we wanted to make sure you got an invitation," Hebe answered. "And we heard your house isn't where time *or* space is. We didn't know that mail could be delivered to where neither time *nor* space are."

"My mailbox is connected through a pseudo-wormhole to a mailbox in southwestern Delaware. You must have known that, seeing as you sent it to the mailbox in Southwestern Delaware instead of my house outside of time or space, so didn't you know?"

"We were worried that you hadn't written back," Hebe rebutted.

"You sent them from 10 PM to 6 AM. I was sleeping."

A little embarrassed, Hebe quickly changed the subject.

"Well, since this is my birthday party, could you tell us all a story or adventure you've gone through?!"

"Sure. Which one do you want to hear?"

"How many stories do you have?"

"$4.361171 \bullet 10^{101}$."

"Oh... Okay. Tell me the first one."

"Really? But don't you wanna hear about $2.578853 \bullet 10^{101}$? It's *reeeeally* interesting."

"OK, tell us about $2.578853 \bullet 10^{101}$."

"No, I'm just joking. $2.578853 \bullet 10^{101}$ is about igneous rocks. I'll tell you number 1 if you want."

Eros cleared his throat and began.

"Long ago, a **beast** roamed the world. It lived in the eternal darkness of space, and it ate darkness, growing big and powerful in a place that was literally made of darkness. Some say that when they were finished with its meals it would creep to the very center of the cosmos, and lay there, blowing, like smoke from his mouth, terrible hatred and malice into the universe.

The beast lived like those for untold ages, for time and space had no meaning at that point.

At one specific point in a non-time-oriented system, the beast slunk back to the center of the universe.

It had been a pretty successful day. The beast had eaten some darkness, eaten some more darkness, and then, as a surprise ending to its meal, eaten some more darkness.

Now it had to go seep evil into the center of the universe, so that anything new would be utterly ruined.

So the beast was just casually running the old grind and dispensing massive amounts of hatred, when-"

"Wait." All eyes turned to Apollo as Eros stopped his story to listen to his question.

"What is it?" Eros asked.

"What is the beast's name?"

"Ah. I was hoping you wouldn't ask me that," Eros responded. He coughed and opened his mouth, almost afraid to say the terrible beast's name. Finally the name slithered off of Eros's tongue.

"**TIM**," Eros said, and the whole group shuddered. After everybody settled down, Eros continued his tale.

"Suddenly, a tiny prick of light entered the world. Infinitely small, Tim looked at it warily. After a while, Tim decided to smell it.

Maybe it's darkness, they thought. *A new, bright darkness that doesn't have the properties of the previous darkness. Yeah, that must be it.*

Right as Tim leaned in towards it, the dot exploded ferociously, hitting them with a flurry of particles and energy that could destroy galaxies upon galaxies in their storm of raw energy.

Tim chose a form for the first time, becoming a monstrous dragon that flew with no air, bit with no teeth, and hid in the shadows with scales as black and durable as the very void of the universe itself.

Enraged, Tim wanted to find its attackers and rip them to atoms in a slow, grueling way.

No, it thought. *If they can hurt me, they can do it again. I must wait for the right opportunity to make them learn pain.*

Tim slunk into the shadows a short ten light years away and watched and waited for the orchestrators to reveal themselves. They soon did, after the quantum soup cooled to a few gazillion degrees.

Humph, Tim thought. *Seriously? These guys?*

The invaders were robed in... well... robes, and wore all sorts of different colors and sizes.

Some were made of the very light that the exploding point was, and Tim shuddered at their appearance.

Some were made of darkness, and Tim licked its lips, swearing to instead eat those ones.

Two of the taller beings wore light and deep blues while one was green and had dashes of purple and yellow on their robes.

Finally, one had tan skin and two golden wings jutting out from behind it, though by what devices Tim knew not.

But nobody cares about that one.

Most prominent of all, Tim saw that they were **gods**. They radiated power, not like the point of light, but like the very vacuum around them that impossibly shook with their strength.

Well, that, and what the winged guy said about thirty seconds after they materialized.[72]

'So, now that we've officially become gods of this reality, what should we do?' Eros asked."

Present Eros was about to continue telling his tale when Athena raised her hand, as was god etiquette, which normal gods[73] generally used to be polite.

"Yes, Athena?"

"Why are you using omniscient third person?"

"Because talking about yourself in the third person is, like, insanely cool," Eros answered.

"No it isn'-"

"Yes it is."

There was an awkward silence and Eros decided it would be best if he continued the story.

"Anyway, Nyx turned to Erebus.

'Good idea. With the Big Bang to destroy anymore, say, primordial beasts lurking in the universe, everything should be just fine and dandy,' Nyx said.

'I'm still worried that we didn't make it powerful enough to destroy all conceivable threats,' Erebus worried.

[72] They were able to do this due to the space-time continuum becoming a thing a few moments earlier.

[73] Who weren't any of the men.

'I'm sure it's fine,' Eros assured. 'I'm just happy that we stopped planning in that stupid pocket dimension. After a billion trillion quadrillion centillion cencentillion google googleplex meetings.'

'Eros!' Hemera objected. 'Rude! First of all, it was *only* a *million* trillion quadrillion centillion cencentillion google googleplex meetings, and second, that pocket dimension was *great.*' Eros frowned.

'Still, I'm sure that all beings that might have been lurking here have been utterly destroyed by now.'

Suddenly, the gods were blitzkrieged with pain as Tim sent darts from its tail straight through their chests, both impaling them and letting deadly poison seep into their essence.

Ichor spilled as the gods fell down in shock and writhed in horrible, ferocious, pain.

Hmm, Tim thought, watching them scream and cry. *Serves them right for not knowing I exist.*

Tim slunk back to the depths of the universe, not happy about the sudden appearance of things intruding on all the nothingness they had so loved before. That stupid ever-expanding singularity just *had* to decide to force itself into reality, probably due to an incursion of other universes.

At least I destroyed those stupid gods, it thought. Tim laughed at the memory of desecrating their fragile minds. *Idiots.*

Its assumption was sadly wrong, though, as there was one fatal flaw in its megalomaniacal plan, which usually works out entirely, as the villains nearly always kill all the heroes quickly and sensibly.[74]

When Tim had attempted to utterly destroy the gods, Eros noticed a tiny little burst of light. Weird. Light usually doesn't occur in a true vacuum outside an expanding new universe.

'That shouldn't be there,' his subconscious muttered to itself. 'There shouldn't be any light or energy being emitted from a true vacuum outside of space, time, and the laws of physics.'

His body simultaneously assured Erebus that everything was fine and going perfectly to plan.

'Hmm. I better keep an eye out for that,' Eros's subconscious thought. 'I have a bad feeling about this.'[75]

The dot was, in fact, a piece of pure energy[76] that had stuck like a piece of gum to Tim's black scales.

When Tim attacked, an on-edge subconscious took over the brain, briefly making an only brain-stem brain[77] [78]. Eros uncontrollably jumped into the air, jetting out of the

---

[74] Not.

[75] Which, of course, came from Eros's subconcious's subconscious

[76] To be specific, it was a antimatter particle that disrupted the cosmic equilibrium and allowed matter to outnumber it, making a significant amount more of the universe into matter, so that matter would always be more prevalent, making it possible for matter to be stable and last without being obliterated. Physics!

[77] The subconcious's home.

[78] It was called SuperStem, until the subconscious saw that there would be a competition called SuperStem in the future, so it stopped and quietly pretended that, "No, there wasn't anything for Eros's subconscious to be sued into oblivion for! Why would you even suggest that utterly preposterous thing!? Of course not!"

universe, and floating in the void.

In that moment, a confused, dazed, and kind of comatose Eros regained control of the brain.

'Thanks, subconscious,' Eros muttered to himself.

Anytime, dude.

Eros looked around and located Tim. Without a word, he shot down to about the middle of his back, landing in a small cave sheltered by huge, black scales pointing towards Tim's head. It appeared to be carved by some quark particles, or possibly leptions.

Better get to work, man, Eros's subconscious told him. *There are 7854925858093 miles until Tim's base. This is gonna be a long ride, but possibly not long enough for your idea. I still have a bad feeling about this.*[79]

Eros waited, itching for some vengeance and, most of all, something entertaining to do. He began his plan.

Much later, Tim returned to its fortress, Utumna.[80] They had raised its walls long ago, prophetically foreseeing that something might come along and ruin his beautiful darkness.

It's good I get to use this, thought Tim, not happy about the reason, but happy that their investment portfolio would get better, you know, since they weren't wasting a fortress.

Tim swooped around a tower of death and blasted open the gates of doom,

[79] See note 75

[80] Which is definitely different then Utumno, and if you've read The Book of Lost Tales 1, ummm, it's different then the way they say Utumno too, so quiet.

reaching a large courtyard that circled around the castle with a stone path[81] imbued with pain and suffering.

The fortress also had a gazebo.

As Tim soared to the front of the throne room, Eros looked up from his work, but could only see darkness.

That's what the castle was, really, just darkness that Tim thought was too

[81] Or, rather, not stone, but slightly lighter darkness.

disgusting, like cauliflower or brussel sprouts.[82]

[82] There are seven types of evil people, this list lists them in rising amounts of evilness from start to finish.

One: The people who consider themselves evil, like people who rob banks or gas stations.

Heroes who defeat them: Normal individual heroes who fight them at the beginning of the comic.

Two: The people who ARE evil, like people who capture small countries, massacre people, or commit genocide.

Heroes who defeat them: A team-up may occur between two or three heroes, resulting in an epic issue.

Three: Planetary threats, who are super powerful and wish to destroy the world and everyone in it.

Heroes who defeat them: The whole team of superheroes will come together, pretending that this is super rare and more dangerous than the other times, even though this kind of thing happens every year or two, sometimes with the same villains.

(See next page)

Four: Universal threats, sometimes from another universe. These beings want to destroy and/or enslave the whole universe.

Heroes who defeat them: All the teams on Earth will band together to defeat their enemy, possibly enlisting alien civilizations.

Five: Multiversal assassins, typically going after a single group or hero, typically a specific kind of hero.

Tim broke the doors of the room wide open and laughed at its marvelous win against those stupid gods, which was kind of destructive, but Tim was just really happy, okay?

Reveling in his success, Tim was about to prepare a feast when its itch acted up again. The itch has been there for the whole time, but now it was particularly itchy. Tim desperately rubbed its back against the castle walls, and as his scales squished together like mail, the itch stopped.

Satisfied, Tim was going to continue preparations for the feast when the itch started again, a little more itchy than before. Tim rubbed its back on the castle walls again, but it knew that would just make the itch worse, and much more annoying and itchy.

After a few more times of scratching the itch against the walls, Tim decided enough was enough. This itch had its chance to be scratched. Now it would be *obliterated.*

Heroes who defeat them: All the variations of that single hero will find each other in an unexplained way, then defeat the big baddy in a huge fight scene where each character will discover they are special.

Six: Threats to the multiverse itself, aiming to recreate it or destroy all but their universe, or rule it, ect.

Heroes who defeat them: The powers and/or abstract entities in the universe will try to stop the villain, but fail in a spectacular way. When all seems hopeless, all the hero teams on Earth and all the hero teams on other Earths will band together and somehow, inexplicably, defeat the bad guy and restore peace.

Seven: The people who make you eat cauliflower and brussel sprouts, claiming they are "Good for you!"

Heroes who defeat them: Sadly, they cannot be defeated. Some heroes are even tricked into telling kids they are good guys. *shudder* They are truly EVIL.

Tim slunk down to its treasuries, grabbing some of the most powerful weapons, including but not limited to:

- The Sword of Darkness
- The Mace of Darkness
- The Staff of Darkness
- The Saber of Darkness
- The Wand of Darkness
- The Bow of Darkness
- The Arrow of Darkness
- The Pepper Spray of Darkness
- The Really Big, Sharp Rock of Darkness
- The Squeaking Rubber Chicken of Darkness

All of them were some of the most powerful weapons to ever have been made. Tim twisted around so they could see where the itch was. Preparing its weapons, to SCRATCH. THAT. ITCH.

Itch, time to die, Tim thought.

One after the other, Tim hit, threw, and smashed the precise spot the itch was, but each weapon was eroded by Tim's impenetrable scales. Each time he hit it, the itch seemed to grow exponentially more painful and annoying, taunting Tim with its inability to beat it.

Stupid itch, Tim thought. *Why can't it just be scratched? It's not as if it's one of those stupid gods or-*

Tim stopped. Was it a god? Tim was so filled with the adrenaline of the moment, what if they missed one? They probably *DID* miss one, didn't they? Tim was growing angrier by the second.

"Hey, itch!" Tim screamed. "If you're going to hurt me, at least do it out here! If I can't kill you by ambush, I can kill you by battle! Come out here and fight me like an animated, conscious being!"

There was a short silence as the itch kept on itching like normal, and no response came.

Tim worried that maybe the itch was just an itch. How embarrassing, yelling at an itch.

Right as Tim was going to try to scratch it again, a splitting pain rocketed up Tim's spinal cord and shook its brain with mind-splitting, shrieking, horrible, terrible pain.

Needless to say, it hurt.

As Tim was still falling to the floor in a daze, the itch started running up its back. Tim barely had time to look up and see a man with golden wings, soaring towards his head, carrying a golden adamantine sword.

Forged in the forge that made the world, cooled in the endless seas that Pontus made before time, with a hilt fashioned from the first tree that grew into green plains of Gaia the sword was awe-inspiring. It was sharpened on Tim's scales for days, and the shocking sensation was one of Tim's scales, tougher than a billion diamonds, being sliced in half.

Created as a worst-case scenario, the sword was named το ξίφος του πατέρα, the father sword, which while flying over Tim's head Eros nicknamed Slicer Slicey Sliceysliceslice, "Slicer" for short.

Able to cut a quark in half and tear time itself to shreds like paper, it was the sharpest sword ever created.

As he fell, Eros jutted the sword down into Tim's head, impaling Tim as its head fell to the floor.

"How's that for an itch?" he said in a super cool way.

Tim and Eros fought for an entire day, striking at each other with more power than has ever been released since. Finally, after tanking enough blasts to incinerate a galaxy, Tim fell, and disappeared into shadow, with just four last words to forebode its return.

"I forebode my return."

Tim, and metaphorically evil and darkness, was vanquished for now, and Eros and metaphorically good and light, I guess, won, so all was good.

Eros stopped and everybody around him sat speechless. Finally Hecate coughed out the question on everyone's mind.

"So...Tim is still out there?"

"Yeah."

"Should we be worried?"

"Well, it's been over 13,800,000,000 years since then so...probably."

Everybody shivered in fear. Unfazed, Eros got up and walked to the cooler, which had been put on the rocks overlooking a gentle slope.

As he reached for a short bottle of mango lassi, the lid slammed shut, revealing a space-black cat with the feeling of darkness emanating from its pointy, flat fur, which was also emanating ACTUAL darkness.

Its eyes were yellow and the pupil slits near impossible to see, but it had such a cold, frightful stare that it was like a million hands reached out from its eyes and encased the gods behind Eros in ice for an awful, unescapable millisecond. The cat opened its terrifying mouth, revealing a row of white fangs, filed to the point with an unnerving precision.

Then it meowed, oh, how it meowed.

Its meow was like the sound of the hopeless dying gasps of a billion billion beings.

Its meow reached into the god's souls and ripped them from their bodies, pounding them into the ground with a crooked, demented joy.

Waking from their small coma, the gods blasted the cat with pure unhinged power, but to their horror the cat was still standing and smiling when the smoke cleared. Exhausted, the gods hid behind their chairs as the cat smiled again and began to talk.

"*Hello.*"

"Hello, daimon."

"*My master says hello. Do you want to know who they are? It'll probably be quite a surprise.*"

"Well, due to the context, I think I know."

"*No matter. My master is...*" the cat paused for dramatic effect. "***TIM***." The gods behind them gasped.

"*Master has been growing strong, yes. Soon they will attack the Realm of Ideals, and nobody will be able to stop them. They have sent me here to... deal with you so you will not be a bother.*"

"And why do they think you will be able to stop me? A vassal you are, and I am their greatest enemy."

"*Because I am an extension of its power, and after waiting so long they have become quite powerful.*"

The cat then extended its claws and pounced at Eros, but he pushed his palm in their stomach, sending it flying through the air and into a stone wall almost a hundred meters away.

"I think they should have waited longer," Eros said in a really cool way yet again, (like, *really* cool).

"*You will never defeat Tim!*"

The cat faded into shadow.

As the stunned gods sat in shocked contemplation, Eros started frantically grabbing his stuff. He whistled, and a dot of black singularity floated over from the woods. Eros threw his things into the dot and it followed him as he began to run off, but Hebe stopped him.

"Where are you going?" she asked.

"To the Realm of Ideals."

"What's that?"

"A metaphysical land full of false gods."

"What?"

Eros sighed. Did he have to explain EVERYTHING to these gods?

"After the universe began, when sentient beings sprouted up, they started believing in gods.

They initially believed in the Greek gods, but soon, others split off and began to believe in others. Other gods.

We considered these people to not be a threat at first, but then, the ideas that they believed in began to manifest into consciousnesses, into new deities. After we discovered them and revealed they were not the true rulers of the Earth, they rebelled and attacked us.

After a long and costly war, I infused myself and some powerful Greek mages with the power of Chaos, and created a pocket dimension, which they were respectfully banished to.

Now and again, we visit them, and they promise to aid us in times of great need. Their universe has grown into a haven for elves, gods, dragons, dwarves, boars, and more.

Tim is almost definitely going there to destroy our reserve forces so we cannot muster a significant force against him. I have to go there to warn them and advise them what to do."

Hebe thought about his story for a minute but then stood up straight and dutifully.

"The Olympians will assist you in this, Lord Eros."

All the other gods behind her stood up straight, slightly afraid but kept by duty to help.

Eros forced out a smile.

"Grrrrreat! I'll just let you follow me, then, and-OMIGOSH WHAT IN THE WORLD IS THAT!"

Everyone turned their heads towards where he pointed, but there was nothing there.

Hebe turned around laughing.

"Oh, you jokester. C'mon, let's-Eros?"

But Eros was already gone.

*   *   *

Eros soared through the blue air majestically, the singularity speeding behind him.

He dove through a wormhole, disappearing from the campsite in Greece and popping into the Aether over Africa's Great Rift Valley, where by a quant river Prometheus made the first bipedal hominids 2,000,000 years ago, after being beseeched to populate the Earth from the image of their rulers, the Titans before their overthrow in the Titanomachy.

Eros scanned the horizon and saw the river, barely a creek now, ruining at the feet of a cave outcropping. Sticking his landing, Eros walked to the cave, but was stopped by an old man with a green spear.

"Stop!" The man said, jutting his spear forwards.

"What are you?" retorted Eros.

"I am Gaufin, and I am the guardian of the entrance into the Realm of Ideals."

"Well, let me in. I have an urgent message. I am Eros Phanes. Here. I've got an I.D." Eros pulled out his local card for the *Cupcaked Club*, the program at that one store that gives you free cupcakes every time you buy there.

Gaufin looked at the I.D. suspiciously.

"How do I know this is yours?"

"What are you talking about? That card is *obviously* loaded with identification. It's even laminated."

"There are no codes, pictures, or bar codes to help, no invisible ink or something. It has the name written on it with a sharpie, but it appears the name was written on in black, but was then scrubbed out, and the name was written again in yellow highlighter."

"They wrote my name wrong."

Gaufin sighed.

"I'm sorry, but I'll need more identification than this if you want to get into the Realm of Ideals."

"Really? What should I do?"

"I dunno. Maybe you could do something heroic. I heard that the closest town, Gadoma, is having some problems."

"Really?"

"Yeah. This monster is terrorizing them. I heard it was like a lion, but with a goat's upper torso erupting from its back, and a snake for a tail. It's the descendant of Echidna and Typhon."

"Oh, is it a Chimera?"

"No, it's something completely different and totally original. Also, the town of Gadoma is a very prosperous town due to its creation of the sword with big chunks of lead stuck on their tips."

"Why don't the people of Gadoma just use the swords with big hunks of lead stuck on their tips *on* the chimera?"

"Try not to think about massive plot holes like that. Also, it's not a chimera. It's a completely original idea."

"Sure."

Eros flew to the river, arriving there in minutes comparable to hours of walking, causing an old guy below him to yell;

"In my day, we used our LEGS to move from point A to point B! Youngsters these days..."

"Alright, young man,[83]" Eros answered, diving to the ground and leaving a small crater. Right outside of Gadoma, Eros quickly strolled into the town center and noticed something.

This town was *really* centered around their trademarked swords with big hunks of lead stuck on the tips.

I mean, everybody had one holstered on their sides or backs and there were swords stuffed in backpacks on the streets.

Some weren't even *in* backpacks, and you had to watch your step in Gadoma for the swords in the street.[84]

Swords with big hunks of lead on their tips were stuck in trees, probably so that the trees could defend themselves.

Squirrels and wildlife picked up swords with big hunks of lead on their tips, and it was not uncommon to hear suspenseful music as two raccoons, or a squirrel and a chipmunk,[85] ducking it out in an all-outback battle with several others standing by the sidelines cheering.

The town of Gadoma had swords with big hunks of lead stuck on the tips coming out of its ears, and for some citizens, that was literally true.

But you know how swords-with-big-hunks-of-lead-stuck-on-the-tips-in-his-ears-Jerry is.

As Eros walked through the streets, he started to hear a big sound growing in

[83] Eros loved calling old humans, "young men," because, when you compared their ages, Eros was much older than them.

[84] In fact, if you looked closely, there was *no* street. Just a bunch of big hunks of lead attached to some not-visible swords.

[85] Who, of course, are sworn enemies.

intensity from the city center.

As Eros was about to turn the corner to the city center when the thumping stopped.

Right as Eros thought it would stop, the ground shook from a terrific roar that rattled wind chimes,[86] shook the street, and caused a flood of people to nearly trample Eros.

As people ran towards their houses and slammed the doors behind them, only leaving Eros in the street, as the monster turned the corner.

Eros staggered at the monster's power. It *was* a chimera, but if you think that chimeras aren't scary, you would obviously never had a giant lion being with a screaming goat on its back, and a hissing snake oozing poison from its mouth by its back, all the while it is belching fire and screaming at the top of its lungs in a terrible, horrible, way.

The chimera screamed in Eros's face, and he could feel death emanating from its mouth.[87]

"Chimera, you will ever harm the people of this fine, swords-with-big-hunks-of-lead-stuck-on-their-tops maker town or its fine people again!" Eros said threateningly. He was about to continue when he was interrupted by a villager poking his head out of the window.

"Actually this monster is distinct from the Chimera in several ways," he helpfully explained.

"Really? Like what?"

"Well...I was hoping you wouldn't ask me that, because I can't really explain the difference."

---

[86] They were near the wind chime store, you see

[87] Some may call it "death breath"

"Well, what did you expect me to say?"

"I just thought you would agree."

"Well, I'm kinda fighting this monster right now, so I was wondering if I could get back to-"

"Oh. No problem." The villager closed the window and Eros and the totally-not-a-chimera went back to fighting.

Eros grabbed a sword with a big hunk of lead stuck on the tip and knocked the chimera in the leg, but it just screamed louder and swiped at him with another foot angrily.

As they battled, Eros noticed the totally-not-a-chimera would charge up its fire blasts, first warming its throat before belching flames.

Hmmm... Eros thought. *That seems familiar. I wonder where I've heard that before Hmmm...*

After about ten to twelve minutes, Eros had an epiphany on what to do.

Bellephorn! Bellephorn defeated the chimera by stabbing a sword with a big hunk of lead on the tip down the chimera's throat! I bet I can do that with the totally-not-a-chimera too, and then it would suffocate!

So, when the time came, Eros hacked his sword at the totally-not-a-chimera, and it soared effortlessly into the totally-not-a-chimera's throat, melting in the intense heat and quickly suffocating it. The totally-not-a-chimera collapsed onto the lead road with a deafening *THUMP*.

As soon as they were sure it was dead, the villagers ran from their homes and cheered around Eros as he stood proudly. The villager from the window reluctantly walked out of his house and stood in front of Eros.

"Just so you know, that was not the Bellerophon/Chimera thing that you did just now."

"Um...I'm pretty sure it was."

"Not."

"Um, yeah, it was."

The villager walked away, grumbling.

"No one is creative in writing these days."

*   *   *

Eros landed back in front of the portal in the way that superheroes do, so it looked super cool.

Then Eros stumbled and fell onto his face.[88]

Whoa, Eros thought. *Maybe I shouldn't have drank those two gallons of sparkling apple juice the villagers had.*[89]

---

[88] The coolness factor was dampened a little bit.

[89] Sparkling apple juice, kids. Not champagne, even though it came from champagne bottles. Champagne contains Alcohol, and alcohol is DANGEROUS.

Gee, Mister Eros. Can't we have some champagne, even though it contains dangerous alcohol? You may be saying.

No, no, kids. You can't have alcohol until you're 45 years old. Even when you're 45, get your parents permission, your doctor's permission, and make sure to contact Homeland Security about it. After all that, only take a milliliter of extremely watered-down champagne a year, and drink two gallons of water afterwards.

There.

After a few minutes of delirious shuffling around,[90] Eros's godly health kicked in and he was healed of the... poison.

Eros walked over to Gaufin.

"You again?" Gaufin said skeptically. "I suppose you got scared of the totally-not-a-chimera and ran back here with your tail between your legs to beg for mercy."

"I don't have a tail. I have wings."

"I suppose you got scared of the totally-not-a-chimera and ran back here with your wings between your...ummm..."

"Shoulder blades?"

"YES! I suppose you got scared of the totally-not-a-chimera and ran back here with your wings between your shoulder blades to beg for mercy!"

"Well, I didn't do that *exactly*." Eros then pulled a scale he had removed from the totally-not-a-chimera's tail and dropped it on the ground in front of Gaufin, who gawked.

"Is this real?"

"No, I just bought it from one of many stores in the huge industrial sprawl around here."

He gestured around at the deserted savannah.

Gaufin shrugged.

"Fair enough. Have fun in the Realm of Ideas, Lord Eros."

That covers my legal troubles.

[90] Due to the sparkling apple juice being.........poisoned! Yup. It was poisoned. No need to look into any of this at all.

Eros took a deep breath, and stepped into the rectangle purple vortex that was the portal.

* * *

As Eros stepped out, he looked around in mild awe. I mean, he'd been there before four years ago, so much of the awe was subtracted from what would have been a lot of awe.

But let's get off the whole 'specified amount of awe' topic.

Eros looked around to see the giant ash tree of Yggdrasil standing ancient and still through the dark sky. Huge branches the size of all the interstates in the world stretched from the trunk to big cities the size of Balkan countries. Other islands hung in the sky, some connected through other ways.

At his feet were hundreds of other portals, each with a sign in front written in an indescribable language known only by the arcane.

Eros walked into the closest portal, and was transported in a rainbows rain to a grassland surrounding a huge city covered in gold towers and silver roads. Rising up from the urban sprawl was a gleaming gold hall that dwarfed all the others and cast a shadow of power over the city.

Eros stepped towards Asgard and hiked through the flowing prairies until he could see the Gate of the Gods, Moronan, for it is said all who wish to break it would be morons.

Made purely of obsidian, the gate was acutely watched by two teams of guards, inhabiting the towers of Stefe, named Barchost and Darchost. The whole gate was supervised by Heimdall, the famous head of the guard, who sees all in the Realm of Ideals and beyond it.

Eros stepped forward but was interrupted by a sonic boom that shook the grass and made Eros cover his ears.

He looked up to see a golden spear twinkling in the light of Sunna's chariot[91], soaring through the sky.

"What in Gaia's green earth[92]-"

The spear struck Eros smack in the face, knocking him down and severely scarring his face. His body collapsed onto a convent piece of grass-less dirt, and his gouged-out left eye and cut open left cheek bled iron-rich ichor into dark ground, as Eros lay in a dazed state of unending pain and suffering which would leave a lasting mark on Eros's fragile psyche for many millennia after, leading to many hours of consistent therapy with...himself.

* * *

EXCEPT NOT.

Eros is a nigh-invulnerable god with higher durability than the nuclear pasta in neutron stars.

The weapon is a solid gold spear.

To add to the reasoning, this book is rated E for everyone, so put two and two together, readers. The spear bounced harmlessly off Eros's face, landing in the grass with a soft *CLANG*.

"That was comically ineffective," Eros noted as several other spears bounced

[91] Which of course, is the representation of the sun in Old Norse mythology. I can't believe you didn't know that. *shame*

[92] Which he was technically not in, so this random burst of religious speech like a member of Gaia's cult, would not apply. I wonder why this random sentence could have possibly occurred. *cough* marketing ploy *cough*

harmlessly off him.

After a short rain of golden spears, leaving them decked around him in a yellow hexagon[93] as they bounced harmlessly off Eros's skin, he heard a commotion just over the next hill. It sounded like metal armor clanking together, and Eros's assumption was proved right when six shouting golden people jumped out from behind a small hill, spears blazing.

"For Asgard!" The tallest golden person yelled, hucking a spear directly at Eros's face.

Eros quickly responded by kicking a spear at his feet into the air, deflecting the spear and sending them both into the dirt.

"The fiend has deflected mine spear! Archers, fire!" The tallest person yelled. A bunch of golden archers began firing upon Eros.

Simultaneously the five spear wielding people whipped spears towards Eros's head, feet, and stomach.

As he was deflecting them easily and completely humiliating the attackers, Eros noticed something.

When the people moved, they moved synchronously with their armor. When they jumped, it was done synchronously with their armor. When they cried in embarrassment that this guy was deflecting their attacks way too easily, it was done synchronously with their armor.

Suddenly Eros had an epiphany. These weren't people wearing armor, they WERE the armor. They were gold automatons!

Now that he thought of it, Odin had once helped Hephaestus with some Urdu forging, and in return, Hephaestus gave him several of his gold automatons to guard the Gate of the Gods.

---

[93] Which are the bestagons, shout-out to CGP Grey

If I'm going to get to the Gate of the Gods, I guess I have to get captured, Eros thought as he held out his hand towards a flying spear, so when it hit, the pressure caused it to melt into a puddle on the ground.

So, when one of the gold automatons lost all their weapons and resorted to punching Eros in the arm, he changed parts of his skin to blood-red, dislocated his shoulder and flipped it behind him, and collapsed on the ground while sticking his tongue out and closing his eyes.

"Our enemy is vanquished!" shouted one of the automatons.

"And after a quick and easy battle!" another added.

"Our enemy may be completely vanquished, but it does not matter how difficult it was, even though it was super easy," said the tall one. "We must bring this one to Heimdall for judgment, like all other ones."

"Yes, my lady," all the others responded.

Eros entered a voluntary unconsciousness until the trip was over.

At the gates, the tall automatan inserted a key into a small key hole, opening a small passage in the sides of the gates.

Climbing some stairs, the company walked out of Barchost across the path over the gate. Right above the gates pinnacle sat a tall man sitting on a gold throne, looking with his misty eyes out towards Yggdrasil.

The man turned as the golden guard walked up, and they threw a tied-up Eros at his feet.

"Master Heimdall, we found this trespasser about twenty leagues from the gate. Luckily, we were able to quickly and easily dispatch him, and anybody who tells you otherwise are fools," the tall guard said.

"Who are you to trespass in the lands of Asgard, which house the greatest gods in the Realm of Ideals?" Heimdall boomed.

"You don't remember me? It's Eros. Eros Phanes. Y'know, the guy who trapped you here all those years ago. It destroyed all your free will, connection with humans, blah, blah, blah."

Heimdall staggered in surprise at this.

"Eros! I did not recognize you! It has been a very long time since you have traveled here through the Bifrost," Heimdall said, his voice suddenly much less threatening.

"It's not the Bifrost, it's a wormhole formed with a broken quantum string and held apart by exotic matter."

"Nah, I'm pretty sure it's the Bifrost." Heimdall waved his hand at the automatons at his side.

"Free him." The tallest automaton recoiled in shock.

"Sir, I must protest. This being is clearly violent and a trespasser, he must be kept under close watch-"

Heimdall grabbed the automaton by her solid-gold[94] ear and pulled her close to him.

"*He could obliterate us all with a thought,*" Heimdall whispered kind of loud. "*FREE. HIM. NOW.*"

Eros was quickly freed of his bonds.

After the guards were dismissed, Heimdall let out a tired sigh.

"So, Eros, why have you come to our fair Asgard today? Is it to try and lift

[94] Which should go without saying, but hey, filler is filler

Mjolnir? Is it to discuss gossip with Lady Sif and Freyja? Is it to sneak into Idunn's garden and try and steal an apple, but not be able to eat it because Idunn comes and slaps it out of your hand, but you do it again and again until she gets so mad that she closes the gardens for a day, only for you to do the same thing over and over and over and over tomorrow? Is it to slap Loki right in the face over and over and over and over and over and over and over and over and over on his punishment tree? All great options."

"No, none of those. I need to talk to Odin about urgent matters as soon as possible."

Heimdall seemed surprised by the request but struggled to keep a straight face about it.

"That's a heavy order, Eros, and an unattainable one too, I'm afraid. Odin is quite busy at the moment."

"Really? With what?"

"Well...he's...he's doing...he's...ummmm...he's defeating mutant termites from digging holes in Yggdrasil."

"That was a lot of confusion for something you probably should have known, considering you see everything."

"Well, I don't have the best memory, so beeeeee...quiet? Plus, I'm the only source you have towards Odin's current location."

"Well, I hoped I wouldn't have to do this, but here goes." Eros whistled and an old sky-black raven popped into existence on his shoulder.

The bird squawked and Heimdall recoiled in shock.

"Recognize him?" Eros asked.

"Yes, that's the raven Munnin, one of the famous pair that tells Odin the ways of the world![95]"

"I thought you might know him."

Eros then turned towards Muninn and twerped a series of clicks and squawks in the tone of a songbird.

Muninn thought about it for a second and then replied likewise in an ancient, raspy voice.

Eros whistled and Muninn disappeared.

"You and Odin recently had a bundt cake party. After eating many bundt cakes, you both passed out on sugar cake. You woke up a half hour ago because you only had ten bundt cakes, while Odin had twenty and is passed out on his throne right now. Or, at least, that's just what the all-knowing raven told me, but who knows if Muninn is even reliable," Eros recollects.

Heimdall scooted back in his seat, frantically trying to deny this. "Well, Muninn must be wrong, because I have absolutely no recollection of this happening, and I think I would remember it."

Eros stared at him skeptically. After a long, awkward silence, Eros put his fingers into the double-hand finger gun position, then leaned his chin into the fingers, the way that philosophers and detectives do.

"You have bundt cake on your chin," Eros finally noted. Heimdall quickly flicked it off, but it was too late.

"Fine," Heimdall sighed. "I will take you to Odin."

[95] He could have asked Heimdall to do it, but it was almost unanimously agreed (well, everyone except Heimdall) that ravens were way cool.

*   *   *

As Eros entered the city, the buildings grew taller and sturdier. He could see some of the great halls of the gods, which were, honestly, not that hard to miss due to being giant palaces.

Eros saw Thor's hall, Bilskirnir, with its 540 rooms, where the mead was ever flowing, laid before the beautiful country plain of Þrúðheimr, where Thor claimed his own long ago.

Next was Sessrúmnir, the palace of Freyja in the beautiful fields of Fólkvangr, where half of all warriors go when they die, to frolic everlastingly in the green meadows and beautiful gardens.

Many places they passed, tall and grand, and small but beautiful, all in some field that also has a name, and written with old weird accents that cannot be written with a traditional QWERTY keyboard. Alas, all of their great names and achievements cannot be fully copy-pasted, else we would still be here when our beards had grown long enough we could trip over them and slide onto a scooter, which would move us forward into a bathtub filled to the brim with bright blue rubber duckies, and we would sink into them and never return.[96]

Anyway, finally Eros and Heimdall reached Valhalla, where the mead was ever flowing.[97] The Vikings laughed and cried at the feasting table, and there was even a new ritual called PunchAJerk™, where they would summon the spirit of jerks from your life from Hel[98], and punch them over and over and over and over and over and over and over

[96] We might all collectively win the Darwin Award, though, so if you want to let your beard grow so long you trip over it and fall on a scooter and then it starts moving and you fall into a bathtub of bright blue rubber duckies to never return, go for it.

[97] Yes, I used this already, but it sounds great, so be quiet. Also, don't ask what mead is, or we'll have to have that whole conversation again.

[98] Or Hek, if you're reading this to kids

and over again.

It was more fun than it sounds.

Finally, they approached the king of all Asgard, Odin, who was...slightly less regal than expected.

Odin was spread across his legendary golden throne Hlidskjalf, on which he was snoring loudly.

His infamous spear Gugnir was laying on the marble floor around a veritable massacre of bundt cake proportions.

His ring Draupnir, which magically duplicates itself ninefold every nine nights, nearly cut off circulation on Odin's left hand, which still clawed at a torn-up bag labeled *Borson's Bundt Cakes.*

Eros and Heimdall waited patiently for Odin to wake up, but when that failed, they resorted to slightly more desperate measures.

Heimdall stepped forward quietly. Right as Eros began to think he would not say anything, words exploded from his mouth.

"Why, is that Loki? And who's that with him? Surtur and Laufey, along with armies of Fire Giants and Frost Giants respectively? And Fenris the wolf and the Jörmungandr the world serpent? And the forces of Hel[99] have carried them all across! Ragnarok must be upon us!"

Odin jumped up, grabbing Gugnir and putting on his "*mean*"[100] face in preparation for the fight.

"Where's Fenrir? Summon the warriors of Valhalla to battle quickly and with

[99] Hek

[100] Heavy quotes and italics here, kids

haste!"[101]

Odin darted his eyes around and listened for the screams of panic and fear, but heard nothing but wind.

"Heimdall? What's going on here?"

Heimdall cleared his throat nervously.

"My lord, Ragnarok has not occurred. I simply needed a way to wake you from your sugar crash."

Odin stared at him angrily.

"That was not very wise. You are dismissed."

"My lord, I-"

"DISMISSED."

Heimdall sighed and shuffled away, leaving Eros alone with a disgruntled Odin, who was trying to subtly scootch some of the bundt cakes behind his throne and avoid embarrassment.

"Are you just going to stand there? Out with it! Who are you and what do you want?" Odin growled.

"I am Eros, Odin. One of the most powerful gods of the Greek Pantheon, if I do say myself. I have come with urgent, but secretive news. You must assemble the Council of Godheads at once."

Odin thought on the news for a moment.

"Eros, eh? I remember you. A few years ago, was it? You came here, humiliated Thor by easily lifting Mjolnir?"

[101] Those two mean basically the same thing, but Odin was in need of talking quickly and with haste

"Four years ago."

"Yes, four years ago," Odin frowned. "Why have you come here, asking me to call the Council of Godheads. Why? What news do you have?"

"Did you just ask *why*, like, three times?"

"WHHHHHYYYYYYY!!!!????"

"I cannot talk about it here. I don't wish to cause a panic, which could then lead to riots, then a civil war, then I would see an entire pantheon burning (metaphorically and literally), at my feet as a consequence of my actions, or, rather, lack of my actions." Eros paused for a moment.

"Again."

"Well, that is a tall order. If you cannot tell me the reason, I will have to answer you no."

Eros frowned. He was afraid something like this might happen. Alright, he'd do it the hard way.

"I wasn't asking," Eros responded coolly.

"Oh! A threat!" shouted Odin, growing more arrogant by the second. "I didn't think you were the threat-giving type!"

"Odin, you have thirty seconds to call a meeting. Or else."

"Or else? Or else WHAT? You'll send the Greek pantheon after me? Easy pickings. The Norse pantheon has grown strong, boy. We are as afraid of you as we are of a spineless porcupine."

"I will trigger the one thing that you fear."

"And what's that?"

"Ragnarok."

The room went silent, but Odin laughed nervously and tried to deny that Eros could do that.

Without a word, Eros snapped his fingers, and a live feed of two fire giants in Muspelheim appeared on the wall.

Scratching his head, the first fire giant turned towards the other casually as the second fire giant sipped some lava punch.

"Y'know what I wanna do right now?" The fire giant said.

"What?"

"Destroy the nine realms in a terrible bloody war that ends in the death of almost every living thing."

The second fire giant thought about this for a second.

"Sounds fun."

"Okay! Okay! I'll cave!" Odin yelled frantically. "I'll do whatever you say! Just don't trigger Ragnarok!"

"Just don't trigger Ragnarok, *sir*." Eros responded smugly. He snapped away the feed of Muspelheim.

"Just don't trigger Ragnarok, sir," Odin fumed.

*　　　*　　　*

After Odin sent ravens to announce a meeting of the Council of Godheads, they sat and waited for a response.

And waited.

And waited.

"What is taking those blasted ravens so long to return!?" Odin shouted, not looking at Eros.

"I don't know. Might be windy," Eros responded.

"That's no excuse. The gods must be lazy," Odin sighed, covering his eyes in tired sadness.

"Who are the cutest little ravens! You guys! Yeah, it's you guys! The cutest little ravens in the whole realm! Yeah, it's true! Yeah, it's true!" Eros said in a high-pitched voice.

"That's a pretty weird non-sequitur," Odin noted, looking over in confusion at Eros.

Eros was standing with his arms spread out, on which stood five black ravens. Eros was nuzzling his face in the feathers of the raven directly to his left, and it chirped happily.

"Eros!" Odin yelled.

Eros turned his face towards him.

"What?"

"Where did you get those birds!"

"Oh, they just flew through the window."

"How long ago?"

"Oh, just after you sent the messenger-ravens out. Isn't that just a delightful coincidence?"

"Give them to me." Eros chirped like a bird and the ravens flew over to Odin, dropping paper messages into his lap and silently flew out the window they had come in earlier.

"What do they say?" Eros asked quizzically.

"They don't understand why the council is being called, but they will come," Odin replied, annoyed.

"When?"

"In two hours, at a knot in Yggdrasil near the main Alfheim branch," replied Odin.

"Good. That gives me time to get Slicer."

"Slicer?"

"A sword. I need it to prevent the utter destruction of this entire plane of reality," Eros explained.

"Ah. You gotta love those weapons that prevent the destruction of entire planes of reality. Where is it?"

"By the oldest lake in the world, Lake Zaysan."

"Which is...where?"

Eros casually ripped a giant quantum string through space-time, creating a stable portal, which he held open with exotic matter. Before walking in, Eros turned back to Odin.

"Kazakhstan. Where else?"

A confused Odin watched as Eros disappeared through the portal.

*   *   *

Eros appeared on the porch of his lake house. Inconspicuous, it was two stories tall and was just about as big as any normal house. There was a short garage with a

Tesla inside, and a canoe, JetSki, and one of those small submarines that you could jump in and out of the water in a really cool way.

Overall, it was what you would expect from a person with almost infinite funds who was trying to be humble.

As Eros opened the wooden front door, he heard snickering and loud noises coming from his kitchen.

Sneaking around, Eros heard wires being ripped and peered through the open door.

The first thing he noticed was the fridge. Rather, he noticed the absence of it, with ripped wires and a small water pipe shooting water onto the floor.[102] Sparks twinkled from the exposed wires.

The second thing Eros noticed was the absence of... everything else. The oven was gone. The microwave was gone. The stove was gone. Eros turned to see the sink was nearly gone, and he saw two blue figures trying to yank it out. Eros tried to step away, but they noticed and turned towards him, offering him just a moment's glance at their darkened faces.

They were Telkhines!

With blue faces and gills on either side, these sea demons were the spawn of Tartarus, and were long since banished from Olympus for practicing evil witchcraft. They forged Kronos's sickle, but since then they had resorted to petty theft and some minor murder.

Not waiting for the Telkhines to catch him, Eros ran up the stairs to his bedroom, where he had left Slicer lying on his bed, even though there was also the option to put it into literally the most secure safe in Kazakhstan.

---

[102] And you don't even want to know how long it took to get the water out of his rug. I'll tell you anyway. Six hours.

As Eros reached his bedroom, he felt for a secret handle to the left of the doorway.

After a minute of searching, Eros gripped the handle and quietly slipped into a small hidden closet. Eros had installed it in case anybody ever unlawfully entered his house.[103]

The closet was connected to a one way-way mirror, and a hidden microphone broadcasted sound from the room. It allowed him to see and hear everything, and Eros gasped at what he saw.

Eight Telkhines were arranged in a circle around Eros's bed, staring at Slicer cautiously. Every minute and a half, one would hiss at the swords or reach towards it, only to yank their hand back quickly.

Across the room was a Telkhine talking on his phone. He was taller in stature than the others, and judging by how much he yelled at the Telkhines for basically standing around, he was the leader of the robbery.

Though he couldn't hear the other side of the call, Eros could pretty nicely guess what was going on.

"No, we can't get it!" the Telkhine screeched at the phone.

The other side screeched back.

"What do you mean, 'just pick it up'?! We TRIED that! The stupid sword reaped four of my minion's souls!"

The other line angrily screamed at the Telkhine and his eyes burned with an evil fury.

"Listen, if you want that sword, you're gonna have to up my pay grade." The Telkhine answered. He shifted into the bathroom, pretty much preparing to literally sell

[103] Or if Hemera ever got in.

his buddies' souls.

When the door slammed shut, Eros quickly kicked open the one-way mirror, which swung on a hinge and hit the wall with a *thump*.

The Telkhines looked at the mirror, alert, but nothing shot or jumped out of the gaping hole in the wall.

"What happened-" One of the Telkhines asked before Eros shot out of the hole like a bullet. Without a word, Eros chinked his gold wings into a sphere, and rolled through the Telkhines like a bowling ball, knocking them unconscious.

"Alright," Eros said to no one in particular. "Now, I just have to slip out of here quickly and quietly." Eros picked up Slicer and was about to jump out the window when the bathroom door slid open.

The Telkhine stood, staring at the frightening scene. A tall, fit, man-bird with golden wings was standing around the unconscious bodies of his companions, holding a sword that reaped souls.

Eros tried to quickly run away, but the Telkhine blew a whistle, and in a second several Telkhines were at the doorway, staring at the two.

Telkhine.

Man-bird.

Telkhine.

Man-bird.

Telkhine.

Telkhine.

Telkhine.

Man-bird.

Man-bird.

Man-bird.

Man-bird.

After a lot of eyes darting between the two, the head Telkhine shouted, "WHAT ARE YOU DOING!? KILL HIM!"

The minions started attacking Eros with lead pipes, lead pipes, and...more lead pipes.[104]

As the strongest Telkhine hit Eros directly in the face with his pipe, it had an effect. It was infinitesimally small, but it had an effect.

A short, stout Telkhine rammed the pipe into Eros's knees, attempting to break his kneecap. It bent out of shape against the skin.

After a short, not very violent fight, Eros asked the Telkhines cradling their bent and broken pipes, "Are you done?"

"Wait," one of the Telkhines said. He banged his pipe across Eros's face, bending it severely. "Now we're done."

"Okay then," Eros responded. He slashed, his sword cutting through space like paper, revealing an endless dirt field filled with green cabbage-like plants. A small stand with a man standing behind it, selling bottles of water, was nearby.

Eros quickly disarmed all of the Telkhines and threw them in. They started milling around the field, depressed about what they were sure was imprisonment, but their leader walked up to the hole in reality.

"Get us out of here or suffer a terrible fate," he said, poking his finger in Eros's face.

---

[104] "If it works for mercilessly beating your enemies into a pulp, use it," an old Telkhine proverb goes.

Eros just shook his head.

"Sorry, I can't. But at least you have water. It's from Tahiti. Well, not from Tahiti, it's tap water from Cleveland, and it's super overpriced," Eros gestured at the vendor, who shook a price tag of 947,860,000,000.00 €. "But, hey, it's 10% vegetarian, so it's healthy."

The Telkhine shook his head. "We have no money. At least we can eat these plants in preparation for your death. What are they, anyway?"

Eros began frantically sewing reality back together as one of the minions looked under the leaves.

The plant was fluffy and large, and had flowers like a white broccoli, except it was in the shape of a cabbage.

"Hey, chief!" he yelled. "This is cauliflower!"

The boss zipped back, checking under all the leaves near him. Cauliflower. Cauliflower. Cauliflower!

IT WAS ALL CAULIFLOWER!

Eros sewed reality back into place as the head Telkhine screamed in terrible agony.

Eros quickly prepared a portal back to the Realm of Ideals.

"These demons seem to get lamer every day," he sighed, and he stepped into the door.

*   *   *

Eros stepped into a giant wood cave. Surrounding him completely, the wood was a pleasant light brown, and the grain flowed like waves around him, with short colorations as thick as Eros's head.

As Eros marveled at the beauty of the cave, Odin cleared his throat in that obnoxiously loud way people do.

Eros turned his head down, finding a wooden table growing from the ground, around which sat six powerful gods.

Eros sat down next to Odin, and quickly examined the Council of Godheads, which had some of the most powerful gods in the entire pocket dimension[105], and

[105] For more fun dimensional names, see this guide:

Universe: Everything in an infinite range

Pocket Universe: A universe inside the boundaries of another universe

Multiverse: A collection of universes with minimal difference from each other, i.e. does Johnny eat from this side of the trail mix bag, forgetting he is allergic to granola and going to the hospital, only to die after seventeen painful hours, or does Johnny eat from the other side of the trail mix bag, forgetting he is allergic to granola and being rushed to the hospital, only to die after seventeen painful hours? Those are two entirely different universes in the same multiverse.

Timelines: This may seem like a different universe, but timelines are possibilities, not realities. They can be accessed by oracles, and flow in the "River O' Possibilities". It's also really fun to white water raft down the River O' Possibilities

Metaverse: A collection of multiverses that share fundamental similarities, i.e. laws of physics, significant events. The universes are usually different via "Big Waves in the River O' Possibilities", like if the moon had never been formed (those metaverses: boring), or if Jupiter was turned into the sun when a random god pressed the wrong button (those metaverses: death), or if Humanity was never a success (those metaverses: awesome) beyond.

From the Egyptian pantheon sat Atum-Ra, the sun god and leader over all of Egypt.

The Hindu representative was Shiva, the wise, powerful god who watches over the Indian subcontinent with his three eyes.

From the Navajo gods came Coyote, where he was a trickster, and Ananse the spider was from the Ghana pantheon, where he was also a trickster.

Finally, directly across the table from Eros, was Sun Wukong, the Monkey King, who was the most powerful demon in Chinese legend, and was the immortal ruler of all the monkeys in China. He was also (surprise!) a trickster.

As Eros looked at the Council, Shiva smiled.

"Why have you called this meeting, Odin?" he said calmly.

"Yeah, I was wondering that as well. I have places to be. Apet won't be stabbed repeatedly in the stomach with a spear himself," Ra said impatiently.

"And I was woken up from my nap for this," Coyote added. "If this isn't important, I'll scale you like a fish."

"Ah, I don't know," Odin answered. "Eros here called this meeting. Said it was important." Odin pointed a finger at Eros.

"What is it?" The Monkey King asked impatiently.

Omniverse: All universes, everything. Is actually a universe that is just nothing but pocket dimensions. But really, you shouldn't think about the omniverse too much because your brain could explode

Megaverse: to all those who said "Oh, of course. Megaverse.", this isn't actually a word. HA!

"Oh, you better sit down for this."

Warily, the council sat firmly into their seats, waiting intently for some kind of an explanation.

"It all began about 13.8 billion years ago..."

As Eros told his story, he detailed the initial encounter with Tim, some of his exploits since, and finally this adventure leading to the meeting. During the story, the council's faces shifted from confusion, to anger, to depression, to a dull acceptance and curiosity.

"...and he'll probably be coming here any second." As Eros finished, a dull rippling sound bugled Tim's arrival.

"Speak of the devil," Eros whispered to himself.

Eros whistled and a small black bird appeared on his shoulder, wearing on his chest feathers a small painted insignia belonging to one of the border patrols near the edge of the Realm of Ideals.

"Caw! Caw caw caw! Chirp chirp caw chirp chirp!" It screeched loudly into Eros's ear, displaying a broken wing and bloody feathers. Eros set the bird down, and it curled into a ball and slept.

"What did he say?" The Monkey King asked, impatient.

"He said Tim has just torn a hole in reality about half a light-year east of here. Tim's minions attacked his patrol, and he is the only one still alive from there. If my calculations are correct, Tim should arrive in about an hour and half. Any ideas on what to do?"[106]

"Perhaps if we just ask Tim to go away, he will," Shiva suggested.[107]

[106] For the next few paragraphs, focus on the imagination picture in your brain with whatever is told.

[107] Now imagine that that picture flashes with the red word "TERRIBLE IDEA".

"Maybe we can gather our armies and just FIGHT Tim!" Coyote added.[108]

Suggestions like these continued for a couple minutes. As they were debating whether to end Tim flying back into the tear in reality via a catapult, Ananse layed a book on the table.

Brown, and with gold pages, everyone turned to see the book, which read: "*Big Book of Convenient Plot Holes.*"

"What is it?" Coyote inquired.

"A book filled with convenient plot holes, of course," Ananse answered. He began flipping through the pages.

After a short time, Ananse stopped at a page detailed with elaborate drawings and poems.

"Aha! The Banishing-Darkness ritual! It takes six high-power gods, which we have, the Wand of Werble, Pot of Potatoes, and the Low-Price Candles of Dollar Tree, all of which I happen to have on me, and it creates a dust that can magically banish all darkness from wherever it touches! We must orchestrate it on the tallest mountain to ever exist, which I happen to know is only an hour away! Isn't that really helpful to our situation?"

Murmurs of agreement spread throughout the group.

"What a convenient plot point," Eros noted.

"That's why it's in the book!" Ananse laughed.

After some short preparations, Eros and the council headed out to defeat Tim, and hopefully save the whole universe.

---

[108] Now it flashes the word "HORRIBLE".

*   *   *

The gods reached the top of Mt. TallTall[109] with about twenty minutes to spare, and set the ritual up, leaving them ten minutes before Tim would attack. That was good. However, the ritual took thirty minutes to complete, which was more than a minor hiccup in the whole stop-Tim-from-taking-over-the-universe thing.

"Well, once you start the ritual you won't be able to stop. I'll guard you from Tim as best I can," Eros explained.

"May the gods be with you, Eros Phanes," replied Shiva, even though the gods were quite literally not with him.

"Have fun dying," Coyote added.

"Ah, not today. I'm not doing anything Wednesday, though. We should arrange something."

Odin looked up, confused.

"What?" he asked. Everyone stared at Eros strangely.

"Nevermind," Eros said quickly.

The gods started chanting a ritual in an ancient language long forgotten, and Eros brandished his sword.

He waited for Tim.

And waited.

And waited.

Right as Eros thought Tim might not come, a blood-curdling roar shook the

[109] Named so for it being tall

ground, knocking boulders down the mountain.

Far in front of him, Eros could see a giant dragon of darkness soaring past the horizon.

Tim had come. And it was terrifying.

*　　　　*　　　　*

When Tim got to be about a mile away, it started to speak, with a dark, deep voice that shook Eros's soul like a... shaking... robot?[110]

Anyway, Tim shouted again and then sneered.

"I FIGURED YOU WOULD COME, PUNY GOD. YOU CANNOT STOP ME FROM DESTROYING THIS PLACE."

"I can try!" Eros answered. He swiped his sword through the air, sending rings of hard light into Tim's stomach. They screamed, and sent vines of darkness shooting at Eros, which missed by a hair and jutted into the rock behind him. Eros quickly turned and sliced at one of them, which was cut off from its vine of darkness. It writhed on the floor and dissipated as Tim screamed. He sent more tendrils after him, and the battle began.

*　　　　*　　　　*

Although the battle began well for Eros, it quickly deteriorated. The two forces of nature clashed brutally, slicing at each other mercilessly, but over time, Eros lost ground, and nearly eight minutes into the fight, he was fighting before the ritual circle

[110] Like a shaker! And yes, that is the proper name for a machine that shakes fluid samples in laboratories.

itself.

I just need to reach the utmost perfection. Eros thought. He had a hint of a very, very, very bad idea, but he just needed more time. More time. More time. How to get more time?

Suddenly Eros had an idea.

"Tim!" he yelled, while simultaneously deflecting an attack with the hilt of his sword.

"YES, PUNY GOD? LAST WORDS, MAYBE?" Tim replied, trying to crush Eros with its wing.

"Say, you wouldn't happen to have a... evil plan, would you? I mean, all the good supervillains have them."

Time seemed to stop as Tim considered the question.

"WHY, YES I DO," Tim admitted. **"I WOULD TELL YOU IT, BUT I DON'T WANNA WASTE THE LAST MINUTES OF YOUR TIME IN THE LIVING REALM."**

"No, it's okay. I would love to hear it. Please?" asked Eros.

Tim stared at him for a minute.

"ALRIGHT, ALRIGHT," they said. **"I'LL TELL YOU MY EVIL PLAN, IF YOU INSIST."**

Tim cleared its throat.

"IT ALL STARTS WITH WALL STREET, WHERE, AFTER TAKING THIS PLACE OVER AND DESTROYING IT, I WILL LAY MY MINIONS, WHO WILL..." Tim monologued.

As they went on about how their minions would incite people to buy into the stock market, then create a bear market, where people would lose their life's savings in stocks, Eros closed his eyes, and his mind floated into the deepest depths of his subconscious.[111]

*   *   *

Eros's astral form formed in a huge dark void. Far in front of him, a single pixel of color identified the area.

Determined, Eros ran towards the color, which grew into definition to a brown massage chair and a short rug. A book case was to the left of the chair, and a TV showed flashing colors as a little car flew past all the other cars in outer space, though keeping steady on a track of brilliantly colored asphalt. Headings on the top revealed it to be called "Rainbow Boulevard", and the car was in first place.[112]

Eros tapped the top of the chair, and a figure sitting in it swerved its head around.

With a fire red snake for a head, the figure had short, stubby wings as an almost imitation of Eros, and like a belt around his waist, the heads of demons breathed white fire.

He also had a shirt with a skull on it, so he was definitely a not-normal guy. In fact, the being was a personification of all of the entropy of Eros's mind, and was a sociopath pessimist.

He was also Eros's roommate.

If Eros let Entropy take over his mind, the monster, named Phanes, would come out, and as was mentioned before, they were a pessimistic sociopath, so it was not really

[111] Yes, we are aware that variations of the word "deep" were used two times in that sentence.

[112] No, this doesn't sound like anything

a good time.

"What?" Phanes asked, not looking up from Mario Krt. "I didn't notice you were stressed."

"I'm fighting an interdimensional monster who is my greatest enemy yet. Why would I be stressed?"

"Well, the last five times you let me out, you tripped over a pebble. I'm just saying, you handle stress in an extremely weird way, man."

"Well, I'm not here about that."

For the first time, Phanes seemed surprised.

"Really? Then what is it?"

Eros sighed.

"To defeat Tim, I need to be perfectly meditated, so I need you to take all of my worries and stuff." He helpfully pulled out a small green oval lid from his pocket, labeled in marker, *Worries and Stuff*.

Phanes recoiled in surprise.

"Really? You know, this will make me stronger. I could gain enough power, and then there could be a repeat of the Cat Cafe Incident, which, by the way, was doused by circumstances that were pitted against me, and all of those circumstances were beyond my control," Phanes assured.

"I know."

Phanes smiled.

"Well, then! I accept!" Phanes grabbed the ball, and Eros instantaneously felt stronger.

"Thank you, Phanes," Eros said dully.

"No, thank you! I'll be seeing you VERY soon!"

Phanes smiled giddily as Eros disconnected from his astral form.

* * *

When Eros's soul returned to his physical realm, he jumped back as Tim's jaws snapped at where he had been a second ago.

"YOU'RE AWAKE!" Tim shouted. **"GOOD. NOW I MAY HEAR YOUR SCREAMS!"**

Tim raised its head up and laughed.

Preparing to shoot tendrils of darkness, Tim looked at Eros. Or, at least, where Eros had been just a second ago. He was gone.

As Tim thought about this, they felt a sharp pain rip through their wing, as Eros dived through the fragile tendons.

Tim slashed at the wing, but Eros quickly evaded the attacks and jumped onto Tim's head, where he grabbed a horn and pulled it, forcing Tom to fly upwards into the air.

"TINY GOD, DO NOT TRY ME!" It flipped its head, and shook Eros off, who without a word encased himself in his wings and landed on the ground with a dull *thump.*

Tim lowered its head, sniffing to see if he was dead, when Eros swung his wings open, sending solid gold feathers straight into Tim's eyes. It screeched in pain as it was blinded.

"YOU'LL DIE FOR THAT, PUNY GOD!"

The fight continued for ten glorious minutes. Eros, perfectly concentrated, was the perfect match for Tim, and their fight shook the stars, melted rock like butter, and made the sun and moon hide in worry.

Finally, Ananse gave a shout as the ritual was completed.

Eros noticed and slid down the wing, using Slicer as a hand hold and digging a deep gash in Tim's scales.

He jumped to the ground, forming a crater, and then ran through the sixty other craters he had made doing the exact same thing.

"This is what we have made," Ananse said quickly, handing Eros a small bag of golden dust. "It is made of pure hope, hope to destroy the darkness. Sprinkle it on your blade."

Eros did so, and Slicer began to radiate power.

Behind him, Tim approached menacingly. The other gods ran away, but Eros stood in front of him like a statue against a raging wind.

"**DO YOU WISH TO DEFEAT ME WITH HOPE, TINY GOD? HA! HOPE WILL WITHER AND DIE BEFORE ME, LIKE ALL ELSE HAS AND WILL.**" Tim laughed.

Eros jumped into the air, rising half a mile into the sky.

"**STILL TRYING, ARE YOU? YOU CANNOT KILL ME.**"

Eros started losing elevation as he dived towards Tim's head.

"**AREN'T YOU GOING TO SAY SOME SNARKY RETORT? ANSWER ME!**" Tim said, increasingly angry about Eros's silence.

Eros was super close to Tim's head when he brandished Slicer and pointed it down.

"**SAY SOMETHING!**" Tim screamed.

Eros hit Tim hard, jamming Slicer down through his skull and impaling his brain. Breaking his concentration, Eros smiled.

"Something." Tim's body went limp and the last breath left his maw as he crashed into Mt. TallTall.

Tim had finally been vanquished.

And you better bet it looked cool.

*　　　*　　　*

Emotion fully returned to Eros's face as Ananse and the rest of the gods excitedly ran up to him.

"That was the coolest thing I've ever seen!" Ananse shouted.

The other gods were less excitable but admitted it was pretty cool.

"It seems we underestimated you," was all Odin said.

"Oh, that was amazing! How'd you do it?" Ananse asked.

Eros quickly explained the situation.

"I see. What didn't you do before?"

Eros's first answer was a long sigh. It was, in fact, so long,[113] Ananse thought that would be his only answer, but then he started talking.

"I didn't want to do it, because it makes Phanes more powerful, and I don't want to repeat the Cat Cafe Incident."

"The Cat Cafe Incident?"

[113] Three minutes and twenty six seconds long, in fact

"Yes. Long ago, I was walking the streets of St. Louis, Missouri, when I saw a cat cafe,[114] which I entered. I paid for an hour with the cats and I ordered some soup. While petting a black and white cat, Phanes suddenly grew powerful enough to take over, after I had needed his help a week earlier. Anyway, long story short, and it is a long, tragic tale, when Phanes had to leave, he attempted to cat-nap the black-and-white kitty, which led to me and him being banned from the entire metropolitan area's worth of cat cafes forever and ever and ever.[115]"

Everybody waited for him to continue, but he remained silent.

Everybody stared at him.

"Is that it?" Ra eventually asked.

"Yeah."

Ananse sighed.

"Did you really risk the lives of everybody in the universe just so you could possibly not get temporarily banned from a cat cafe?!"

Eros looked at him like he was overreacting.

"I have a coupon for a cat cafe. If I get banned, it will expire in three months. You're making a big deal about this."

Ananse sighed deeply

"Writing these days..."

[114] A cafe where one eats one's food while cats are just hanging out all around you. It's better than it sounds.

[115] For six months

Epilogue

The epilogue. The part of the book where the book is *over*, but not, like, **over**. This is the part of the book where you've read the whole book, then realize you have to read the appendices. And they are *long*. So I'm going to keep this short. I'm not going to write a long description on how writing this was a "literary adventure" or any or that stuff. We already did that in the prologue. So I shall just write my publisher mandated page about the main character (me), reflecting on his adventures.

*   *   *

Eros stepped onto the pebbly beach near his summer home in Mycenia. He picked up a rock and skipped a rock. As it hit the water and bounced into the sunset, it reminded Eros of his adventures in a way that will never be explained.

"My adventures," Eros said in a weird voice that was kinda sad. "That was so long ago." He reminisced by staring into the sky profoundly. "Precisely twelve years ago. Ah, twelve years ago me. Blah blah blah blah blah blah blah blah blah blah blah blah blah blah blah blah blah blah blah. Blah blah blah blah blah blah blah blah blah blah blah blah blah blah blah blah blah blah blah. Blah blah blah blah blah blah blah blah blah

blah blah blah blah blah blah blah blah blah blah. Blah blah blah blah blah blah blah blah blah blah blah blah blah blah blah blah blah blah blah. Blah blah blah blah blah blah blah blah blah blah blah blah blah blah blah blah blah blah blah. Blah blah blah blah blah blah blah blah blah blah blah blah blah blah blah blah blah blah blah. Blah blah blah blah blah blah blah blah blah blah blah blah blah blah blah blah blah blah blah. Blah blah blah blah blah blah blah blah blah blah blah blah blah blah blah blah blah blah blah. Blah blah blah blah blah blah blah blah blah blah blah blah blah blah blah blah blah blah blah blah blah. Blah blah blah blah blah blah blah blah blah blah blah blah blah blah blah blah blah blah blah blah blah blah. Blah blah blah blah blah blah blah blah blah blah blah blah blah blah blah blah blah blah blah blah blah blah blah. Blah blah blah blah blah blah blah blah blah blah blah blah blah blah blah blah blah blah blah.” Then a random lady walking on the beach by him walked up to Eros.

“Wise one, you cannot reminisce about your adventures like this. That was long ago. Blah blah blah blah blah blah blah blah blah blah blah blah blah blah blah blah blah blah blah. Blah blah blah blah blah blah blah blah blah blah blah blah blah blah blah blah blah blah blah. Blah blah blah blah blah blah blah blah blah blah blah blah blah blah blah blah blah blah blah. Blah blah blah blah blah blah blah blah blah blah blah blah blah blah blah blah blah blah blah. Blah blah blah blah blah blah blah blah blah blah blah blah blah blah blah blah blah blah blah. Blah blah blah blah blah blah blah blah blah blah blah blah blah blah blah blah blah blah blah. Blah blah blah blah blah blah blah blah blah blah blah blah blah blah blah blah blah blah blah. Blah blah blah blah blah blah blah blah blah blah blah blah blah blah blah blah blah blah blah. Blah blah blah blah blah blah blah blah blah blah blah blah blah blah blah blah blah blah blah. Blah blah blah blah blah blah blah blah blah blah blah blah blah blah blah blah blah blah blah. Blah blah blah blah blah blah blah blah blah blah blah blah blah blah blah blah blah blah blah. Blah blah blah blah blah blah blah blah blah blah blah blah blah blah blah blah blah blah blah. Blah blah blah blah blah blah blah blah blah

blah blah blah blah blah blah blah blah blah blah. Blah blah blah blah blah blah blah blah blah blah blah blah blah blah blah blah blah blah blah. Blah blah blah blah blah blah blah blah blah blah blah blah blah blah blah blah blah blah blah blah. Blah blah blah blah blah blah blah blah blah blah blah blah blah blah blah blah blah blah blah. Blah blah blah blah blah blah blah blah blah blah blah blah blah blah blah blah blah blah. Blah blah blah blah blah blah blah blah blah blah blah blah blah blah blah blah blah blah. Blah blah blah blah blah blah blah blah blah blah blah blah blah blah blah blah blah blah blah blah. Blah blah blah blah blah blah blah blah blah blah blah blah blah blah blah blah blah blah blah blah. Blah blah blah blah blah blah blah blah blah blah blah blah blah blah blah blah blah blah blah blah blah blah. Blah blah blah blah blah blah blah blah blah blah blah blah blah blah blah blah blah blah blah blah blah blah blah blah blah. Blah blah blah blah blah blah blah blah blah blah blah blah blah blah blah blah blah blah blah blah blah blah. Blah blah blah blah blah blah blah blah blah blah blah blah blah blah blah blah blah blah blah blah blah blah blah blah blah. Blah blah."

"Random lady, you always know best. Blah blah blah blah blah blah blah blah blah blah blah blah blah blah blah blah blah blah blah. Blah blah blah blah blah blah blah blah blah blah blah blah blah blah blah blah blah blah. Blah blah blah blah blah blah blah blah blah blah blah blah blah blah blah blah blah blah blah blah blah. Blah blah blah blah blah blah blah blah blah blah blah blah blah blah blah blah blah blah blah. Blah blah blah blah blah blah blah blah blah blah blah blah blah blah blah blah blah blah blah. Blah blah blah blah blah blah blah blah blah blah blah blah blah blah blah blah blah blah blah. Blah blah blah blah blah blah blah blah blah blah blah blah blah blah blah blah blah blah blah blah blah. Blah blah blah blah blah blah blah blah blah blah blah blah blah blah blah blah blah blah blah blah blah blah blah blah. Blah blah blah blah blah blah blah blah blah blah blah blah blah blah blah blah blah blah blah blah blah blah. Blah blah blah blah blah blah blah blah blah blah blah blah blah blah blah blah blah blah blah blah. Blah blah blah blah blah blah blah blah blah blah blah blah blah blah blah blah blah blah blah blah blah blah blah blah blah blah blah blah blah blah blah blah blah blah. Blah

blah blah blah blah blah blah blah blah blah blah blah blah blah blah blah blah blah blah. Blah blah blah blah blah blah blah blah blah blah blah blah blah blah blah blah blah blah blah. Blah blah blah blah blah blah blah blah blah blah blah blah blah blah blah blah blah blah blah. Blah blah blah blah blah blah blah blah blah blah blah blah blah blah blah blah blah blah blah. Blah blah blah blah blah blah blah blah blah blah blah blah blah blah blah blah blah blah blah. Blah blah blah blah blah blah blah blah blah blah blah blah blah blah blah blah blah blah blah. Blah blah blah blah blah blah blah blah blah blah blah blah blah blah blah blah blah blah blah blah. Blah blah blah blah blah blah blah blah blah blah blah blah blah blah blah blah blah blah blah blah blah. Blah blah blah blah blah blah blah blah blah blah blah blah blah blah blah blah blah blah. Blah blah blah blah blah blah blah blah blah blah blah blah blah blah Blah blah blah blah blah blah blah blah blah blah blah blah blah blah blah blah blah blah. Blah blah blah blah blah blah blah blah blah blah blah blah blah blah blah blah blah blah. Blah blah blah blah blah blah blah blah blah blah blah blah blah blah blah blah blah blah blah. Blah blah blah blah blah blah blah blah blah blah blah blah blah blah blah blah blah blah blah. Blah blah blah blah blah blah blah blah blah blah blah blah blah blah blah blah blah blah blah. Blah blah blah blah blah blah blah blah blah blah blah blah blah blah blah Blah blah blah blah blah blah blah blah blah blah blah blah blah blah blah blah blah blah. Blah blah blah blah blah blah blah blah blah blah blah blah blah blah blah blah blah blah blah. Blah blah blah blah blah blah blah blah blah blah blah blah blah blah blah blah blah blah blah. Blah blah blah blah blah blah blah blah blah blah blah blah blah blah blah blah blah blah blah. Blah blah blah blah blah blah blah blah blah blah blah blah blah blah blah blah blah blah. Blah blah blah blah blah blah blah blah blah blah blah blah blah blah blah blah blah blah blah. Blah blah blah blah blah blah blah blah blah blah blah blah blah blah blah blah blah blah. Blah blah blah blah blah blah blah blah blah blah blah blah blah blah blah blah blah blah blah. Blah blah blah."

*   *   *

Okay, that might have been longer than I thought.

Author's Note

Let's get real. Writing a book is super easy. Super, super easy. NOT. Writing a book is sitting down, determined to write. Then you procrastinate. Then you get determined again, and focus on getting completely distracted. Then you say, "No, I have to write." Then you get distracted again. Repeat until you get a sudden burst of inspiration and write ten pages. Continually do that for at least a year on end. Boom! You have a book! Now you just gotta print it-NOPE! Now you must contact an editor. The editor will say they love your book, they like the theme, the characters, the dialogue. They have a few minor suggestions, though, if you don't mind. The editor will then scrutinize every tiny bit of your story, having you change so many things that you'll have to spend every waking minute of the day fixing them. Then, exhausted, you'll crawl on your hands and knees to the editor, tiredly delivering the second draft.

Then the editor will tell you that they "forgot" to mention about a billion other things that you need to do. This will continue until the editor looks upon your sad, shriveled body, and takes pity on you. They will tell you it's time to look for a publisher (dramatic music plays).

The publisher website will say, "We love this! You get full customization. Just import your files." You will, and you'll get an error which will take weeks to resolve.

When you're done, you can finally go to pricing, where you'll learn that you will gain at most fifteen cents from each purchase. And then there you go. A big book, you crammed stress into and a few coins in profit.

Acknowledgments

For being so crucial to the writing process, I'd like to thank Elisha Dukes, my editor. I'd also like to thank Harry VanDernoot, the person who dodged countless traps and lava pits[116] to rescue the scrolls I wrote these memoirs down on. I'd also like to thank J.R.R. Tolkien for being J.R.R. Tolkien. Thank you to Meagen Bowersox for motivating me to start writing these. Thank you Hadley Skouby for the cover design. Thank you to Ingramspark for distributing the book and absolutely nothing else. Thanks to Sam Guthrie, who is a monster when it comes to grammar, and became particularly helpful near the end when Elisha Dukes became white and intangible. READ: A Ghost. As in "ghosting" people. LAUGH. More thanks to Hadley Skouby for helping proofread, and for leaving a suggestion for her own acknowledgment ("Except for one of the best humans I have come across, Hadley Skouby. They swooped in when I needed a hand proofreading.") There. That's it. Absolutely nobody else gets a mention!

[116] None of which WORKED, for some reason.

The Appendices

Appendix A

On Primal Gods

Eros Phanes

God of Love

Eros Phanes was born before the dawn of the time when the god of nothingness, Chaos, burped. He formed with his brothers and sisters, Tartarus, Nyx, and Erebus.[117] He invented love soon after. When the gods met to decide how the universe would work, Eros summoned some mystical power from Chaos to form birds.[118] To this day, they bear wings on their backs, in honor of their ancient creator. They were first made, before all other animals, in the pit of Tartarus, of which they were so desperate to get away from

[117] Hesiod, Theogony 116 ff (trans. Evelyn-White) (Greek epic C8th or C7th B.C.). This text fails to mention both Nyx and Erebus, so Hesoid's soul probably isn't doing well in Hades.

[118] Aristophanes, Birds 685 ff (trans. O'Neill) (Greek comedy C5th to 4th B.C.). Not completely correct either. It's part of a play, so some muse must be willfully uninformed.

that they first learned to fly.[119] When Uranus was usurped, Eros's essence in Uranus fell to sea. It started forming Aphrodite. After that, he mostly performed his duties as god of love. At one point, Zeus, knowing Eros' power, asked him to aid him in the crisis with Typhon.[120] Eros thought it was petty and would draw some anger from Gaia, so he did nothing. Born from the burp of Chaos, Eros's close family is comparatively small. Besides his siblings, Eros's only children are birds,[121] and Aphrodite, who formed from sea foam when his center of power in Uranus fell into the ocean.

Tartarus

God of the Pit

Tartarus was born before the dawn of time when Chaos burped, along with his siblings. For most/all of his life he housed prisoners and spawned monsters. He had Typhon with Gaia,[122] along with the giants.[123] He had the Telchines with Nemesis.[124] Most primal monsters were formed from the primordial ooze of Tartarus. That's it. He's not a very interesting guy.

[119] It really hurt Tartarus's feelings.
[120] Nonnus, Dionysiaca 1. 400 ff (trans. Rouse) (Greek epic C5th A.D.)
[121] Actually, he has a rather large family if you count all birds.
[122] Hesiod, Theogony 820 ff
[123] Pseudo-Hyginus, Preface
[124] Bacchylides, Fragment 52 (from Tzetzes on Hesiod's Theogony) (trans. Campbell, Vol. Greek Lyric IV) (C5th B.C.)

Erebus

God of Darkness and Hades

Erebus was born before the dawn of time when Chaos burped along with his siblings. He had children with Nyx.[125] for most of his life, he fulfilled his duties as darkness and the upper underworld. Also with Nyx, he had Moros, the spirit of doom; Geras, the spirit of old age; Thanatos, the spirit of peaceful death; Ker, the spirit of violent death; Sophrosyne, the spirit of restraint; Hypnos, the god of sleep; the uncountable Oneroi, the spirits of dreams; Epiphorn, spirit of shrewdness; Eris, goddess of discord; Oizys, the spirit of misery; Hybris, spirit of bad behavior; Nemesis, goddess of revenge; Euphrosyne, one of the Charities; Philotes, spirit of friendship; Eleos, goddess of mercy; Styx, goddess of the river Styx and the spirit of hatred;[126] Dolus, spirit of trickery; Ponos, spirit of hard labor; Momos, spirit of criticism; Apate, spirit of lies;[127] and the Furies.[128] Needless to say, he had quite a few children.

Nyx

Goddess of the Night

Nyx was born before the dawn of time when Chaos burped along with her siblings. She had Aether and Hemera with Erebus. See Erebus for her other children.

[125] Hesiod, Theogony 115 ff (trans. Evelyn-White) (Greek epic C8th or C7th B.C.)
[126] Pseudo-Hyginus, Preface (trans. Grant) (Roman mythographer C2nd A.D.)
[127] Cicero, De Natura Deorum 3. 17 (trans. Rackham) (Roman rhetorician C1st B.C.)
[128] Virgil, Aeneid 6. 250 ff (trans. Day-Lewis) (Roman epic C1st B.C.)

Hecate may be her child, but the wording is unclear.[129] She held the scepter of the universe for a little bit.[130] Like others, Nyx spent her life mostly performing her duties as the embodiment of night, but she does have more adventures than most other primal beings. One time, she brought baby Hypnos and Baby Thanatos into her chariot for a midnight ride.[131] During the high political unrest of the Trojan War, Hera came up with a dirty trick. She had Hypnos put Zeus into a deep sleep. She then threw Zeus in the ocean. Her plan was to anger him, but also, on some accounts, to use the time to drive Dionysus insane.[132] Zeus woke up and got mad at Hypnos. He chased him around until Nyx saved him. At one point, Nyx built a house for her and Hemera so they can see each other for about three seconds every twelve-hour period.[133] Sometimes, Nyx would help some sailors with sailing.[134] When Eos's son Memnon died, Nyx felt bad for her.[135] When Helio's son was stupid and died, leaving the sun unattended, Nyx helped out and started the night early, messing up everyone's sleep schedules.[136] Around this time, Nyx

---

[129] Bacchylides, Fragment 1b (trans. Campbell, Vol. Greek Lyric IV) (Greek lyric C5th B.C.) states:

"Torch-bearing Hekate (Hecate), . . [missing text] holy . ., daughter of great-bosomed Nyx ." It seems that it means Hecate is the daughter of Nyx, though some sources identify her as a titan. The missing text could mention someone else. The answer is lost to history. *Author's Note:* I asked both Hecate and Nyx about this, and they didn't tell me anything. And if you're gonna say that since I'm omniscient I should know, I shut omniscients off from my thinking brain so I wouldn't be a drag.

[130] Orphica, Theogonies Fragment 101 - 102 (from Proclus) (trans. West) (Greek hymns C3rd - C2nd B.C.). This text reads Eros as Phanes, but that was because the authors were "convinced" (READ: threatened) by Phanes to do so.

[131] Pausanias, Description of Greece 5. 18. 1 (trans. Jones) (Greek travelog C2nd A.D.)

[132] Nonnus, Dionysiaca 35. 276 ff (trans. Rouse) (Greek epic C5th A.D.)

[133] Hesiod, Theogony 744 ff (trans. Evelyn-White) (Greek epic C8th or C7th B.C.)

[134] Aratus, Phaenomena 405 ff (trans. Mair) (Greek astronomy C3rd B.C.)

[135] Quintus Smyrnaeus, Fall of Troy 2. 549 ff (trans. Way) (Greek epic C4th A.D.)

[136] Philostratus the Elder, Imagines 1. 11 (trans. Fairbanks) (Greek rhetorician C3rd A.D.)

completed her night cycle for the one trillionth time. She celebrated by spending six months straight in Antarctica, which replaced the budding new ecosystem with ice, snow, and penguins.[citation needed] One time, Zeus was hanging out with Semele and asked Nyx what time that dawn will be.[137] She was like, "Time for you to get a watch!" and Zeus was so ashamed and it was great! In recent times, Nyx has been involved in numerous prayers, most perpetrated with her oracle in Megara, the head city of Megaris.[138]

Aether

God of the Heavens

Aether was born from Erebus and Nyx before time. For most of his life, he simply did his job. With Gaia, he had the Algea, spirits of pain; Lyssa, spirit of madness and fury; Penthos, spirit of grief; the Pseudologoi, the spirits of lies, who worked for Apate; Horkos, spirit of punishments; the Amphilogiai, spirits of disputes; Lethe, spirit of the river Lethe and god of forgetfulness; Aergia, spirit of laziness; and the Hysminai, spirits of combat.[139] Prometheus once called Aether to his prison to see how much of a jerk the gods were.[140] He was really honored, and then he realized Prometheus had basically invited everyone.

---

[137] Nonnus, Dionysiaca 7. 280 ff

[138] Pausanias, Description of Greece 1. 40. 6 (trans. Jones) (Greek travelog C2nd A.D.)

[139] Pseudo-Hyginus, Preface (trans. Grant) (Roman mythographer C2nd A.D.). It's wrong on some fronts, but right on others.

[140] Aeschylus, Prometheus Bound 1091 ff (trans. Weir Smyth) (Greek tragedy C5th B.C.)

Hemera

Goddess of Day

Hemera was born from Erebus and Nyx before time. For most of her life she just was day. That's it. She didn't even have any children. It's crazy.

Pontus

God of Water

Pontus is the son of Gaia.[141] For his entire life, he mostly just hangs out in the water. With Gaia, who was his mom, so eww, he had Nereus, the old man of the sea; Thaumas, the promotional man for the sea, who told everyone how great it was; Phorkys, god of the deep parts of the sea; Keto, goddess of sea monsters; Eurybia, who represented power over the sea;[142] and Aigaios, god of storms.[143] When it became time to populate the world, Pontus created fish to live in the seas.[144] When Prometheus cried for the lands to witness his torment, Oceanus reassured him that he and Pontus thought it was a pretty mean thing to do.[145] When Jason and his argonauts set sail for Corinth, they played a song and Pontus thought it was very soothing.[146]

---

[141] Hesiod, Theogony 106 ff (trans. Evelyn-White) (Greek epic C8th or C7th B.C.)

[142] Hesiod, Theogony 233 ff

[143] Eumelus of Corinth or Arctinus of Miletus, Titanomachia Fragment 3 (from Scholiast on Apollonius Rhodius, Arg. i. 1165) (trans. Evelyn-White) (Greek epic C8th or C7th B.C.)

[144] Pseudo-Hyginus, Preface (trans. Grant) (Roman mythographer C2nd A.D.)

[145]Aeschylus, Prometheus Bound 431

[146] Philostratus the Elder, Imagines 2. 15 (trans. Fairbanks) (Greek rhetorician C3rd A.D.)

Appendix B[147]

On the Underappreciated Gods

Hebe

Goddess of Youth

Hebe was born in bliss. After their wedding, Zeus and Hera were happy for hundreds of years, bringing into the world Hebe, Ares, and Eileithyia.[148] When she was just seven days old, the Olympian gods competed about who could give her the best gift. Athena gave her toys made in the palace of Poseidon. The others followed suit. Soon, little Hebe was drowning in playthings more precious than gold. Apollo, seeing the quarrel, asked the muse Phoebus to play some beautiful music. She did, and Hebe

[147] I'd also like to mention Morpheus, the king of dreams, who almost made it onto this list, except he only has one significant mention. Ovid, Metamorphoses 11. 585 ff (trans. Melville) (Roman epic C1st B.C. to C1st A.D.). Check it out.

[148] Hesiod, Theogony 921 ff (trans. Evelyn-White) (Greek epic C8th or C7th B.C.)

picked her gift.[149] Then, everyone noticed that Hebe wasn't a very powerful goddess, so they stuck her with being their cupbearer, and a part-time handmaiden of Hera. They didn't think much of Hebe, but secretly she was hugely influential, keeping their immortality safe and stopping them from withering away.[150] When this prince of Troy, Ganymede, and Zeus started dating, Zeus made him immortal, bringing him to Olympus to become his cupbearer.[151] This was actually good for Hebe, because you may notice that Zeus isn't the most emotionally stable guy. Hera needed to use her chariot once and Hebe cleaned it in a record two seconds.[152] Hera then rescued Ares from a battle where he got hurt and Hebe healed him.[153] Hebe eventually got married to Hercules after he finally died and became a god.[154] She had with him the gods Aniketos and Alexiares, who were in charge of helping people fortify their cities. When Dionysus was becoming a god, he asked Hera if he could marry Hebe. Hera explained that Hebe was married to Hercules, right as they both came into the room.[155] It was incredibly awkward. When Iolaus, Hercule's nephew, was dying, Hercules wished he would live. Hebe had been told by the titan Themis that Hercules would be her husband one day, so she granted his wish and made Iolaus young again. This caused a lot of grumbling amongst the gods, and Hebe said she wouldn't do it again.[156] She then helped Medea rejuvenate Jason's

[149] Callimachus, Iambi Fragment 202 (trans. Trypanis) (Greek poet C3rd B.C.)

[150] Euphronius, Fragment (from Scholiast on Aristophanes) (trans. Campbell, Vol Greek Lyric IV Bacchylides, Frag 41)

[151] Nonnus, Dionysiaca 25. 430 ff

[152] Homer, Iliad 5. 720 ff (trans. Lattimore) (Greek epic C8th B.C.)

[153] Homer, Iliad 5. 905 ff

[154] Hesiod, Theogony 950 ff (trans. Evelyn-White) (Greek epic C8th or C7th B.C.)

[155] Nonnus, Dionysiaca 35. 333 ff (trans. Rouse) (Greek epic C5th A.D.)

[156] Ovid, Metamorphoses 9. 396 ff (trans. Melville) (Roman epic C1st B.C. to C1st A.D.)

father in secret.[157] As for her cult following, she as an temple at Athens,[158] Sicyon,[159] and another, unnamed location.[160] When Romulus was thinking of month names, Hebe tried to convince him to name June after her, instead of Hera. She failed, and Hebtember wrote to be.[161] [162]

Eileithyia

Goddess of Childbirth

Eileithyia was the last to be born from the bliss of Hera and Zeus's honeymoon. Born in the cave of Dictaean in Crete,[163] Eileithyia became the goddess of childbirth because people began to notice childbirth hurts. When Leto cleverly decided to give birth on the floating island of Delos, all the gods begged her to allow Leto to have her children, but Eileithyia wanted to stick with her mother Hera's decision. This dutiful appreciation of her mother's wants went flying out the window, however, when she was offered a gold necklace as a totally-not-a-bribe. Apollo and Artemis were born soon

---

[157] Ovid, Metamorphoses 7. 241 ff (trans. Melville) (Roman epic C1st B.C. to C1st A.D.)

[158] Pausanias, Description of Greece 1. 19. 3 (trans. Jones) (Greek travelog C2nd A.D.)

[159] Strabo, Geography 8. 6. 24 (trans. Jones) (Greek geographer C1st B.C. to C1st A.D.)

[160] Aelian, On Animals 17. 46 (trans. Scholfield) (Greek natural history C2nd A.D.)

[161] Ovid, Fasti 6. 65 ff (trans.Boyle) (Roman poetry C1st B.C. to C1st A.D.)

[162] I know this seems like a lot of stuff about Hebe, but if you think she isn't under-appreciated, go to your local bookstore, buy a children's Greek mythology book, and if you can find a significant mention of Hebe, you get a cookie. I'll wait... I didn't think so.

[163] Nonnus, Dionysiaca 8. 178 ff (trans. Rouse) (Greek epic C5th A.D.)

after.[164] Eileithyia again honored Hera's wishes when Hercules was about to be born and subsequently named King of Mycenae. Hera told Eileithyia to let Hercules's cousin, Eurystheus be born prematurely.[165] Eileithyia was then told to stop Alcmena, Hercules's mother, from giving birth, which she did. Galinthias, a maid for Alcmena, saw her sitting by, not doing anything and worried that the mother and children would both die. She shouted that the twins had been born, which surprised Eileithyia, making her release her power on Alcmena for just long enough that the twins could be born.[166] [167] Eileithya basically has helped people give birth ever since. She had the child Sosolpis, god of the city of Elis, with an unknown person.

Eris

Goddess of Strife and Discord

Eris was the goddess of the strife. She was also the goddess of discord, and brought all the fighting in the world about. The discord between gods. The discord between kingdoms. The discord of Melkor. She did it all. The child of Nyx, she was a demented being. But she was still underappreciated, so here she is. As I mentioned, she was the child of Nyx and Erebus. Hesiod states that all of the spirits on Pandora's jar were Eris's children, but those daimons mostly are parented by Nyx and other daimons.

---

[164] Homeric Hymn 3 to Delian Apollo 89 ff (trans. Evelyn-White) (Greek epic C7th - 4th B.C.)

[165] Diodorus Siculus, Library of History 4. 9. 4 (trans. Oldfather) (Greek historian C1st B.C.)

[166] Antoninus Liberalis, Metamorphoses 29 (trans. Celoria) (Greek mythographer C2nd A.D.)

[167] This made Hera so mad that she made Galinthias into a weasel. Hecate took pity on her, so now Hecate has a weasel as one of her attendants.

Sometime in her life, she was not allowed in a wedding. Zeus let her in though, after planning with Theitis for this incident to incite the Trojan War. When Eris got in, though, she got mad that no one would let her have any fun, i.e. orchestrating chaos and destruction. When Hephaestus stopped her from lighting fires for the ninetieth time, she got mad and threw a golden apple into the crowd, shouting "For the Fairest!". The apple rolled up to Hera, Athena, and Aphrodite, and they all tried to pick it up,[168] [169] [170] but that's a story for another time. During battles, Eris would ride in on Ares's war chariot and wreak havoc.[171] This one time Hercules was walking along a path when an apple was on the road. Hercules got angry that, I dunno, the road inspectors hadn't seen it, and tried to smash it with his club. When he hit it, though, it grew two times bigger. He kept hitting it until it grew so large it blocked his path. When Hercules strove to get around it, Athena told him that it was Eris's trickery. It was supposedly a metaphor for how fighting something makes the problem bigger, but it was still pretty funny when he first realized what was happening.[172] Eris is even on the Aegis because of how scary strife is.[173] When everyone was ordered to stop interfering in the Trojan War, Eris was allowed to stay and watch.[174] Eris was generally just escalating everything, so Zeus said she could continue. She influenced many people to do terrible things on numerous occasions. As he passed through the underworld, Aeneas, the future founder of Italy, jumped, like, eighty feet when Eris surprised him.[175] It was great. Hephaestus was once

[168] Stasinus of Cyprus or Hegesias of Aegina, Cypria Fragment 1 (summary from Proclus, Cherstomathia 1) (trans. Evelyn-White) (Greek epic C7th or C6th B.C.)

[169] Pseudo-Apollodorus, Bibliotheca E3. 2 (trans. Aldrich) (Greek mythographer C2nd A.D.)

[170] Pseudo-Hyginus, Fabulae 92 (trans. Grant) (Roman mythographer C2nd A.D.)

[171] Homer, Iliad 4. 441 ff (trans. Lattimore) (Greek epic C8th B.C.)

[172] Aesop, Fables 534 (from Chambry 129) (trans. Gibbs) (Greek fable C6th B.C.)

[173] Homer, Iliad 5. 738 ff (trans. Lattimore) (Greek epic C8th B.C.)

[174] Homer, Iliad 11. 73 ff

[175] Virgil, Aeneid 6. 268 ff (trans. Fairclough) (Roman epic C1st B.C.)

crafting a necklace with an evil curse on it, and Eris helped him with the spell.[176] When Dionysus was striving to invade India, and, seeing an opportunity for immense pain and sadness, Eris disguised herself as Rhea and told Dionysus to invade, which he did.[177] Eris was sent by Hera to disrupt a marriage.[178] This book is rated E for everyone so let's move on. In her free time, Eris guards Ares's palace in Thrace.[179] So yeah. She's not a very nice person.

Hecate

Goddess of Magic

Hecate was the goddess of magic, daughter of Perseus, titan of destruction, and Asteria, titan of falling stars and the island of Delos,[180] though some say she was the child of Nyx. Medea, the wicked wife of Jason, was her student.[181] Hecate never had any children, which she said was due to some philosophical reason. If you ask me, though, and I was the one who orchestrated this decision, so listen up, Hecate was just too cool for school to get married to any of those idiot boys.[182] She allied herself with the gods in the Titanomachy, and Zeus was super nice to her.[183] I know. It's INSANE. Hecate again

[176] Statius, Thebaid 2. 286 ff (trans. Mozley) (Roman epic C1st A.D.)

[177] Nonnus, Dionysiaca 20. 35 ff

[178] Antoninus Liberalis, Metamorphoses 11 (trans. Celoria) (Greek mythographer C2nd A.D). This story is so terrible it cannot be repeated here. Look it up on Theoi.com and read the terrible details yourself.

[179] Statius, Thebaid 7. 64 ff

[180] Hesiod, Theogony 404 ff (trans. Evelyn-White) (Greek epic C8th or C7th B.C.)

[181] Ovid, Metamorphoses 7. 74 (trans. Melville) (Roman epic C1st B.C. to C1st A.D.)

[182] Lycophron, Alexandra 1174 (trans. Mair) (Greek poet C3rd B.C.)

[183] Hesiod, Theogony 404 ff (trans. Evelyn-White) (Greek epic C8th or C7th B.C.)

helped the gods against the giants in the Gigantomachy. In the fighting, she killed the giant Clytius with her two flaming daggers.[184] It was super cool. When Persephone was kidnapped, Hecate heard from her cave and tried to investigate. When Demeter came by nine days later, an unsuccessful Hecate told her she thought Persephone had been kidnapped. Demeter took Hecate to Helios's palace, where the story progressed further.[185] After some time, when Persephone was returned, Hecate took up a job as Persephone's attendant, and magic was easier to perform in Erebos than in a smelly old cave, so it was a win-win.[186] During her time as an attendant, Hecate threw a duck into a cave. When Persephone picked it up, a river sprouted from the rock. The river was named Herknya, after another name for Hecate.[187] Yeah. It was *really* random. One time, this witch Gale asked Hecate out and Hecate got mad because Gale should've known about how Hecate swore to never date, and so Hecate transformed her into the first pole-cat.[188] When the Greeks captured Troy, Odysseus captured the Queen, Hecuba. On the way back, Hecuba killed a Thracian king, and the locals started throwing rocks at her. Hecuba prayed to the gods for help and they turned her into a black dog. Hecate then took her as her familiar.[189] To this day, Hecate still practices magic, which is why when you might see something weird and unexplainable, just know it's probably Hecate messing around with you.

---

[184] Pseudo-Apollodorus, Bibliotheca 1. 34 - 38 (trans. Aldrich) (Greek mythographer C2nd A.D.)

[185] Homeric Hymn 2 to Demeter 19 ff (trans. Evelyn-White) (Greek epic C7th - 4th B.C.)

[186] Homeric Hymn 2 to Demeter 436 ff

[187] Pausanias, Description of Greece 9. 39. 2 (trans. Jones) (Greek travelog C2nd A.D.)

[188] Aelian, On Animals 15. 11 (trans. Scholfield) (Greek natural history C2nd A.D.)

[189] Lycophron, Alexandra 1174 ff (trans. Mair) (Greek poet C3rd B.C.)

Hypnos

God of Sleep

The son of Nyx and Erebus, Hypnos was the hypnotizing god of sleep. That whole thing with Hypnos and Nyx and Hera happened. See Nyx for more information. Zeus's son Sarpedon died in the Trojan War. His dead body was getting all mangled, and stuff, so Zeus sent Hypnos and Thanatos down to get him. They buried him in Lycia.[190] Selene once fell in love with this mortal named Endymion, and sent Hypnos to find a way to make him immortal. Endymion and Hypnos brainstormed for a long time, but then they started playing some games. After a while, Hypnos and Endymion clapped hands and declared they were "BFFs!"[191] Hypnos then had an epiphany and lured Endymion into sleeping forever, so Hypnos and Endymion could play games for all eternity. This made him immortal, so I guess Selene got what she asked for, but something tells me that wasn't what she was thinking of.[192] After killing a giant named Antaeus, Hera sent Hypnos to make Heracles fall into a deep sleep. When Antaeus's followers, the Pygmies, tried to avenge him, Hypnos showed up to wake Heracles and show him his role (and Hera's) in the event.[193] In the end, Hercules escaped, so don't worry, Hercules fans. He's fine. One time, this person named Gorgias of Leotini was so tired that he began to die. Falling asleep, Hypnos saw him and was like, "Whoa. This guy is gonna die any second. Here you go, Thanatos." Hypnos handed Gorgias to

[190] Homer, Iliad 16. 681 ff

[191] And possibly lovers too, but don't tell Selene about that part though, 'kay?

[192] Licymnius, Fragment 771 (from Athenaeus, Scholars at Dinner) (trans. Campbell, Vol. Greek Lyric V) (Greek lyric C4th B.C.)

[193] Philostratus the Elder, Imagines 2. 22 (trans. Fairbanks) (Greek rhetorician C3rd A.D.)

Thanatos, and he died peacefully.[194] Once, this man named Ceyx died in a shipwreck, and Hera told Iris to go tell Hypnos to break the news to his wife, Alycone, through a dream. Iris delivered the message, and he put his best man, Morpheus, on the task. He broke the news in the form of Ceyx, and everything worked out great for everyone.[195] Except for Ceyx. And Alycone. And Ceyx's shipmates. But beside those guys, everything worked out great for everyone. When the gods got mad at the people of the island of Lemnos, they sent Hypnos and Thanatos to do their dirty work. Hypnos appeared, in the dead of night, wearing his magic hood that sent every man on the island into a deep sleep. Thanatos then sent a wave of madness towards all the women, so that they slaughtered their husbands in their sleep.[196] It was a pretty terrible thing, but they each got four Ambrosia cookies, so it was definitely worth it. One time, there was this crazy party, and Hypnos had to leave because they thought "Sleep is for the Weak,"[197] which, as luck would have it, would later become the motto for video animators. Sometimes insomniacs would pray to Hypnos, asking for sleep,[198] and if he liked you he would cure you. If he didn't, he would make your insomnia worse. So it was a double-edged sword. Hypnos has temples in Sicyon,[199] Troezen,[200] and Sparta.[201] Well, nobody wants a temple in Sparta. It was covered all in bones and stuff.

Gross.

[194] Aelian, Historical Miscellany 2. 34 (trans. Wilson) (Greek rhetorician C2nd to 3rd A.D.)

[195] Ovid, Metamorphoses 11. 585 ff (trans. Melville) (Roman epic C1st B.C. to C1st A.D.)

[196] Statius, Thebaid 5. 155 ff

[197] Statius, Silvae 1. 6. 90 ff (trans. Mozley) (Roman poetry C1st A.D.)

[198] Statius, Silvae 5. 4. 1 (trans. Mozley) (Roman poetry C1st A.D.)

[199] Pausanias, Description of Greece 2. 10. 2 (trans. Jones) (Greek travelog C2nd A.D.)

[200] Pausanias, Description of Greece 2. 31. 3

[201] Pausanias, Description of Greece 3. 18. 1

Appendix C

On Missing, Unidentified, or Miscellaneous Articles

Oracle, On the Land of Australia Fragment 15 (from Oracle, On the Land of Terra) (trans. VanDernoot) (Greek Oracle C3rd B.C.)

"And when you see them [the kangaroos] ... you shall sing the "Ballad to Kangaroos" which they [the Aboriginals] sing till Meanface (Day) [Hemera], awful goddess, leaves and Nyx brings dreary Hypnos to lay them into rest."

[C.N. The description of Hemera as "Meanface" is connected with Eros. He is believed to be the voice behind the oracle.]

Oracle, On the Land of Australia Fragment 33

"And then ye shall do the 'Kangaroo Hop', which entails ... [Missing Text] ... and then ye shall have done the 'Kangaroo Hop'."

Anaximander, Description of Terra 478 ff (trans. VanDernoot) (Greek travelog C3rd B.C.)

"And to get to the land where the kangaroos hop, head south east at ... [missing text] ... and travel 2439 leagues [sic], and then you will be there."

[C.N. This travelog is believed to be the companion piece to On the Land of Terra.]

Eros Phanes, Journal 8. 13. 19. (trans. VanDernoot) (Greek Diary C2nd A.D.)

"*May 22nd, 10,256. Calendar: Pseudo-Gregorian*

Today I held a bake sale. I don't need money, but what was I going to do with all that stuff I baked? I was bartering with Hermes, trying to sell him a rhubarb pie, when Meanface (Day) [Hemera] materialized. I quickly sold the pie for two gold coins and ran over to her.

"What are you doing here?" I asked. Meanface laughed.

"I heard you were holding a bake sale," she scoffed.

"So?"

"I didn't want to miss the show." And so, without a word, Meanface sat down in a lawn chair. I shrugged. Meanface could be Meanface, but I would still hold my sale. I began to show Athena a series of breads that increased your dexterity, and Meanface scoffed at my offer of trading Athena one of her tapestries.

"Even with Eros's stupid breads, you couldn't make a good tapestry if your life depended on it, Athena. Also, did I mention my opinion on Eros's bread? Just to reiterate it, I think his bread is stupid." Athena knew to keep her cool, but I'm not so proud to say that this made me a little angry. But, no, I couldn't let this ruin the day. I could still sell some more baked goods. But the cycle continued. I tried to sell Zeus a bunch of croissants.

"If taste could kill, those croissants would be serial killers."

I tried to sell Aphrodite a banana cream pie.

"What a banana cream sigh."

Apollo wanted a cake.

"Hold your nose, Apollo, because that cake *stank*."

Finally I couldn't take it anymore. I walked up to Meanface with an apple pie in my hand.

"What do you want, Eros?" she said accusingly. "I have to get back to teasing you."

"Oh, you can get right back to doing that after this one thing." And with a great thrust of my arm, Meanface was ApplePieface.

"WHAT ARE YOU DOING!?" she screamed. "You ... [missing text]! You are such a ... [missing text] ... you ... [missing text]! I hate you so much, ... [missing text]! See you never, ... [missing text]! [missing text]!" And Meanface stormed off. All in all, it was a pretty successful day.

Oracle, Legendarium of the Gods 80 ff (from Mnemosyne, Book of All Knowledge) (trans. VanDernoot) (Greek Epic Before Time-Present)

"And, the god who took the fairest [name]; Eros, whose mother Aphrodite, daughter of the primordial Eros, who first tamed evil. His father ... [missing text] ... and that is all you need to know about Eros's father."

Eros Phanes, What's Up with those Romans? 168 ff (from Mnemosyne, Book of All Knowledge) (trans. VanDernoot) (Podcast Minutes C20th A.D.)

"And this one time, Apollo tried to take Helios's job, and Artemis tried to take Selene's job. The Titans stopped the gods pretty quick, but *of course* that was the day the Romans were watching."

[C.N. The Book of All Knowledge is a composition of all information in the universe. It is collected by the titan Mnemosyne, who is in charge of memory. Mnemosyne is very proud of the book, which contains infinite pages. It is held in the heart of an unnamed Oort Cloud object, keeping it secret and hidden. You don't want to know how much paperwork is required to get a single page of information from it. You're welcome.]

Eros Phanes, What's Up with those Romans? 234 ff

"And then it was Crazy Name Day. So, for Spirits Week, all the gods used crazy names like 'Jupiter' and 'Mars'. It was totally waka-doodle! But *of course* that was the day that the Romans asked what the god's names were."

Eros Phanes, What's Up with those Romans? 329 ff

"This guy Aeneas, the Romans thought he was *sooooo* great. He thought the gods loved him and brought him on adventures. The [Romans] thought that the gods took Aeneas to Olympus to become a god. And they did do that. They *did* take him to Olympus after he went on all those adventures. But it was only a visit. Aeneas drank nectar and ate ambrosia. But right as the gods were about to [show him the door], he was talking with Hermes as they walked down a great hall.

"Thanks for bringing me here, man," he said, his brain a little loopy from all that nectar.

"Anytime, bro," Hermes replied. "Well, not anytime, only when we invite you, but you get what I mean."

"Dude, before I go, can I just, like, play in the clouds?" Aeneas looked out at the fluffy white clouds that circled Olympus. "I've always wanted to do that."

"Um, I don't think you should," Hermes answered, cautiously. "I think the whole 'playing in clouds' thing is just for paintings."

"Oh, I'm sure it'll be fine," slurred Aeneas, and he strode towards a cloud right outside the walls.

"Dude, I'm pretty sure clouds are gasses. I don't think they're very tangible," Hermes warned, but Aeneas had stepped onto the cloud already.

"Shouldn't I be falling, then?" he asked.

"It's cartoon physics," Hermes told Aeneas. He didn't want to make his friend fall, but rules were rules. "Here, hold this sign behind your back."

"Why?" Aeneas asked, grabbing the sign.

"Not important. Now look down."

Aeneas did as he was told, and the cloud parted to reveal the thousands of feet of nothing but air below his feet.

"Now hold out the sign." Aeneas took out the sign, a red arrow pointing down that read, "UH-OH!"

Then Aeneas fell. He died, and was sent to the fields of Elysium.

"What a tragedy," Zeus sighed. "What will we tell his followers?"

"We could tell them that he ascended to godhood," suggested Persephone, who was in town for spring. "I mean, we've done it before."

"Good idea, daughter," Demeter smiled. "But what should he be the god of?"

"How about Jupiter Indiges?" Zeus suggested.

"What does that mean?" Hera asked.

"Nothing. But it was one of the contenders for my name on Crazy Name Day, and it sounds kind of fancy."

"Then it's settled," Poseidon finished. "I'll get a river god to pretend to wash away his mortal essence, and we'll be good."

And that is how Aeneas came to be known as a god, and not a person who steps on clouds and falls like Wile E. Coyote."

Eros Phanes, Analysis on Godhood 30 ff (from Mnemosyne, Book of All Knowledge) (trans. VanDernoot) (College Paper Before Time)

"If Chaos [is a god then], so are Gaia, Eros, Tartarus, Erebus, and Nyx
If they [are gods then], so are Aether and Meanface
If Aether and Meanface [are gods then], so are Uranus and Pontus
If Meanface [is a god then], life is not fair"

Eros Phanes, Analysis on Godhood 354 ff

"A god is believed to be a conscious being with power over nature or the universe. Most gods bleed ichor and are immortal, at least, they will not die of cell death due to old age, or minor wounds. With the exception of only Hercules [sic],[citation needed] the gods are part of one, big, huge, ginormous family. Gods traditionally don't have the same family values, and the tremendous amount of inbreeding that occurs is probably what makes them so horrible."

Eros Phanes, The Complete Passage of the Scepter of the Universe 10 ff (from Mnemosyne, Book of All Knowledge) (trans. VanDernoot) (Current Event Article C20th A.D.)

"The Scepter of the Universe has passed through the hands of those who control the cosmos for an untold number of years. This is the order in which the scepter has passed.

Firstly, Phanes, in his first take over of Eros's body, created the scepter to assert his control over the universe.

When Eros[202] took back control, he did not want to rule, so he gave the scepter to Nyx. Nyx ruled fairly yet strongly for thousands of years. So, of course, someone had to mess it up.

Shortly after the Titans were born Uranus forcibly seized the scepter. Nyx was angered by this little upstart taking her status and power. Nyx told her servants to throw big projectiles at Uranus. They did, and that's why the sky is littered with stars. The servants took the stars from a pocket of space far away,[203] and Uranus's spirit still burns with the heat of a thousand stars today.

[202] Who was super cool, and spoke in the third person, which is also super cool.

[203] The Eridanus Supervoid, to be specific.

Kronos took power and the scepter through a story that I won't make you have to hear for the 467th time.

Zeus took power and the scepter through a story that I won't make you have to hear for the 765th time.

Now, according to most narratives, the story ends there. Zeus still holds the scepter today and is High Lord Over the Universe. But there's one nuance in this particular theory.

Prometheus.

Prometheus stole fire and gave it to humans, even though Zeus specifically told him not to.

That was bad.

But when Zeus chained him to a rock in the Caucasus Mountains, with an eagle eating his liver out every day, somebody was like, "That's a little extreme". And then everybody else thought, "It *is* a little extreme. Zeus could just strip him of his immortality for a year or two, like he had done with Poseidon and Apollo when they revolted. Why is he being so harsh?" The reason, even though Zeus will never admit it, was simple.

Zeus was paranoid.

You see, Zeus was worried about losing control of the universe. Before him, Kronos was usurped by his youngest son, Zeus. Before that, Uranus was usurped by his youngest son, Kronos. Before that, Nyx was usurped by her youngest, *um*, nephew, Uranus.

Forget about that part.

The point is, Zeus thought the cycle would continue, and he thought his youngest godly son would overtake him. Years ago, he sat at his throne thinking. He looked suspiciously at Dionysus, who was with Apollo. They were both drinking non-alcoholic wine,[204] and were laughing and smiling like idiots.

"You can't do a cartwheel!" challenged Apollo. "You're too dizzy!" Apollo's face then grew very serious and stern. "Though not because you are intoxicated, because this is non-alcoholic wine." Once that was cleared up, Apollo resumed his giddy smile and laugh.

"Yes I can!" Dionysus yelled at an unnecessary volume. "Here I go!" Dionysus did a pseudo-cartwheel straight out of the palace, falling off of Olympus. There was a faint yell and a *thump* as he hit the ground. A second later, a bruised Dionysus got back up standing on a grape vine.

"That was CRAZY, man!" Apollo yelled.

"TOTALLY crazy!" Dionysus agreed.

"Can I have a try now!?"

"Yeah!"

The next hour was spent with Dionysus and Apollo repeatedly doing pseudo-cartwheels until Artemis and Hestia, who had been watching, both sighed and led them to their apartments to take a nap and clear their heads from the, again, non-alcoholic wine.

[204] Ah-HAH! You can't censor me now, can you, overly sensitive people? - A.N.

"A future son," Zeus assured himself. "If the cycle were to continue, it would be through a son that has not been born yet. Unless any of my other godly sons turn out to overthrow me."

Zeus looked over and saw Ares acting in a blind rage about the fact that one of his acolytes left a single grain of dust inside his temple, because Ares had stepped on it and it got onto his sandal.

"I. AM. BEING. COMPLETELY. REASONABLE!!" he yelled, annihilating the city and wiping it from everyone's memory.

"Not Ares," Zeus noted. "What about Hephaestus? I always thought he was a little underrated."

Zeus looked over to see Ares, now a little cooled down from his unhinged rage, walked over and draped his arm over Aphrodite's shoulder. She giggled and smiled at Ares, who was still wearing his intimidating war helmet and his smoldering spears he had used to destroy the city.

"Hey, babe," he said. "How's your day going?"

"It just got better," Aphrodite replied. She smiled and then strutted over to Hephaestus, who was standing nearby.

"Husband, I must retire to Ares's mansion," she said. "He has just destroyed a city and I must bring love to the survivors."

"Okay, dear," Hephaestus said. "Be back for dinner."

"I will try, husband." Aphrodite began walking back to Ares. "But I can't make any promises."

As Aphrodite and Ares walked away, Zeus sighed at his son's ignorance. Hephaestus heard and walked over to Zeus, who was sitting on his golden throne, depressed.

"Father!" Hephaestus said. "I didn't see you there! Did you see Aphrodite and Ares over there?"

YES! Zeus thought. *THEY'RE PROBABLY...NO,* ***DEFINITELY*** *LEAVING TO GO ON A DATE!*

"Yes, Hephaestus," Zeus spoke out loud. "Sure is nice of them to go help those survivors."

"Yeah, Aphrodite's great,"[citation needed] Hephaestus said. "Y'know, when we got married, I thought Aphrodite would take secret mortal boyfriends."

YES, LIKE ADONIS, PHAETHON, ANCHISES, BOUTES, ECT.! SHE HAS ***SO*** *MANY MORTAL SECRET BOYFRIENDS!*

"I thought she would have some secret godly boyfriends," Hephaestus elaborated.

LIKE HERMES, DIONYSUS, HERMES, OR POSEIDON[205]*? WORRIED ABOUT ANY OF THOSE GUYS, HEPHAESTUS?*

"Or maybe one main godly boyfriend."

LIKE ARES.

"But so far, none of that has happened yet. Don't you love how committed to the institution of marriage she is? Anyhow, that's all I really wanted to say. See you around, father." Hephaestus walked away.

---

[205] Zeus conveniently forgets about being Aphrodite's secret boyfriend at one point.

"Well," noted Zeus. "Not Hephaestus. What about Hermes? He delivers messages better than Iris. Without him, the souls of the dead wouldn't reach Hades. None of my messages would leave Olympus and the mortals would be completely deprived of my wisdom."

As Zeus was thinking, Hermes ran into the room with an urgent message, judging by how much he was sweating.

"Pop! I have news! BIG news! HUGE news! GIANT news! PLANETARY news! GALAXIAN ne-"

"That's enough, Hermes."

"What is your news, Hermes?" asked Athena, who came into the room when she heard yelling.

"The Giants are gathering! They could attack us at any time!"

Zeus and Athena gasped.

"We must prepare for war! Let's go, Hermes!" Athena ran towards the war room and Hermes followed her.

Hmm. That was useful information, Zeus thought. *Without Hermes, we would be doomed. Maybe he is a bit more of a threat than I thought he was. I had better keep watch against him.*

Right then, Hermes tripped on his shoelaces, and rolled, falling out of the place and off of Olympus.

Zeus checked his name off.

So Zeus knew that if the cycle were to continue, it would definitely be from a new godly son.

So what did this all have to do with Prometheus? It was connected through the fact that Prometheus was a deity, so he must be the deity of something. But Prometheus wasn't the deity of water or air or something lame. He was the deity of forethought. Basically, he could see the future.

He could see so far into the future, that he could probably tell who was going to replace Zeus.

So when Prometheus stole fire, Zeus was happy to get rid of him and stop him from telling people.

And the eagle was happy to eat a bunch of liver.

And Prometheus was… not happy about any of this.

"So what?" You may be saying. "So he knows who could overtake you. Stop being paranoid, Zeus."

Oh, I forgot to mention that Métis told him that her second child would overthrow him.

And Thetis's child was prophesied to be greater than their father, and Zeus always forgot about that part when talking to Thetis.

…

…

…

…

...

Maybe he had the right to be paranoid.

Appendix D

A Short[citation needed] Family Tree

Index

If you can't read that blurry, small picture, which I can't actually use, due to printing issues, just know that it's really hard to make those, and I spent like twenty hours on it!

Chaos, via tripping on a rock, had Gaia.

Chaos, via a burp, had Eros, Tartarus, Nyx, andErebus.

Eros, using Chaos's power, created Birds.

Pontus, using Chaos's power, created Fish.

Nyx and Erebus had Aether, Hemera, Moros, Geras, Thanatos, Ker, Sophrosyne, Hypnos, the Oneroi, Epiphorn, Eris, Oizys, Hybris, Nemesis, Euphorsyne, Philotes, Eleos, Styx, Dolus, Ponos, Momos, Apate, Allecto, Tisiphone, and Megaera.

Eros, via Uranus's essence falling into the sea, had Aphrodite.

Gaia had Pontus and Uranus.

Gaia and Tartarus had Typhon.

Gaia and Aether had Alega, Lyssa, Penthos, Pseudologi, Horkos, Amphilogia, Lethe, Aergia, and Hysminai.

Gaia and Pontus had Keto & Nereus & Eurybia and Aigaios.

Gaia and Uranus had Oceanus, Koeus, Krius, Hyperion, Themis, Tethys, Rhea, Kronos, Iapteus, Theia, Mnemosyne, Brontes, Arges, and Stereopes.

Oceanus and Tethys had the uncountable Oceanaids and the fifty Nereids.

Eurybia and Krius had Astraios, Pallas, and Perses.

Zeus and Mnemosyne had Calliope, Clio, Erato, Euterpe, Melpomene, Polyhymnia, Thalia, Terpsichore, and Urania.

Koeus and Phoebe had Leto and Asteria.

Hyperion and Themis had Eos, Helios, and Selene.

Eos and Astraios had Anemoi and Astra.

Stx and Pallas had Nike, Kratos, Bia, and Zelos.

Aphrodite, via an unknown parent, possibly Ares or Hermes, had Eros the Younger[206].

Kronos and Rhea had Hestia, Demeter, Hera, Hades, Poseidon, and Zeus.

[206] And lamer.

Maia and Zeus had Hermes.

Metis and Zeus had Athena.

Semele and Zeus had Dionysus.

Leto and Zeus had Artemis and Apollo.

Dionysus and Aphrodite had Priapos and Iakkhos.

Themis and Zeus had Clotho, Lachesis, Atropos, Thallo, Karpo, and Auxo.

Ares and Aphrodite had Phobos, Deimos, and Harmonia.

Hera and Zeus had Ares, Hebe, and Eileithyia.

Hera, all by herself, just for spite, had Hephaestus.

Poseidon and Aphrodite had Rhode and Herophile.

Poseidon and Demeter had Aerion and Despoine.

Aphrodite and Hermes had Hermaphroditos.

Bibliography

- For all the great information they provide, Theoi.com. Seriously. It's better than you could imagine.
- Thanks to Mermaid.js for helping me make the family tree you really can't read.

About the Author[207]

Author

Eros Phanes is a writer, artist, and primal deity. Author of countless memoirs, when he's not writing, Eros enjoys video games, reading, and bringing order to the entire universe. He lives in a timeless void.

Compiler

Harry VanDernoot is a writer, reader, and treasure hunter. When he's not hunting for ancient scrolls, he enjoys reading, writing, studying a variety of topics, and researching Tolkien. He has nearly died exactly 58,478 times obtaining this information. He lives in Bridgeton, MO.

Editor

Elisha Dukes is a writer, reader, and computer scientist. When he's not designing his latest scheme to take over the world, he enjoys reading, studying quantum physics, and reading the works of J.R.R. and Christopher Tolkien. He lives in Missouri. These are the main reasons why he edits Eros's works.

---

[207] , Editor, and Compiler.

www.ingramcontent.com/pod-product-compliance
Lightning Source LLC
LaVergne TN
LVHW081547070526
838199LV00061B/4240